A·W·O·L·
ENT WITHOUT LICENCE

ALSO BY ANDREW LANE

Young Sherlock Holmes
Death Cloud
Red Leech
Black Ice
Fire Storm
Snake Bite
Knife Edge
Stone Cold
Night Break

Lost Worlds
Lost Worlds
Shadow Creatures

Crusoe
Dawn of Spies
Day of Ice
Night of Terror

A.W.O.L.

AGENT WITHOUT LICENCE

ANDREW LANE

Piccadilly
P R E S S

First published in Great Britain in 2018 by
PICCADILLY PRESS
80–81 Wimpole St, London W1G 9RE
www.piccadillypress.co.uk

A CIP catalogue record for this book is available from the British Library.

ISBN: 978-1-84812-663-3
also available as an ebook

1

This book is typeset using Atomik ePublisher
Printed and bound in Great Britain by Clays Ltd, Elcograf S.p.A.

Piccadilly Press is an imprint of Bonnier Zaffre Ltd,
a Bonnier Publishing company
www.bonnierpublishing.com

Dedicated to Kieron Furnell, Ryan Mellor and Bradley Marshall-Smith, for allowing me to use bits of their names. You might not want to read it yourselves, guys, but you can wait until the film comes out . . .

Dedicated also to the staff and boys at Summer Fields School, Oxford, where I spent a hugely enjoyable week as Writer-in-Residence and wrote Chapter 7 of this book (but not in lessons. Obviously). (And a special shout-out to Eliot. Sorry about that dedication . . .)

CHAPTER ONE

'So, how are we going to get past security?'

Kieron Mellor grimaced. That was going to be the really tricky part.

'We could . . . pretend to be roadies,' he said hesitantly. 'Go in round the back.'

Sam shook his head. A purple lock of hair, bright among the otherwise coal-black strands that hung down over his forehead, whipped across his eyes and he blinked. 'That would be a dumb move,' he said. 'The roadies will all have security passes, and besides, they'll all be middle-aged blokes with bald spots, ponytails, beer guts and tight black T-shirts with sweat stains under the armpits.' He gestured at his scrawny frame. 'I don't know about you, but I don't really fit that stereotype.'

Sam's T-shirt *was* actually black – he'd bought it at a band merchandise shop elsewhere in the mall – but at his size, rather than confidently hefting a 300-watt guitar amp around, he was more likely to be crushed underneath it. His tight black jeans, ripped at both knees, and the massive boots covered with rivets that he always wore didn't scream

1

'roadie' – even though they were large enough that they could have belonged to a construction worker twice his size. Kieron wasn't much better – the two of them could have been brothers, although Kieron was taller and filled out his T-shirt more.

He glanced around the mall, looking for inspiration. They were in the food court on the basement level, surrounded by a cluster of metal tables and chairs. Three levels of balconies towered above them, lined with shoe shops, lingerie shops and places to buy strangely flavoured chocolates or weirdly patterned ties. The levels were linked by wide escalators that moved so slowly that you were stuck there, going up or down, for what felt like forever, with everyone watching you. The shops along the other side of the food court, opposite the counters selling coffee, pastries, pizza slices and burgers, were mainly newsagents, mobile-phone retailers or places to buy e-refills. There was, however, a laptop repair and mobile-phone unlocking unit, and that gave him an idea.

'What about hacking the ticket website and putting our names on there? When we get to the front of the queue we can tell them we lost our tickets, but we're on the list as having paid for them. They'll have to comp us, get us inside for free.'

Sam shook his head. 'The names on the database will be tied to barcodes on the tickets. I can't just invent two barcodes out of nowhere cos they're all issued from a separate allocation, and if I copy ones that are already on the database then it'll be obvious that they've already been scanned through.'

'Not if we're at the front of the queue,' Kieron pointed out. 'Whoever has those barcodes will be behind us, and by the time they get scanned we'll be inside and in the mosh pit.'

Sam opened his mouth to say something, but a sudden shout of 'Emo scum!' from the far side of the food court surprised him into silence. It was followed by a rain of plastic knives falling near them. 'Why don't you use these to cut yourselves?'

Kieron stared across to where a group of teenagers in baggy tracksuit bottoms, polo shirts and baseball caps were staring at them challengingly. Heads turned all around the food court – mothers with kids, elderly ladies with shopping trolleys, a couple of men in work overalls, all of them glancing reflexively at the teens, then over at Kieron and Sam, with frowns on their faces. One of the elderly ladies started tutting at them.

'Why don't you –' Sam shouted, clenching his hands on the arms of his chair and starting to lever himself out.

Kieron grabbed a handful of Sam's T-shirt and pulled him back. 'Don't give them the satisfaction.'

Sam fell back into the chair and crossed his arms defensively over his chest, clutching onto his elbows. 'I could take them. You think I couldn't?'

'I'm sure you could, but the mall Nazis are watching.' Indeed, a bulky uniformed guard was already moving towards the feral teens.

'Then why don't they *do* something?'

'It's a free country. Apparently.'

Sam's hands were rubbing his forearms now. Kieron had

seen the thin red scars on his white skin, but he had never raised the subject. He'd not needed to; Sam knew that he knew. If Sam wanted to talk, he would.

'Free for insults and oppression directed at anybody who's different from the norm,' he muttered. 'It makes me sick. I wouldn't mind, but they can't even tell the difference between emos and greebs.'

Kieron glanced again at Sam's black hair, black T-shirt and clumsy New Rock boots, and then down at himself. Apart from the fact that his T-shirt was supporting a different screamo band to Sam's and he was a head taller than his friend, he could have caught sight of Sam in a shop window and assumed he was seeing his own reflection. Pointing out to him that greebs were setting up their own norm and their own look, just like chavs, probably wouldn't go down too well.

He wondered briefly what the collective term for a bunch of greebs was. 'An isolation of greebs', perhaps. Or maybe 'a sadness'.

Sam still looked gloomy and angry. Kieron looked around, trying to find something to distract his friend with, when he noticed a rack of newspapers in front of one of the newsagents. 'We could be reporters,' he said. 'Doing an interview with the band.'

'For the school newspaper!' Sam shook his head. 'We haven't even *got* a school newspaper.'

'We could be bloggers!'

'I *am* a blogger,' Sam pointed out quietly, but dangerously.

'Yes, but we could be bloggers with more than thirty

followers.' Kieron saw his friend wince, and cursed his lack of subtlety, but kept going. 'There are bloggers out there with *thousands* of followers. *Tens* of thousands. We could pretend to be one of them.'

'Way to make a friend feel special,' Sam muttered.

'They'd go for it – interview before the gig and then we can watch from the side of the stage. At the very worst, we'll be inside the hall rather than outside.'

Sam shrugged. 'Might work, I suppose. How do we get in touch with them?'

'There'll be a publicist. We can find them through the band's website.'

Sam thought for a moment. His expression suggested that he might just be buying in to the idea. 'I could even fake a blog with lots of posts, just temporarily – take someone else's site, copy it and put my photo on it. If the publicists don't recognise it and haven't met the blogger before, we'll be OK.'

'*Our* photos,' Kieron pointed out quietly.

'Hey, this isn't about you!' Sam smiled to show that it was just banter. 'That's actually what I meant. Worth a try, anyway.'

'Who knows,' Kieron said, 'we might even get invited to the after-gig party.'

He glanced surreptitiously over to where the group of teens were drifting away from the security guard like iron filings being repelled invisibly by a magnet. One of them turned to look at Kieron as he went, and raised his middle finger derisively. Kieron waved back and smiled. The boy snarled, wrinkling his lips and nose like a pit bull. It was amazingly easy to annoy them – you just had to be cheerful. They seemed to be born annoyed, and brought up in a way that just exacerbated the mood. 'An annoyance of chavs', then. Was that better than 'an insult'?

He was about to turn back to Sam and ask him, when he noticed the man at the next table. He'd been the only person not to look at the two of them when the chavs had kicked off. He had a bushy beard and wore chinos and a striped business shirt with the sleeves rolled up. A light grey jacket was slung over the back of his chair. His boots, Kieron noticed, were of a good, comfortable walking design. He'd wanted boots like that for his outdoor-education week away in Wales, but he'd had to make do with his old trainers. His mum didn't earn that much at her job.

The man stood out because he wasn't looking disapprovingly either at Kieron and Sam or the others, and because he was talking to himself, chatting away as if there was someone on the other side of the table, making small gestures in the air as if he was trying to describe something to an invisible friend. He wore glasses, but they stood out because of the unfashionably thick frames and the slightly smoky look to the lenses. The man suddenly turned his head, revealing a black, curved device nestling just behind the curl of his ear – a Bluetooth earpiece.

'Why's he waving his hands around?' Kieron asked. 'Whoever he's talking to can't see him. He must know that.'

'Maybe he's just very physical.' Sam shrugged slightly, and stared at the table. 'Some people are. They put hands on their friends' arms, and stuff. And hug, at random. You know.'

'It makes him look like an idiot,' Kieron said.

'I wave my hands around all the time when I'm talking to you on the phone.'

'Not on Skype, you don't.'

'Skype's different.'

Kieron glanced back at the man in the glasses. He was pausing now, head cocked slightly to one side as if he was listening. 'Actually,' he said, 'when you're Skyping you zoom the camera right in on your face. You could be wearing a creepy clown costume and I wouldn't know.'

Kieron noticed two men heading for the table where the man with the Bluetooth earpiece was still waving his hands around. He assumed they were friends, but there was something about their body language that started alarm bells ringing in his head. They were dressed similarly to the seated man – loose chinos, Ben Sherman shirts, loose Harrington jackets – but they both had blond hair cut close to the scalp. And they were coming at the man from different directions – one angling in from behind the man's left shoulder, one in from the right.

And they weren't slowing down.

As Kieron watched in surprise, the two newcomers grabbed the man by his arms and hauled him backwards out of his chair. They must have both hit a nerve somewhere in his armpits, because the man's face creased up in agony. His left foot kicked out, catching the table, but it didn't fall over. One of the men reached around and pressed hard beneath their victim's jaw. He folded up, unconscious, and they carried him away between them like two blokes supporting a friend who'd had too much to drink. His chair fell over backwards with a clatter as they dragged him off. Within a few seconds they were clear of the tables and heading for the lift to the car park. Only a few heads turned as they passed. Most people just ignored the ruckus. Typical, Kieron thought. Two greebs sitting doing nothing get tuts and dark glances, but an abduction gets nothing.

'Did you –?'

Sam's face was the perfect picture of Manga shock: all wide eyes and gaping mouth. 'That was a *kidnapping*!' he said. 'They just picked him up and took him!'

'I know!' Kieron glanced around, looking to see if anybody else was doing anything, but everyone was minding their own business. 'Was it, like, a stunt of some kind? Someone filming it for YouTube, you think?'

Sam shrugged, his eyes still wide. 'I don't know.' Kieron looked around the food court, then scanned the balconies above. 'I can't see anyone with a camera. Not even a mobile or a tablet. If they *are* filming, then they're keeping it really under wraps.'

'Maybe they're using the mall security cameras.' He tried looking for the security Nazi, but he seemed to have vanished. Maybe he was still tailing the chavs.

'That wouldn't be very radical and underground, would it?' Sam pointed out. 'Getting a video feed from some corporate office.' He glanced up at the balconies. 'None of the cameras are pointed over here, anyway.'

'Which is odd in itself.' Kieron followed his gaze. Sam was right: all of the cameras appeared to be pointing randomly off into corners. 'Do you think they've been moved?'

'What, deliberately, so there was no record of that bloke being taken?' Sam frowned. 'It wouldn't take much to hack the software controlling the camera motors and point them away from particular areas. Failing that, you could just knock them with a broom handle.'

'Old skool – I like it.'

The three men had bypassed the lift doors and were pushing their way through the meagre crowd to the stairwell that led down to the car-park level.

'Should we tell someone?' Sam asked.

'Before we do that, I want to see what they do when they get to the car park. If they throw the man into a police car or an ambulance then we'll ignore it; if they put him in the back of some anonymous black executive car then we'll tell someone.'

As Kieron sprang to his feet Sam said: 'And if you find him badly beaten or dead in the stairwell?'

'Then you're my alibi. Wait here; I won't be long.'

As he moved past the table where the men had been sitting, Kieron noticed that the man's Bluetooth earpiece and dark glasses had fallen to the floor in the brief scuffle. He bent down and scooped them up as he went past. If the man was OK then he might want them back. If he had vanished, well, the stuff might fetch a few pounds at one of the shops Kieron knew in the old High Street, no questions asked. Maybe he could afford those gig tickets for himself and Sam after all.

The stairs to the car park were over by a 99p store where everything in the window looked like 99p was an extortionate amount to pay. Kieron pushed the door open against its springs and hesitated. What if the men were just inside, waiting to see if anyone was stupid enough to follow them? Several of the fluorescent light tubes were broken and one flickered erratically, but there was enough light for him to see that the balcony and the first flight of concrete stairs were empty. From somewhere down below he thought he could hear footsteps: hard rubber scuffing on concrete.

He glanced back over at Sam, who gave him two thumbs up, and a smile. Emboldened, he moved into the stairwell.

It smelled like someone had been using it as a toilet, despite the fact that the mall had some very nice toilets about ten yards away. There were also some stains on the walls that he didn't recognise and didn't want to think about. He headed down the stairs, trying to breathe through his mouth rather than his nose.

The car-park levels were designated not with numbers or letters but with the names of animals. It had probably seemed like a cute idea to the planners. The first level was Antelope, with a silhouette of something that looked more like a small pony with a TV aerial on its head painted crudely onto the wall. Kieron pushed the door open and took a quick glance into the low-roofed concrete expanse. In the middle ground an SUV drove slowly between rows of parked cars, but the thugs who had grabbed Bluetooth Man couldn't have got to a car, opened it, thrown their captive in, climbed in themselves and started it up in the few seconds they'd been out of his sight.

He let the door close and kept going, down to the next

level. The silhouette on the wall by the door looked like a hunchbacked cow, but apparently it was meant to be a buffalo. The door was just swinging closed as he got to it. He pushed it open a crack and stared through.

The two blond-haired men were standing by a black van. Japanese – probably a Delica. Kieron's dad had driven a Delica, which is how he recognised the silhouette. He'd driven it out of Kieron and his mum's life three years ago, loaded up with his stuff. Funnily enough, he missed the van a lot more than he missed his dad.

One of the crew-cut thugs had an arm around the chest of the unconscious man and was holding him up. He was looking around the car park, checking to see if anyone was showing undue interest in them. The other man was unlocking the side door of the van and sliding it back.

Kieron felt trapped between two courses of action – either racing out into the car park to help the unconscious man or ignoring it all and walking away. Skulking there, peering through the crack between the door and its frame, seemed *wrong*. He ought to commit himself, one way or the other, but if he interfered then the two blond men would probably make mincemeat of him. So he stayed there, hiding and watching and cursing himself as a coward, as the men threw their captive into the back of the van, slid the door closed, checked one last time for anybody watching them, then climbed into the front and started the engine.

As the van pulled out of its parking space, Kieron pushed the door open and moved into the cross-hatched area marking out the stairs and the lifts. He watched as the van moved slowly along the row and turned at the end, past the ramp leading down to Camel, Duck and Eel, and continuing on towards the ramp leading up to Antelope and then to daylight. As it turned onto the ramp he could see its number plate clearly. He pulled a battered Sharpie from the pocket of his jeans and wrote the number down on the inside of his forearm. He wasn't sure why, but it seemed like a good idea. Maybe the police would want to know, if this was ever reported.

Not that there was anybody apart from him and Sam to report it. That level of the car park had been as empty of people as the one above.

He moved back into the stairwell and began to climb the stairs back to the food court. Thoughts were racing around his head. He tried to imagine himself going into a police station and reporting this, or even just stopping a policeman in the street – if he could find one – and telling them what he had seen, but the conversation in his head hit a brick wall when the imaginary policeman checked his file and found that he'd been given several warnings for spraying graffiti on the walls of a deserted warehouse near where he lived, for loitering around the bus station, and for making prank calls. Oh, and he'd been banned from the bowling alley, along with Sam and some friends, for bouncing the balls rather than rolling them. The police wouldn't believe a word he said now.

He emerged on the lowest floor of the mall and glanced across to where Sam sat watching something on his mobile. He looked around for the security guard. Maybe Kieron could tell *him* about what had happened. The problem was that he'd banned Kieron from several audio-equipment shops up in the higher levels already, after Kieron had used the Bluetooth functionality on his own phone to play the *Thomas the Tank Engine* theme tune through all of the shops' wireless speakers at full volume, a few months back. He would remember Kieron. In fact, that's what he'd said. 'I'll remember you,' had been his exact words, accompanied by a glare that would have been menacing if he hadn't been slightly cross-eyed. No, Kieron suspected that there wouldn't be any help coming from that direction either.

Looking across the food court, Kieron suddenly thought about how small and vulnerable Sam looked. He took things very personally, Kieron knew, and he thought deeply about stuff. Kieron was able to shrug bad things off, pretty much, but Sam took it all to heart: internalising the pain and nursing it.

He walked towards towards Sam. As he went, he glanced up at the security cameras that were screwed to the first balcony level. Usually they covered the entire food court with their electronic footprint apart from a small but well-known area over near the newsagents where the kids sometimes gathered to swap things they'd shoplifted, or to have a quick smoke. Now, however, he saw that all of the cameras there had been turned away too, facing sideways along the balcony wall. They'd definitely been interfered with.

'What?' he said as he walked towards his friend.

'What *what*?' Sam responded.

'You were looking at me strangely.'

'I look at everyone strangely. It's the way my face goes.'
Sam glanced over at the door to the stairway, then back at
him. 'What happened?'

'When I got down there, they were bundling that guy
into a black van, then they drove off.'

'You got the licence plate?'

Instead of replying, Kieron just raised his arm.

'Purple,' Sam said approvingly. 'I like.' He held out his
mobile. 'I managed to get some shots of them as they were
dragging him away. Might be useful.'

Kieron sat down and took a drink from the large plastic
cup on the table. Everything in the food court was plastic –
the plates, the cups, the cutlery and, arguably, the food. He
often wondered what the people who ran the place were
scared of. It wasn't like an aircraft: nobody was going to
hijack the food court.

'What are we going to do?' Sam asked. Kieron suppressed
a smile. Sam was always the practical one.

'Not sure. It was definitely an abduction, right? I mean,
we didn't misunderstand what was happening?'

Sam shook his head. 'No, it was definitely an abduction.'

'And it wasn't a couple of friends mounting a fake
kidnapping as the start of a booze-fuelled stag weekend
in Bulgaria?'

Again, Sam shook his head. 'You saw the way they
incapacitated him with their thumbs in his armpits. They
knew exactly where to hit to get the nerves. That goes well
beyond playful physical banter.'

'Right.' Kieron thought for a moment. 'They didn't take

his wallet and abandon him in the car park, so it's not a mugging. It was definitely *him* they wanted.' He shrugged. 'Maybe it's a gang thing. He trespassed on their territory, so they had to do something about it.'

Sam looked uncertain. 'I suppose, except that as far as I know the local gangs are pretty small, and the mall here is like neutral territory. It has to be, otherwise they'd never get their shopping done. Those guys looked seriously mean.' He thought for a second. 'What kind of van were they driving?'

'Like something surfers would use to get down to a beach in Cornwall. Four-wheel drive, bull bars, smoked-glass windows.'

'Not the kind of thing the local gangs drive. They prefer pimped-up Mondeos and Astras – usually with the entire boot taken up with a sound system. Vans aren't their thing.'

Sam was right. Everything about the two blond men suggested that this was something verging on a professional operation. 'What if he was a terrorist and they were Special Forces?'

Sam considered the suggestion for a few moments. 'That kind-of explains what actually happened, but he didn't look like a terrorist.'

'You mean he wasn't obviously a Muslim?' Kieron challenged.

Sam scowled. 'That's not what I meant. If anything, they looked more like the bad guys and he looked more like a good guy. They reminded me of the neo-fascists you get at rallies. Shaven heads and boots. They probably had tattoos all up their arms.'

Kieron couldn't help himself. 'You'd have tattoos up your arms if you could afford it, and if your dad would let you,' he said.

Sam automatically bristled. 'Yeah, but Celtic knots and Maori stuff. Not swastikas. Though actually the swastika is an ancient symbol that got adopted by the fascists. They weren't even bright enough to come up with their own branding.

'Anyway . . . what shall we do?' Sam reverted to his original question. 'There's only one security guard, and he's so overweight he walks around with his laces undone because he can't bend over to tie them. What use is he going to be when a man's been kidnapped?'

'Call the police?' said Kieron.

'With our records?' Sam pointed out.

Kieron sighed. 'Maybe we could send them a text, or leave an anonymous message.'

'No such thing any more,' Sam said, shaking his head. 'The government can track any message or any text back to who sent it. Don't you know anything?'

'I know you're paranoid,' Kieron said.

'With good reason,' Sam protested. 'We're living in the most heavily observed society in the world!'

'You shouldn't believe everything you read on the Internet.'

'I don't,' Sam said. 'The Internet's been completely penetrated by the CIA, the NSA, MI5 and GCHQ. Half the sites that are up there on the dark web advertising guns or drugs are actually phishing sites trying to lure people in so they can be arrested.'

A sudden thought struck Kieron. 'Hang on – I've got that bloke's earpiece and glasses. Maybe there's something there that will tell us who he is.'

'Not without his mobile,' Sam pointed out. 'If that earpiece really is Bluetoothed to his phone then it's not going to tell us anything, because his phone will be out of range by now.' He thought for a moment. 'Oh, except that you can give labels to Bluetooth equipment. If we pair it to one of our mobiles then it might have a name attached to it.'

'Knowing our luck it'll just say "Paul's Phone" or "Steve's Mobile", which will be no use whatsoever.' Kieron reached into his pocket and pulled out the stuff he'd scooped up from the floor.

As Kieron put the earpiece and the glasses on the table, Sam leaned forward. 'Actually,' he said, 'I take it back – that's not a standard Bluetooth earpiece.' He slid it across the metal surface of the table, avoiding the sticky lemonade and cola stains that had survived the last cleaning. 'I guess it might be next-gen Bluetooth, or maybe WiFi Direct.' He popped the earpiece apart with his thumb. 'The battery isn't a standard make either.' He looked at it more closely. 'In fact, it's not a battery at all – it's a miniature fuel cell.' He gave a low whistle. 'That's clever.'

'I'll take your word for it,' Kieron said. He took the earpiece from Sam and examined it. The way the thing was sculpted, and the soft silicone feel of it in his hand, made him revise his estimate of the price upward by a significant chunk. This wasn't your bog-standard supermarket own-brand kit – this was something special. High-end audio.

Curious, he picked up the glasses and looked them over. No obvious trademark or logo, but again they *felt* expensive. On a whim, he slipped them on and looked at Sam with a mock-serious expression on his face. 'And in other news tonight . . .' he said.

Sam laughed.

It occurred to him that he could see Sam's face without blurring or distortion. 'Hang on – these things are plain glass!'

'Photochromic sunglasses?' Sam asked, 'Just clear at the moment because they're out of the sun?'

He was about to answer when glowing words appeared at the bottom of his visual field.

User detected. Powering up from sleep mode.

'There's something –' he started to say, but then he was looking at an image of a different world in a rectangular box that seemed to be projected in the air about ten feet in front of him. It was like looking at a widescreen TV, except that he could see Sam *through* it.

And on the screen, in the image, he could see a bright blue sky and a white arched building. Oh, and a hand, holding a glass of cola, positioned exactly as if it was his hand. Except that it wasn't. It was a girl's hand, with a thin gold watch on the wrist and gold rings on the fingers.

'Bradley,' a female voice said, 'stop feeding your face. I need your help.'

CHAPTER TWO

'Bradley – stop feeding your face. I need your help.'

Bex Wilson reached up and tapped the button on the side of her sunglasses, wondering if she'd accidentally managed to turn the volume down while brushing her hair out of her eyes. Or maybe a trickle of sweat had got into the electronics and short-circuited something important. She wouldn't be surprised – the kit was meant to be military-grade, hardened against environmental and climatic conditions, but accidents happened, and the heat here in Mumbai was more oppressive than anything she had ever experienced. It was like something you'd feel if you opened an oven door after you'd been baking a potato for an hour. The humidity was just as bad: so much moisture hung in the air that her sweat had nowhere to go, so it just stayed on her skin. What with the heat *and* the humidity combined, Bex felt as if the entire atmosphere, in a column from where she stood all the way up to the edge of space, was pressing down just on her.

Glancing around the open space outside the hotel, she wondered why nobody else seemed to be feeling it. Or maybe they were, but they just weren't showing their discomfort.

Maybe, once she got used to it, she would be all right. She wasn't putting any money on it though.

She was sitting on a stone bench on the edge of an area of paved ground with a can of cola in her hand. Behind her the ornate and impressive Victorian edifice of the Taj Mahal Palace hotel rose up, where rich tourists stayed in glorious, air-conditioned luxury. Ahead of her sat a massive square basalt building with an arch in the centre that Bradley had told her was called the Gateway of India, and beyond the arch the grey water of Mumbai Harbour rolled greasily.

The sky above her was grey as well – dark clouds swelling like dirty sheets hanging from washing lines high above.

Bradley had warned her about that water. *Don't swim in it,* he'd said. *Don't even touch it. Apparently it's like raw sewage.*

That's why she had Bradley on the end of a virtual line – to provide information like that. And, of course, to get her out of trouble.

The area in front of the arch heaved with people. Some of them were tourists from abroad wearing backpacks and holding cameras or guidebooks. Some of them were tourists from elsewhere in India, wearing saris or baggy linen shirts and trousers, and with two, three or four kids running around them. Some of them were locals selling cans of drink, cheap sunglasses, postcards and maps. One of them – Bex – was an undercover intelligence agent. And every single one of them seemed to be ignoring the fact that it was so hot that they could all have cooked eggs on the paving slabs.

Bex had spent a lot of time in America, from Death Valley to Florida, and she'd thought she knew all about hot weather. This, however, was nothing like anything she had ever felt. This, as her gaming friends would say, was a level up from her previous experiences.

Speaking of gaming friends, she tapped her earpiece again in frustration. As far as anyone looking was concerned, she was just making a call. Which, in effect, she was. 'Bradley? Are you there? What's going on?' She didn't make any attempt to disguise the fact that she was talking to nobody – everyone in the world these days knew what Bluetooth and Wi-Fi were. It wasn't suspicious.

For a moment she heard nothing but the seashore-hiss of background static, but then a tentative voice said: 'Hello?'

'Bradley?' she asked. It didn't sound like him.

'No, my name's Kieron.'

She frowned. She and Bradley had never noticed any interference with their communications before, but she wasn't that experienced with the technology and she supposed there had to be a first time for everything. 'I'm sorry,' she said politely, 'I think we've got a crossed line. Can you cancel your call and try again? I'll do the same.'

'Wait,' the voice in her ear said urgently, 'I need to ask you something. Are you looking at a massive arch thing made of stone?'

'Ye-es,' she said.

'And have you got a can of cola in your hand?'

'Yes.'

'It's not a game, or something?'

'No. Are you saying *you* can see the arch and the can too?'

This was wrong. Somehow this Kieron had accessed her encrypted communications with Bradley. Maybe he had even hacked it. Instinctively her hands rose to her sunglasses. Making it look like she was just pushing them back on her nose, she covered up the miniature cameras on each side, just in front of the hinges where the arms met the lenses.

'Hey,' he said, 'it's gone dark! What happened?'

So he *was* seeing what she was seeing. This *was* wrong. She had to tell her bosses in SIS-TERR – the Secret Intelligence Service's Terrorist Technology-Enhanced Remote Reinforcement team – but first she had to find out what had happened to Bradley. Maybe he was trying to get through to her on another channel and finding it blocked. She hoped so, anyway.

She lowered her hands before it looked too odd.

'Are you wearing something like those cameras you see on cyclists' helmets?' the kid asked.

'Something like that,' she replied noncommittally. 'Look, kid, you need to disconnect now, OK?' She tried to pitch her voice like an air stewardess telling a passenger that they can't have another glass of wine. 'It's a protected link. You could get into trouble.'

'I think trouble's already happened,' the voice said. He sounded young. Maybe just a kid. Not that she was much past her twentieth birthday herself, but she *felt* older. She'd lived through a lot in the past couple of years, even if most of it had been training and simulations.

'What do you mean?'

'This bloke – he got taken away. He left his stuff behind. I'm using it now to talk to you.'

Bex felt as if a bucket of cold water had been poured all over her. It was like stepping into an ice-cold shower. For a second she shivered, but then the Mumbai climate enveloped her again like a warm, wet duvet. 'What bloke?' she asked urgently. 'What did he – I mean, what *does* he look like, the man you're talking about?'

A pause on the other end, then the kid – Kieron – said: 'Early thirties, long blond hair and a beard. I'd say he was wearing thick glasses, but I'm wearing them now and they're just plain glass. Not prescription lenses at all. Dressed like someone's hipster dad – chinos and an ironed shirt.'

'You've got his glasses and his earpiece?' Bex asked urgently.

'Yes, that's what I'm saying.'

Oh, this was getting worse and worse.

'Where are you exactly, right now?'

'I'm in the basement of a shopping mall in Newcastle.'

Newcastle. She felt a sick feeling welling up in her stomach. That was where Bradley had been operating from. There was some connection between her mission in India and that city, but it wasn't clear what the link was. Bradley's job had been to investigate that link when he wasn't providing Bex with support.

'Tell me exactly what happened.'

'He was just sitting here, when two men came over and grabbed him. They dragged him away, down to the car park. They threw him into a van and drove away.' His voice rose in tone while he spoke, as if he was reliving the events and feeling shocked all over again. Bex had been trained in listening unemotionally to people's voices and picking up undercurrents of emotion and meaning, but now she was feeling shock along with this Kieron.

'And he just left his kit on the table?' She couldn't believe what she was hearing.

'It fell off.' He sounded defensive. 'I just picked it up and, you know, kind of tried it on, and realised I could see, like, a high-def 3D image projected on the lenses somehow so I can see what's happening *here* but I can see what's happening *there* as well. That's some really sick technology.'

'What about security? Didn't anyone try to stop them?'

'Nobody noticed.'

Bex thought she heard a voice in the distance saying, 'Or cared!' For a moment she thought it was someone near her, but she realised that it came from her earpiece: another boy's voice. Kieron had friends. Or *a* friend.

She took a deep breath. She felt a flutter of panic in her chest that she couldn't seem to get rid of, like a butterfly that she'd accidentally swallowed.

She was about to say something, although she wasn't entirely sure what it was going to be, when the kid said: 'So, should I call the police or something?'

'No,' she said quickly. That wasn't a good idea. SIS-TERR should be handling this, not the police.

She had to think. She looked around, seeing the tourists and the hawkers of maps and gifts but not really focusing on anything; letting it all blur together while her thoughts raced.

The problem was that it would take time to get through to SIS-TERR and brief them on what had happened, and then even more time for them to arrange to have her transferred to another agent handler – probably one she'd never even met before – and get the mission back on track. And by then there probably wouldn't be a mission any more.

She felt sick. She and Bradley were independents, working under top-secret contract to the Secret Intelligence Service. Up until now they'd successfully handled every mission that had been thrown their way, but if they screwed this one up then the chances were they'd never get a contract again.

'Are you sure this isn't a game?' Kieron asked suddenly.

'This is definitely not a game.' She thought she detected something strange in his tone of voice, despite the thousands of miles that lay between them. 'Why do you ask?'

'Because a little box has come up in the top of the picture. It says "Security Alert – Threat Detected".'

Somebody had turned that ice-cold shower back on again. '*Where?* Tell me!'

'Look,' he said, 'this is getting too weird. Really, it is. I'll just hand the stuff in to the Information Point here at the mall, assuming there's anybody there, and we'll call it a day, OK? You can pick your friend's stuff up there.'

Her gaze flickered across the open space, resting on faces for a moment before checking out body postures, looking for something she recognised or something that screamed *threat!* but nothing stood out. 'No, wait. Kieron – it was Kieron, wasn't it? – just tell me: is there a thin yellow line leading from the corner of the box and pointing at something?'

'Yeah. It's pointing at some bloke.'

'Describe him for me.'

'Medium height, Indian by the look of him, standing with his back to the arch and staring kind of past your left shoulder. He's got a camera in his hand. One of those old-fashioned ones, with the chunky lenses. Not a smartphone or a tablet. When he moves, the box moves with him.'

His description was spot-on. She quickly isolated the man she thought he had described. 'Thin moustache? Sideburns? Blue shirt?'

'Yes.' A pause. 'Who is he? Why is this thing labelling him as a threat?'

'You tell me,' she said.

'I don't know!'

'OK, listen to me. This is important. Raise your right hand and touch the air where the threat box has appeared.'

A pause, then: 'Oh wow! This thing has gesture recognition built in, as well as facial recognition? What kind of processor is running the code?'

'Focus. Tell me what's happened.'

'Another box appeared. This one says: "Shakeer Saryadhi – minor agent – Indian Counter-Terrorism Centre", and underneath it says: "Possible surveillance threat".'

Unlikely to be a threat to my mission, she thought, relaxing slightly. The Gateway of India was a prominent landmark in Mumbai. It would be more than likely that India's top counter-terrorism organisation was maintaining 'eyes-on' the location: Lashkar-e-Taiba, a terrorist group based in Pakistan, was still active, and relations between India and

Pakistan were still highly unstable. If this was a surveillance operation then it wasn't directed against her. The Indian Counter-Terrorism Centre hadn't been told that she was there.

'Hey,' Kieron's voice said, 'this thing is like Wikipedia! I can click on words and it'll give me more detail.' He paused, then: 'You're in Mumbai? In India?'

'Yes.'

'So this thing is communicating via satellite? With no lag? Sweet.'

He sounded intelligent. 'Kieron, be quiet for a minute. I need to think.'

She thought she heard him having a muffled conversation with the boy who'd spoken earlier, but the majority of her mind crunched through facts, assumptions, speculations, predictions, options and courses of action. OK: fact one – her controller, Bradley, had been taken captive by bad guys of some kind. This of course was based on *assumption* one – that this Kieron was on the level and telling her the truth about what he'd seen. Fact one also led to speculation one – that Bradley's kidnapping was connected in some way to their joint mission, otherwise why take him there and then, in a shopping mall? That then provided her with *prediction* one – whoever had taken Bradley would be coming back for his glasses and his earpiece when they discovered that he hadn't got them on him. The tech – known as Augmented Reality Computer Capability, or ARCC – was new and secret, based on Google Glass, Oculus Rift and the HTC Vive but way in advance of those commercial applications,

27

but rumours got around fast in the intelligence and terrorist communities. These particular bad guys would know that he had *some* way of communicating with her, and would want to get their hands on it. 'Kieron,' she said urgently, 'you need to get away from wherever you are! The people who took . . . my friend . . . might come back looking for the tech kit you've got!'

'Already done,' he said reassuringly. 'Sam suggested we relocate to somewhere a bit more secluded. I'm walking and talking at the same time.'

'Good thinking.' Sam – that must be his friend.

The heat of the sun, soaked up by the stone bench on which she sat, made her legs itch. She put her can down and shifted to a more comfortable position. While she thought, she let her gaze wander across the various sights and sounds of the bay area she was in: the tourists, the locals, the boats and the spectacular architecture. Her gaze caught on a man standing off to one side: black hair and neatly trimmed black beard. He wore a three-piece pinstriped suit, which seemed odd considering the temperature. Maybe he was a businessman, there for a meeting. He turned and met her gaze, somehow aware that he was being watched. Bex smiled at him, and looked away.

Speculation two – the bad guys would keep Bradley alive while they worked on getting his communications link, and using it to trace her. Not a fact, of course, just a speculation, but she had to believe they would keep him alive otherwise she would be pitched into despair.

Two options – continue with the mission if possible,

without Bradley but making sure she got Kieron out of harm's way and stopped the kit falling into enemy hands, or pause the mission and notify SIS-TERR of events.

Fact two – her mission in Mumbai, guided supposedly by her handler Bradley back in Newcastle, was time-critical. Hence prediction two – if she paused to seek help from SIS-TERR then things would rapidly go pear-shaped, and they might lose their contract, and all further work.

It was pretty clear what she had to do. She couldn't go on by herself, without a handler, and she couldn't involve this kid, Kieron. She had to notify SIS-TERR and let them make the call on scrubbing the mission.

She was just about to tell Kieron to walk away and leave the kit at the information desk as he had suggested when he came back on line.

'I forgot to say – I wrote down the licence plate of the van that took your friend away.'

That would be something to give Control. 'Good work,' she said. 'If you raise your right hand, can you see a blue button appear in your field of view?'

'Yeah.'

'I know it's not there, but make out like you're pressing it.'

'An empty box appeared. Oh, and a virtual keyboard beneath it.'

'Either type the licence plate into the virtual keyboard, or just say "verbal input on", then say the licence plate out loud. The microphone's pretty sensitive. It'll pick up a whisper.'

'OK.' A pause, while Bex held her breath. 'Right – I typed it in. There's a little icon like a brain that probably means it's thinking. What is this – like an eighth-generation chip or something?'

'Don't worry about that now.'

Bex heard the other voice in the background again, then Kieron said, 'Sam wants to know how the chip keeps itself cool? Oh, hang on, the brain icon has vanished, and there's a box that says: "Mitsubishi Delica Stargazer, registered owner Three Cornered Square Communications Ltd". Does that help?'

'Not really,' she said bleakly. A leaden lump sat in her stomach. It hadn't been there a few seconds before. Unfortunately, she knew the name 'Three Cornered Square Communications'. It was a shadow company, owned and run by SIS-TERR. It was one of the ways they could register vehicles and properties and pay wages without anyone being able to trace it back to them. Except that Bex had seen that same company listed on top-secret accountancy spreadsheets.

Bradley had been taken by SIS-TERR. Or by someone working for SIS-TERR. But that didn't make any sense.

Maybe the bad guys were trying to make it *look* like Bradley had been taken by his own employers in order to destabilise Bex, put her off her stroke. Or perhaps there was a traitor, a double agent, supposedly working for SIS-TERR but actually working for the terrorists, or for an inimical nation. There were a whole load of assumptions and speculations right there, but she didn't want to think about them right now. The only thing she knew was that, right now, reporting back to SIS-TERR wasn't really an option.

But she had no resources, nothing to fall back on.

Despair rooted her to the spot and infiltrated its tentacles through her mind, stopping her from thinking properly.

'What's your name?' the boy back in Newcastle asked. His voice had an undertone of concern.

'Bex,' she said automatically. 'Short for Rebecca.'

'And you're what? A secret agent, on an actual mission in India?'

'Something like that.'

'And this guy Bradley, who has been kidnapped, is looking after you – feeding you information, analysing stuff and identifying threats while you pretend to be a tourist?'

'That's pretty much it.'

'And now he's gone, you're on your own and you don't know who to trust?'

'Exactly.' She smiled bitterly. 'You've got a pretty analytical brain, Kieron.'

'I read a lot. Oh, and I'm teaching myself programming, which is all about breaking a problem down to a series of steps and solving each step, one at a time.'

Bex had started to feel strangely protective of this kid. He'd fallen into something much bigger than he was used to, and she felt as if she had to shield him from any dangers that might arise.

'Have you changed location, Kieron? Where did you go?'

'We walked up two levels in the mall to the ice-cream shake place.' He paused. 'I've got a "Super Salted Caramel" and Sam's got a "Very Berry Explosion".'

Bex felt a sudden and unexpected sob welling up in her

chest. It was all so normal, so ordinary. Bradley would do that when he was talking to her – tell her what he was eating, or give her a running commentary on what the people around him were doing. He would also randomly tell her that there was a cafe nearby that sold *the best* lassi, or whatever local drink was appropriate, or that some famous person had stood exactly where she was standing: details gleaned from the computer processor in his glasses. Yes, it kept her grounded, kept her from getting sucked into the detail and the tension of the mission, whatever it was, but that was his character. That was what he did. Or had done.

'How old are you, Kieron?' she asked suddenly.

'Old enough,' he said guardedly.

'What colour is your hair?'

'Why?'

'Because I'm telling you all kinds of things that I shouldn't, and I realised that I don't have a mental picture of you. Tall or short? Sporty or academic?'

After a pause he spoke again, sounding suddenly tense. 'I'm nearly six feet tall, I've got black hair, and my skin looks like I've got a tan. I haven't – my dad's from Mauritius – but that's the only thing about me that looks Mauritian. Everything else I get from my mum. I identify as a greeb, but looking at me you'd say I'm an emo or a goth.'

'What's the difference?'

'Goths are attracted to the darker side of things, but they're not necessarily depressed or suicidal. They dress mainly in black, or purple if they're girls. Emos are really sensitive and depressive – they overreact to anything that happens, and they deal with it by self-harming or locking themselves in their room, curling up into a ball and listening to really loud music. Greebs reject any fashions or trends, and that's the difference between us, emos and goths. Being emo or goth *is* a fashion.' He paused. 'And the natural enemy of the greeb, the emo and the goth is the chav. They're the ones wearing tracksuit bottoms tucked into their socks, new white trainers and baseball caps, and have plenty of bling around their necks and on their fingers and wrists.'

'Sounds very tribal,' she said, smiling.

'I suppose it is,' Kieron said in a quieter voice, 'but actually that's not important right now. I've just seen one of those two blond guys again. We're sitting in the window of the ice-cream shake place on the second floor of the mall, and we're looking down into the food area. We can see our table, and the table your friend was sitting at. The bloke who's come back is looking around as if he's dropped something.' A pause, then, 'Now he's going across to the nearest rubbish bin. He's opened up the flap and he's looking inside. He probably thinks that one of the cleaners cleared the table and threw all the rubbish away.'

'Don't let him know you're watching him,' Bex said decisively.

'We won't. We're two levels up, and there's a window between him and us. There are four other people sitting in the window and looking out. He can't tell that there's anything special about us.'

'He would have noticed you,' Bex pointed out. 'He would have been trained to spot everything around him.'

'Not us,' Kieron said. His voice sounded angry and frustrated. 'Nobody sees kids like us. We're invisible, except to chavs and old people.'

'What's happening now?'

'He's talking to one of the cleaners. He looks like he's getting annoyed. OK, the cleaner's turned away now and he's trying to walk off. The guy has grabbed the cleaner's shoulder, and he's pulling him back. OK, he's holding his hands up in an apology, and he's taking a wallet from his jacket pocket. It looks like he's offering the cleaner money, but the cleaner is backing away and shaking his head.'

Bex could visualise what was going on as if she was actually there. Kieron was a good talker.

'You know how you got the information on the guy you saw here in Mumbai?'

'Yeah.'

'Try doing the same with the man you're looking at. Raise your hand until your forefinger is over his face and pretend that you're tapping a key on a keyboard, but twice.'

'OK, I'm – wow! So I can get information on things *I'm* seeing as well as things *you're* seeing!'

'What's happening?'

'His face is outlined with a yellow border, and that brain symbol has appeared again. Right, the bloke has walked out of sight, but there's a text box that's just appeared in mid-air. This one is blue, not yellow like last time.'

'What does it say?

'"Searching for known terrorists". Oh, it's changed to "Searching for known terrorist associates". That one's gone now, and it says: "Searching for known criminals". Ah, it's found something. It's saying: "Identified as Kyle Renner. British citizen; aged twenty-three. Convictions for grievous bodily harm and for assault. Linked to right-wing group Blood and Soil." There's a reference number and a whole series of links as well. Whoa, this guy is seriously dangerous.' He paused, then said, 'This thing isn't just accessing the Internet, is it? This isn't just Wikipedia. It's checking government stuff as well – classified databases.'

Bex didn't want to make the tech sound too attractive in case Kieron ran off with it, never to be seen again, so she kept quiet. She wished that she could access the information that he could, right now, so she could check him out. The problem was that field agents weren't allowed to do that, only their handlers. Partly it was so they had access to information when they were undercover and couldn't wave their arms about without attracting suspicion. Partly also it was so that secret information didn't fall into the hands of the bad guys. Agent in the field; handler in a safe place. That was the rule.

'Let's say it accesses a whole load of data that isn't generally available.'

'I know – I just pulled up all the blueprints for the mall, just by waving my hands around and miming clicking on things. Alarms as well – where the alarm boxes are, where the cables are routed and information on the codes that will turn them off. This thing is incredible. Oh, hang on, I've got the employment records of the employees now.' He suddenly sounded more muffled, as if he was talking to his friend – Sam. 'That security guard was apparently dishonourably discharged from the Army for stealing a handgun and some live ammunition. And he's on medication for stress – something called propranolol.'

Bex heard Sam say something like: 'Get wrecked! That's a beta-blocker. He wouldn't have admitted that to his employers!'

'No,' Kieron agreed. 'I followed a link and got access to his medical records. Does this thing access the Deep Web as well? I bet it does. And the computer systems of other nations? It's wicked!'

'Probably. It's just a tool as far as we're concerned.' She thought for a second. 'What's this Kyle Renner doing now?'

'He's talking to the security guard who patrols the mall. It looks like he's learned his lesson from what happened with the cleaner – he's being a lot more reasonable now. Yeah, he's offering the guard some money. They're walking away together now.'

'That's bad,' Bex said without thinking.

'Why?' Kieron sounded nervous. Bex couldn't really blame him.

'Because if I was Renner, if I knew something important had gone missing from a public place and I knew that it hadn't been cleared away, then the next thing I would do is check the recordings from the security cameras.'

'That's not going to help,' Kieron sniffed.

'Why not?'

'Because they'd all been turned away so that the table where your friend was sitting couldn't be seen.'

Bex laughed in relief. She was impressed how the kid had been so observant. 'You're right. They are intellectually challenged.'

'Does that mean we're safe?'

'Probably. For the moment.' With the threat in the mall suspended, Bex's thoughts turned back to her own situation. What could she do?

'I don't want to worry you,' Kieron said suddenly, 'but another box has come up at your end of the link.' He sounded as if he was talking through a mouthful of ice cream.

'What colour is the box?'

'Green.'

'That's a mission-related one.' She let her gaze roam around the plaza, just like a tourist. Nothing seemed to have changed: the crowds were still milling around the Gateway of India, taking selfies and looking impressed. 'What's it indicating?'

'There's a man over to your right. He's wearing a suit. Dark-skinned, bald on top but long hair around the back of his head falling down over his collar. Middle-aged.'

She could see him now. He stood still, looking around as if he was expecting someone. He held a briefcase defensively in front of him. Local vendors and impromptu tourist guides approached him expectantly, but he just waved them away. 'What's the system saying about him?'

'It says: "Target One identified – Fahim Mahmoud, Sub-Director, Pakistani Atomic Energy Commission". So what's the deal with him?'

'I can't tell you,' she said. '"Need to know".'

'Never mind.' Kieron sounded smug. 'I've accessed a sub-menu. He's meeting someone in order to hand over atomic information, isn't he? You know, from phone intercepts passed to the UK by the American National Security Agency that he's selling secrets to but you don't know who or what for. You're there to find out who he's meeting. Terrorists is the best guess.'

'I can neither confirm nor deny that,' Bex said stiffly, but inside she felt a little glow of admiration for this kid she'd never met.

'Oh, that's interesting,' Kieron added. 'The phone intercepts weren't between this bloke and his potential customer; they were between two numbers that couldn't be traced, but they *mentioned* him and this meeting. The closest you could get to finding out who had been talking about it was that one of the numbers was near Newcastle.'

'Again,' she said, 'that's just pure speculation on your part. I'm not going to comment on it.'

'But it says so, right here!'

As she watched, a man approached Mahmoud: Indian, young, with cheeks marked by smallpox scars. He had a rucksack in his hand.

The two men were shaking hands now.

'Can the system identify the second man?' she asked. As she said the words, the man with the rucksack turned his head to scan the crowd. To avoid meeting his eye and rousing his suspicions, Bex turned around and looked at the ornate bulk of the Taj Mahal Palace hotel behind her. She let her gaze scan across it idly while she counted to twenty.

'The system doesn't know who he is,' Kieron said hurriedly, 'but you've got a bigger problem to worry about.'

'What's that?'

'A red box has just appeared, with a line pointing to the hotel's roof.'

'What does it say?'

'Oh God! You need to get out of there! It says: "Danger! Retro-reflection from telescopic sight detected! Sniper on roof, preparing to fire!"'

Bex's immediate reaction was an urge to whirl around and scan the roof of the hotel behind her, but she stopped herself. That would give her away to the sniper immediately. Instead she casually raised her camera as if taking a photograph. Keeping the camera pointed low, she peered over the top of it and let her gaze travel across the top of the building.

The roof of the hotel was a complicated mix of red tiles, little white spires and three large red domes – one on either end and a larger one in the middle. There was a lot to look at, and no immediate clue as to where the sniper might be located.

'Give me a pointer,' she said quietly to the kid on the other end of the ARCC kit, holding her camera in front of her mouth so nobody could see her lips move.

'See that middle dome?'

'How could I miss it?'

'Look to the right of the dome – about twenty feet.'

She let her gaze wander away from the dome while keeping the camera stationary. Yes, there! A black shape in the shadow of one of those white spires. It was the only flaw in the Christmas-cake perfection of the hotel's facade; like a fly on white icing.

'Got them. Too far away for me to do anything.' She lowered the camera and glanced back at where Mahmoud and the Indian man were now shaking hands warily. They separated, and the man said something to Mahmoud. The Pakistani man nodded, and held the briefcase up. The Indian man nodded as well, and slid the rucksack from his shoulder.

It looked like the exchange was about to take place: Pakistani nuclear secrets for cash. Bex's instructions were to observe but not interfere, and to follow the person who took the nuclear secrets. Mahmoud was known to MI6; the person buying the secrets was not. Her job was to follow him to wherever he was using as a base and try to identify him. The problem was that the unexpected presence of the sniper confused the issue massively. Were they there to kill Mahmoud, or the Indian man? Or were they there just to watch, and kill anyone who tried to interfere with the exchange?

Or, Bex considered with a chill, were they there to kill her?

She felt a tingle right between her shoulder blades, as if a pair of crosshairs was already centred on her fifth thoracic vertebra.

If she moved, if she tried to hide or duck or get out of the way, then the two men exchanging nuclear secrets for cash would immediately know that something was wrong, and they would run for it. She just had to stand there, feeling like a spider was crawling around on her back, and pretend that everything was all right.

'Turn around!' the boy on the other end of the ARCC kit said in a panicked tone of voice; 'I can't see the sniper.'

'More important things to think about,' she murmured. 'I've got a job to do.'

As Mahmoud took the rucksack in one hand and prepared to relinquish the briefcase with the other, the rucksack suddenly seemed to explode. In her earpiece, Kieron gasped in surprise. Scraps of cloth flew everywhere, along with a spray of brightly coloured banknotes that fluttered like butterflies in the hot breeze.

Mahmoud staggered backwards in shock, releasing the rucksack. It fell towards the ground. The other man, the Indian, gazed around in horror, trying to work out what had happened; how the secret meeting had suddenly gone so public and so wrong. He held the briefcase in both hands in front of him, like a shield, obviously worried that the next shots would hit him.

The crowd near them took a few steps back, the way any crowd did when something strange happened. Well, the entire crowd except for two people who actually stepped forward. For a second Bex thought they had spotted the falling cloud of banknotes before anyone else and wanted to get hold of some for themselves. Instead one of them grabbed the briefcase while the other took the Indian man by the back of the neck and squeezed.

As the Indian man fell to the ground with an expression of agony on his face the briefcase was wrenched from his grasp. The two people turned to leave. It was only then that Bex saw them clearly: young, one male and one female. The

41

man had short blond hair while the woman had her blonde hair pulled back in a plait. They were wearing anonymous clothes of the kind you could get from any camping store: lightweight jackets and loose canvas trousers.

'They look like the men who took your friend,' Kieron said suddenly. 'They could all be part of the same family.'

'Or the same organisation,' Bex said quietly. Her mind raced, sorting facts, possibilities and speculations.

The whole situation was in flux anyway, so she felt no compunction about turning around and staring at the hotel's facade. Where previously she had seen something that might have been a person's head, and possibly a gun, now there was nothing. The sniper had vanished.

CHAPTER THREE

The young blond-haired couple – the man and the woman – were almost at the edge of the crowd surrounding the great arch of the Gateway of India now. Kieron could only work out where they were because the glasses had thoughtfully put two arrows above their heads, like something in a computer game, so that he could keep track of them. Threat markers, he thought. If only real life came with something like that. It would be nice to go into a skate park, or a shopping arcade, and immediately have all the chavs and the bullies marked out so he could avoid them.

'Where are they?' Bex asked urgently.

'Heading past the corner of the hotel, towards the road,' he replied.

Bex's vision suddenly shifted, making Kieron feel sick. There must be a trick to this, he thought. Maybe travel-sickness tablets. She was looking along the line of the hotel roof now. The sniper had vanished. There wasn't even a threat marker to show that they might have ducked below the roof line. Actually, Kieron realised, if the camera in Bex's glasses hadn't been pointed at the sniper for a while then the computer system would have no idea where they might have gone. It did have its limitations, then. It wasn't magic – just technology.

'I was right,' she said, looking back towards the edge of the crowd. 'It *was* a diversion. I need to get after them.'

She started moving, but the picture in Kieron's glasses suddenly shifted as if she'd tripped again, or been grabbed. She looked around. The man who, until a few seconds before, had been holding the rucksack stood behind her, his hand on her shoulder. He'd obviously only been unconscious for a few seconds. Now he looked angry and scared, as well as in pain. Kieron wasn't surprised. The man had just lost what was almost certainly atomic secrets belonging to the Pakistani government, and he hadn't even got any cash in return in order to start a new life for himself in hiding. His life was probably going to be very short and very painful if his bosses got hold of him. If Kieron had learned one thing from action movies, it was that.

'Where did they take the briefcase?' he said, his voice high-pitched. 'I have to get it back!'

'It's gone,' Bex's voice said. She reached up and casually moved his hand off her shoulder. She must have been putting pressure on a nerve, because Mahmoud winced.

'Please,' he said, 'you do not understand. If I do not get that briefcase back –'

'Let's be clear – you were giving the briefcase to your terrorist contact,' Bex said. 'The only thing you've lost is that envelope full of rupees. Or was it dollars? So much easier to spend, dollars. So much easier to take out of the country if you're starting a life somewhere else, which I'm guessing was your next step.'

On the screen Kieron was watching, a beige box appeared. The text in the box read: *The Indian rupee is named after the silver coin, rupiya, first issued by Sultan Sher Shah Suri in the 16th century and later continued by the Mughal Empire. The current exchange rate is 81.06 Indian rupees to the pound, or 66.71 India rupees to the dollar.*

This thing would be so great for doing his homework. This thing would be brilliant. Then again, it obviously had a problem in deciding what information was relevant and what wasn't.

Bex's words interrupted his thoughts. 'Who was your contact?' she said. Kieron swiped the currency information away, conscious that in the real world of the shopping mall he actually sat in it probably looked like he was trying to swat a fly.

'I don't know what you mean!' Mahmoud said defensively, trying to pull away. She still held his hand tightly. Kieron could see his skin turning pale under the pressure. His thumb seemed to be twisted back at a strange angle as well.

'Your name is Fahim Mahmoud and you work for the Pakistani Atomic Energy Commission,' she continued. 'You made a deal with a terrorist group to hand over your country's nuclear secrets for cash, but they've just betrayed you. The secrets are gone and the money is gone. I want to know which terrorist group recruited you, and who your contact is.'

'My people will kill me if I go back!' he squealed.

'Not actually my problem, but I can arrange for the British government to take you in. Just give me the group and the contact.'

Mahmoud's face was slick with sweat. 'I honestly do not know. They sent me a text from an unidentified mobile phone. They offered me money – so much money! – for just a little information. Not even information on our atomic energy programme –'

'Your atomic *military* programme,' Bex corrected.

'– but just some geographical locations. Places where these devices were stored.'

'And you agreed to it?' There was frank disbelief in Bex's voice. 'What are you – some kind of moron?'

Mahmoud succeeded in looking sullen and embarrassed at the same time. 'I have an American girlfriend,' he said. 'I wanted to have some work done on my teeth, and –' he indicated his receding hair – 'perhaps some of those implants I read about in magazines.'

'You *are* a moron,' Bex said, releasing his hand, 'but we can use you.' She indicated the hotel behind her with her thumb. 'Get a room in there under the name . . .'

She trailed off suddenly, as if waiting for something. Kerion suddenly realised she was waiting for him, or, rather, for Bradley to give her information.

His fingers rippled in the air as he typed *Find name of Pakistani footballer* into the virtual keyboard. He didn't know why he'd thought of footballers – he hated football – but it was better than just trying to make a name up, or getting the computer to make one up.

Another beige screen appeared in Kieron's field of vision. *Mohsin Ali: Pakistani national squad. More information?*

'Mohsin Ali,' he said.

'Mohsin Ali,' Bex repeated. 'Wait there. Someone will contact you.'

She gave Mahmoud a little push on the shoulder. He staggered away, staring back at her with fear.

'Thanks for that,' Bex muttered. She swung around again and glanced towards the edge of the crowd. 'Can you still see the two with the briefcase?'

There were still two arrows pointing at a couple of figures standing by the side of a fence that seemed to run around an area of grass. One of them had a hand raised. 'Yes, just. I think they're trying to hail a taxi.'

'Then I'd better get after them. They're the only real leads we've got. Can you stay with me?'

A thrill ran through him. 'Of course.'

Something touched his arm in the real world.

'Just let me sort something out,' he added. 'Go towards that park ahead of you. I'll keep you updated.'

It was a strange mental adjustment to look through the images that were projected onto the lenses of the glasses, but he managed it. Sam was staring at him.

'Where are you?' he asked. 'When you've got those things on?'

'I can't tell you,' Kieron said, 'but there's someone on the other end of these glasses who needs my help.'

Sam raised a sceptical eyebrow. 'Did you actually hear what you just said?'

Kieron nodded, smiling weakly. 'I did. But it's true.'

'And so's that.' Sam nodded his head towards the window of the ice-cream shake place they were in.

Outside the window, a man with close-cut white-blond hair stood against the balcony. It was the man that the computer had identified as Kyle Renner. He was looking around the multi-storey open area inside the shopping mall, letting his gaze run over the balconies opposite and the escalators. He seemed to be staring at everybody, checking them out for something.

Checking out whether they were wearing tinted glasses, making strange waving gestures in mid-air and talking to themselves, perhaps. Or, if he had managed to take a look at the mall security recordings, maybe he was looking specifically for the person who had taken the glasses and the earpiece from the floor just after he and his friend had kidnapped Bex's friend, Bradley. Either way, Kieron was in trouble.

'You should go,' he said to Sam.

'Are you talking to me or to her?' Sam asked.

'You, moron.'

'No, seriously, which one?'

He sighed. 'I'm talking to Sam.'

'OK then. No – I'm staying here.'

Sam had that look on his face – that stubborn look that said, *No, I'm not leaving the skate park to go home even though it's dark and my mum and dad will be worried, and No, I'm not going to put this cat down even though it's hissing and clawing at me, and No, I'm not going to pause*

48

the game to go to the toilet even though I've drunk an entire two-litre bottle of soda and my bladder is shortly going to explode. That look.

Kieron had to try anyway. 'This could be dangerous. I don't want to see you hurt.'

Sam folded his arms. 'I don't want to see you hurt either. That's why I'm staying.'

Kieron nodded, and turned his attention back to the glasses. Bex was moving through the crowd towards the two blond-haired briefcase thieves. A taxi had just stopped for them.

'They've got a taxi,' he said urgently.

'Who are you talking to?' Sam and Bex said simultaneously.

'You. Bex.' He took a deep breath. 'Right, Bex – I'm going to have to go offline for a while. The man who took your friend has come back. The couple you're following have just got into a taxi. The licence plate is black with a yellow background, which means it's like an Uber. The number is DN-1L-4262. I'll be back as soon as I can.'

'Wait!' Bex said urgently in his ear. 'There's a security protocol built into the system. If the glasses aren't being used for more than a few minutes they shut down, and you need a passcode to get back in. Type in "MyLittlePony1983".'

'Seriously?' Kieron yelped.

'Bradley's idea. He said nobody would ever guess it.'

Outside the ice-cream shake place Renner suddenly turned around and stared through the window. Kieron barely had time to sweep his hand across his face, taking the glasses off and hiding them beneath the counter. He turned his head sideways to hide the earpiece, then raised his hand and scratched his ear. The earpiece dropped into his palm. He slid it into a pocket along with the glasses.

'Come on,' Kieron said to Sam, 'let's go.' He felt an almost irresistible desire to meet the gaze of the man outside. That would be fatal – literally, he suspected.

The two of them ambled towards the door. As they got there Renner turned and moved towards them, raising his arm. Kieron had to pinch his thigh through his black jeans to stop himself from flinching, but instead of hitting him or trying to grab him Renner took hold of the door. As Kieron and Sam walked away he went into the ice-cream shake place.

'That was close,' Sam murmured. 'Where are we going to go?'

'I think we should go home,' Kieron responded.

'Yours or mine?'

'Your dad's going to be at your place, in front of the TV, and your sisters are going to be around. Not much privacy. We'll go back to my flat.'

'What about your mum?' Sam asked.

'She's working. Won't be back until late.' He could hear the undertone of bitterness in his voice, and he hated it. He sounded – and felt – a lot more grown up than he should be. Than he wanted to be.

Kieron had lost track of time, given all the excitement of connecting with Bex in Mumbai, so when he and Sam left the shopping centre he was surprised to find it was late afternoon. The sky was an overcast slate-grey. The mirrored glass panels that clad the concrete block of the shopping centre reflected the light from the sky. Only the dark edges of the panels were visible, making the block look like the skeleton of something that hadn't been built yet.

He and Sam walked away from the shopping centre and towards the nearby River Tyne. As they crossed the bridge that linked Newcastle to Gateshead – the waters below them only a shade or two darker than the sky – Sam spoke.

'So, this person you're talking to – she's in India?'

'Yes.'

'And she's on some kind of mission – like a secret agent?'

'Yes, exactly like a secret agent.' Kieron slipped the glasses back on, put the earpiece in. Waving his hands in mid-air he summoned up a virtual keyboard that hung in front of his eyes and moved as he walked. He typed the password that Bex had given him into it, feeling slightly embarrassed as he did so. 'I can probably find something out about her and the people she works for with this thing. Give me a moment.'

'You look like a nutter,' Sam said. 'People are staring.'

'We're greebs,' Kieron pointed out. 'People are always staring.'

He was so caught up in reading the text on the virtual screen that he tripped and pitched forward. The real world and the virtual screen and keyboard swirled in front of his eyes. He raised his hands to cushion his fall and felt grit burning his hands as they hit the ground. The air suddenly left his lungs as his full body hit the deck.

'Are you OK?' Sam's voice was full of concern. Kieron could feel Sam's hands trying to turn him over. He brought

51

his own hands up to check that the glasses and the earpiece were still there. Fortunately they hadn't fallen off.

With Sam's assistance he stood back up. The heels of his hands were grazed: shredded skin and little beads of blood.

'Ouch,' he said.

'You need to be careful,' Sam pointed out.

Kieron nodded. 'These things should come with a health-and-safety warning. I'll wait until we get back to my place before I do anything more.'

'You haven't damaged them, have you?'

'I think they're military grade. Probably unbreakable.'

'That's what you said about your iPhone,' Sam muttered.

The rest of the walk took them twenty minutes, past Saltwell Park and into the old red-brick terraces of Low Fell. The houses had once been grand affairs occupied by well-off families, but now they had been separated into flats – ground floor, first floor and sometimes a second floor, with the imposing front doors replaced in many cases by two narrower doors side by side. In some cases the floors of the houses had been subdivided into individual one-room flats, with shared bathrooms and kitchens. He and his mother were lucky enough to have one complete floor of a house: two bedrooms and a small lounge, as well as their own narrow kitchen that you had to walk through to get to the tiny bathroom. The bathroom door slid across the doorway and locked with a sliding bolt that was missing half its screws. Every time Kieron had a bath or used the toilet he worried that his mum, or one of her friends when they came over to share a bottle of wine, might pull too hard on the door handle and wrench the bolt completely off.

His mother wasn't home. He and Sam climbed the stairs to the hall that linked all the rooms together. Ignoring the lounge, they went into his bedroom.

The funny thing about going into a room in your own house with someone else, Kieron thought ruefully, was that you saw it through their eyes rather than your own. He was suddenly painfully aware of the fact that the carpet was invisible: covered with discarded T-shirts, several pairs of black jeans, a couple of coffee mugs and three or four plates with half-eaten meals on them. He suspected there were another couple of plates hidden beneath the bed, but he really didn't want to think about what might be growing on them.

Sam stared at the Fatal Insomnia poster blu-tacked to the wall behind his bed.

'We never did finish working out how we were going to get into the gig,' he pointed out.

'Stuff happened.'

'Yeah.' Sam nodded. 'Strange stuff. You got any cans in the fridge?'

'I think there's some cola. Go and get a couple, will you? And some cheese, if there's any.'

While Sam was gone, Kieron quickly summoned up a keyboard and screen again, partly to check that the system still worked after his fall but also to complete the search he'd been making. By the time Sam came back with two cans and a plastic bag of grated cheddar he'd found what he was looking for.

'OK,' he said, 'the woman I've been talking to is

Rebecca Wilson. Her friend – the one who got taken from the shopping centre – is Bradley Marshall. They're both freelance operatives working under contract to something called SIS-TERR.'

'Does that make her your big SIS-TERR?' Sam asked, raising an eyebrow.

'Shut up,' Kieron said. 'SIS-TERR stands for the Secret Intelligence Service Technology-Enhanced Remote Reinforcement Unit. It looks like the two of them ran a start-up to develop the glasses and the earpiece, demonstrated them to the Secret Intelligence Service – which is what MI6 is really called, apparently – and then got employed full-time on missions. Bex was in the Army for a while, so she's got the training. She goes undercover, and Bradley supports her with information.'

'From a shopping centre in Newcastle?'

'From wherever he wants to be. Or needs to be.'

'Kind of like high-tech mercenaries,' Sam pointed out.

'Yeah, but working for the good guys full-time, it looks like.'

'And can you still see what she's seeing right now?'

Kieron shook his head. 'It's switched off now. I guess if she needs me, she'll call.'

'Needs you?' Sam shook his head sadly. 'Look, mate, she might be working for MI6, but you're not. You know that, don't you?'

Kieron knew that Sam was trying to help, but the words stung. 'She needs help,' Kieron pointed out defensively, 'and her friend has been kidnapped. I don't think she knows who to trust any more. I'm the only person who can feed her the information she needs.'

'You're her last, best hope?' Sam snorted. 'She's in trouble then.' He frowned. 'Hey – if that thing can access top-secret databases, you might be breaking the Official Secrets Act right now. What if her bosses in MI6 can track you back here?'

'I don't think that's going to happen.' Kieron felt less convinced than his words and his tone of voice suggested, but he didn't want Sam to know that. 'The reach-back into the MI6 computers is limited. As far as I can see, I can only access classified stuff related to the mission they've been contracted to do, plus lots of unclassified but difficult to get hold of things like licence plates, blueprints of buildings and personnel records for various companies and organisations. Kind of like a super-Wikipedia.' He waved Sam towards his games console. 'Why don't you play for a while. I want to check on what's happening to Bex.'

'Why do you get to have all the fun?' Sam wanted to know, irritably.

'Hey – at least you'll be able to control where you move, and you can fire guns and stuff at zombies. I'm just a passenger in this thing.'

Sam didn't seem mollified, but he started booting up the console while Kieron reactivated the glasses and earpiece, and yelled as he was suddenly jerked backwards and thrown into a world of vivid colours, blurred, jerky motion and the high-pitched whine of a two-stroke engine.

'Are you OK?' Sam called, concerned.

'Just – acclimatising,' Kieron said tightly.

It looked as if Bex was in a car. No, Kieron corrected himself as she briefly glanced down and he saw her hands gripping a pair of handlebars, she was on a motorcycle. She was driving down a road lined with open shopfronts piled high with baskets of fruit and vegetables, tottering piles of books wrapped in transparent plastic, rolls of brightly printed cloth and all kinds of other things that Kieron couldn't even identify. Her motorcycle – probably a moped, he thought – wove back and forth between various cars – some dusty and battered, some polished and expensive – which were just parked in the road while their drivers negotiated with the shop owners. Up ahead was the taxi that Kieron had seen the two blond-haired thugs get into earlier. Bex held back, keeping them in sight without, hopefully, alerting them to her presence.

'Where did you get the moped from?' he asked, activating his microphone with a small gesture of his hand.

The picture he was watching shifted abruptly as the moped swerved.

'Don't do that!' Bex snapped in his ear.

'Sorry. I wasn't thinking.'

'Where are you now?' she asked. 'Are you safe?'

'We're back at my mum's flat.'

'Is she there?'

'No, she's at work. She won't be back for a couple of hours.'

'What does she do?'

'She works in Human Resources for some big company here in Newcastle. Her department used to be eight people. It's only three now, but the work is still at the same level, so everyone's working massive amounts of overtime, and she doesn't get paid for all of it.'

'That's a shame,' she said, veering around a man just standing in the middle of the street talking on his mobile phone. He gestured angrily at her as she passed, and shouted something.

'It is what it is,' Kieron said philosophically.

'And your dad?'

'Walked out a few years ago.' He laughed, but there was no humour in the sound. 'Mum said he got a better offer from a younger, blonder woman. Actually, "woman" wasn't the word she used.'

'I'm sure.' Bex paused for a moment as she negotiated a cloud of dust thrown up by the wheels of a lorry between her and the taxi.

'So – this moped?' Kieron asked again, not wanting to continue the conversation about his dysfunctional family situation.

'Yes. Someone had left it by the side of the road.'

'Just left it? Really?'

Bex edged her moped sideways so she could see around the lorry. Ahead, the taxi was turning a corner. 'Well, I say "left". They were standing beside it. My need was greater than theirs. Look, I'll leave it somewhere when I've finished with it. The police will return it.'

'Or someone else will steal it,' Kieron pointed out.

'What are you – the voice of my conscience?'

He laughed. 'Just call me Jiminy Cricket.'

'Oh, you've read *Pinocchio*?'

'Seen the film.'

Kieron watched as Bex's hand twisted the accelerator on the handlebar of the moped and undertook the lorry with a burst of speed, then braked as she got to the corner. The lorry driver blared his horn at her.

'The old Disney one?'

'No,' he said. 'The new live-action and CGI remake, with Johnny Depp as Pinocchio.'

'I suddenly feel old,' she muttered.

Ahead, the taxi slowed to a halt. Bex drove casually past it, then came to a stop by an open shopfront stocked, bizarrely, with cages filled with kittens, puppies and small birds. Kieron found himself hoping that it was a pet shop, not a food shop.

Bex set the moped back on its stand. 'Right,' she said, 'let's see what these two are doing.'

CHAPTER FOUR

The Mumbai street was a riot of colour and scent. Wherever Bex looked, people were wearing brightly coloured shirts or saris. Behind them were open shopfronts stacked up with fruit and vegetables, tottering piles of books wrapped in plastic sheeting, and animals – kittens, puppies and parrots in tiny cages. The shops competed with each other to have the most attention-grabbing awnings, and above them were massive posters advertising beauty products, electronic devices and, strangely, local politicians with gleaming white smiles. Or perhaps they were toothpaste adverts; it was difficult to tell. But while her eyes were being dazzled by the confusion of sights, her nose was being assaulted by the smell of a hundred different spices – some of which were piled up in heaps in bowls in front of the shops, so vivid they almost glowed. The symphony of spice scents overlaid but didn't quite disguise the smell of rotting vegetables and sewage that seemed to characterise that part of Mumbai. And – she frowned – she thought she could smell . . . yes, fresh laundry. Washing powder. How strange.

The street to which she'd followed the briefcase thieves

was clogged with traffic: a combination of battered old cars, shiny new ones and three-wheeled motorised auto-rickshaws. They had an enclosed cabin to keep off the rain, but no doors, and there was only room for the driver up front. In the back the passengers sat on a padded bench.

She looked around, trying to seem like a tourist while the two blond-haired thieves paid their taxi driver, but genuinely fascinated by the whole look and feel of the city. She'd travelled widely in Asia during her gap year, but she'd missed out on India – replacing it with Indonesia and Thailand. This, from what she could see, was the *real* Mumbai – not the old Victorian part left behind by the English when they pulled out of India or the pretty bits that the visitors wanted to see, but the areas where the people who actually called the city home lived their day-to-day lives.

She could hear, above the cries of street vendors and the buzz of motorcycle and moped engines, a regular slapping sound. She couldn't see what was causing it. Still distracted by the smell of washing powder, she crossed the pavement from where she had left her moped (well, the moped she had temporarily borrowed) towards a chest-high brick wall plastered with posters telling anyone who passed about local dance festivals, religious events and concerts. It was the kind of wall that, in England, would have given a view of a train track or a river below. That's what Bex expected now, but what she saw was so unusual, so Indian, that she couldn't help but smile.

It looked like a river probably did flow down there, at right angles to the street, but it was almost impossible to see it thanks to the hundreds of lines of washing that had been strung across it. They receded into the distance, looking like some bizarre spider's web in which various scraps of coloured paper had been caught. Bex could just about make out, through the flapping clothes, sheets and pillowcases, that the slanting banks of the river had been covered with concrete. Where the water should have been was a mass of soapy bubbles, and the concrete thronged with women, all dressed in saris, who were busy dipping more clothes and bedding into the soapy water, pulling them out, twisting them into ropes and then hitting them against the concrete as hard as they could to expel the water. That explained the slapping noise she had heard. Once the women had got as much water as they could out of the clothes, they hung them up on the lines to let them dry in the heat, although given the humidity Bex suspected that there was almost as much water in the air as in the massive outdoor laundry she had found. Seeing the preponderance of sheets and pillowcases, Bex assumed that most of the hotels in Mumbai probably sent their dirty washing here to be cleaned. It certainly made her wonder if the sheet she had slept on the night before – the sheet she had assumed had been through a thorough wash since the last hotel guest had slept on it – had actually been dipped in a soapy river and hit against concrete to get it clean.

India. What a country.

She turned her head to glance towards the two blond thieves, but a small man with mahogany-coloured skin and jet-black hair stood in front of her. Most of his front teeth were missing.

'You need a tourist guide?' he asked in accented English. 'I show you the best places. I show you the places that nobody else knows about. I get you in everywhere. Many friends in many museums and art galleries.'

She smiled, and held up her hand, palm outward. 'No thank you,' she said firmly. 'I know where I am going.'

She tried to step past him, towards where the taxi was pulling away from the kerb, but the man caught her arm.

'Nobody better than me in Mumbai!' he said. 'Best tourist guide ever.'

'No,' she said firmly. She pulled her arm away and kept moving, turning her head slightly so she could see out of the corner of her eye what he was doing. He started after her for a moment, an ugly snarl flashing across his face, then shrugged and moved on, looking for another victim.

Begging seemed to be a constant thing in Mumbai – or, at least, in this area. Women in saris and shawls moved along the road from car to car, extending their hands and beseeching the drivers for *'bahkshish!'* – which, she assumed, meant 'money'. Some of them were holding babies, while others had burns on their arms or scars on their faces.

A voice in her earpiece surprised her. 'They look like they're begging for themselves, but they're almost certainly part of a gang.' It was Kieron. The sound of a familiar voice made her feel slightly less alone and vulnerable. It also reminded her of Bradley. The action of the past hour or so – the theft of the briefcase of atomic secrets, the following of the taxi and now the reconnaissance here – had pushed the thought to the back of her mind, but now she had a moment of relative peace it was right at the front again. She had to find Bradley, and get him away from the people who had kidnapped him, but how? She couldn't tell her bosses back in SIS-TERR because the abductors appeared to have a link to them. And, to make it worse, she was stuck here in Mumbai on a mission with only a teenage stranger back in England to help her.

'Where are you?' she said in the end.

'Still at my flat.'

She asked the question that bothered her the most. 'Any sign of the guys who took Bradley? Did they actually come back to look for you?'

'One of them did. We managed to evade him.'

She breathed a sigh of relief. At least that was something. Deciding what to do about that could wait until the present business was complete.

'Looks like you're in a market,' Kieron said through her earpiece. 'Is that where you followed your two suspects?'

'They aren't suspects,' Bex pointed out. 'They actually stole the briefcase. I saw them. But yes, I've followed them here.'

'Let me just –' Kieron said, then: 'Oh, this thing's like the best guidebook ever. I can call up details of the best-value cafes, local customs, things to avoid saying or doing – it even has a translator function!'

'I don't want a cafe,' she pointed out. 'Not yet, anyway.'

She heard a snort of astonishment through the earpiece. 'Oh, that's just wrong.'

'What's that?' The two blond thieves had moved off the

pavement now, and she walked along the row of shopfronts towards where they had been.

'Apparently those women begging can actually rent babies to carry around with them so they get more sympathy and more money! What kind of mother would rent her baby out to be carried around the streets?'

In the background Bex thought she heard another voice – the mysterious Sam? – say: 'My mum would.' She winced, hoping it was a joke.

Up ahead, set back a little from the road, and raised above it by a handful of wide steps, Bex suddenly saw something incredible. It was so out of place, so garish, that she caught her breath. It had to be a place of religious worship, but it looked more like something out of a flu hallucination than any church she was used to. The columns and arches in front of the wide-open main door were, she supposed, a bit like the gothic architecture of St Paul's Cathedral or Westminster Abbey, but they were painted in pastel colours – soft pink, calm light blue, gentle lavender and marine turquoise. They also had figures carved into them, but not the gargoyles or religious figures that a church in England would have. No, these looked like dancers in skimpy costumes, ready for a party.

The tops of the arches were scalloped instead of smooth, as if someone had gone around with a huge hole punch and taken semi-circular chunks out of the stonework every few inches, and most of the upper floors glittered and gleamed with gold paint. The windows on the upper floors were narrow, like those in a castle, and as she looked further up she could see that the entire edifice ended in a series of domes. They weren't the regular, hemispherical domes you'd get in Western buildings though – they were taller, thinner at the base, more like the shape of some poisonous toadstools. They too were painted gold.

With some difficulty, Bex pulled her gaze back to ground level, and she realised that nothing she had just seen could compare with the sheer bizarreness of the fact that on either side of the temple sat a statue of an elephant.

The statues were about three times her height – so probably life-sized. The skin of the creatures had been painted a greyish blue, but they were draped in sculpted blankets, painted red and gold, that fastened underneath their bellies with sculpted buckles. Their eyes didn't look anything like the eyes of elephants she'd seen on television, and once on a trip to Africa. Normal elephants had small, orange eyes set in wrinkled and cracked flesh. The eyes on these statues were like exaggerated human eyes – white corneas surrounding bright blue irises and black pupils. They even had lashes – huge lashes, like something from *Strictly Come Dancing* or an early Disney movie – and a cheeky little gleam.

'I do not believe it,' Kieron's voice said in a hushed tone.

'It's real,' Bex said, although she wasn't completely convinced.

'Apparently this is a Jain temple. Hey, I didn't know any of this, but the information's coming up now. Jainism is an ancient religion, mainly in India but with offshoots around the world. Jains believe in non-violence and love towards all living beings, open-mindedness and non-attachment to possessions. They believe so much in non-violence that they are all vegetarians and they'll even pick spiders up and take them out of their houses rather than kill them. Some Jains won't eat potatoes and carrots and stuff, because they think that the vegetables feel pain when they're pulled out of the ground.' After a pause, he added, 'Somehow, I don't think Jain fundamentalism is a thing. I doubt there are any Jain terrorists.'

'Then why have two probable terrorists just gone inside?' Bex asked.

'The computer says it has no idea.'

Two middle-aged Western tourists – a man and a woman – emerged from the open main doors as Bex arrived there and stopped. They were both carrying cameras. They stopped and bent down, and Bex realised they had left their shoes outside while they looked around. That was probably a mark of respect, but at least it told her that she could go inside and not look out of place. 'I'm going to go in and see what's going on,' she said.

As she walked up the steps and got to the door she bent down and slipped her trainers off.

'It's well worth it,' the man who had just emerged from the temple said to her as he straightened up. He spoke with an American accent.

'It's beautiful!' the woman said. 'So much care and attention devoted to it!'

Bex smiled briefly and moved on.

Just inside the doorway she saw a life-sized statue of a

man sitting cross-legged on a pedestal. The statue had been painted to give him dark brown skin. His eyes were closed and his hands were folded in his lap. For a moment she'd thought the man was real and alive, until she saw the gleam of varnish and the cracks around the neck and forehead. Bex stopped for a moment, feeling a sudden urge to bow her head respectfully. As she did so, a woman in white robes who entered just behind her smiled and nodded. She, too, bowed her head to the statue, and Bex thought she heard the woman whispering, 'Nishihi, nishihi, nishihi.'

The inside of the temple was large and airy, and surprisingly cool compared to outside. Monks in white or orange robes moved silently across the tiled floor. The walls and columns inside were as colourful as those outside, and when Bex glanced up she saw the interior of one of the domes, patterned with small multicoloured tiles that made it look like the inside of a kaleidoscope.

She moved around the inside of the temple, trying to look like a tourist but keeping watch for the two thieves. Whenever she passed one of the monks they bowed politely to her, and she bowed to them. Strangely – or perhaps not, given the nature of the place – several hens also strutted around as if they owned the place. In a city the size of Mumbai, with something like twelve million hungry inhabitants who considered cows sacred and pigs dirty, this was probably the only place they felt safe, Bex thought.

The inner space of the temple had a colonnade around its edge. Doors in the walls gave access to other rooms. Bex checked several of the rooms, looking as innocent and touristy as she could. The first few she tried seemed to be meditation spaces, with people kneeling or sitting cross-legged with their eyes closed. Or perhaps they were more statues; she couldn't tell. Another door gave access to a large but secluded garden area, with paths of cracked paving slabs and dry-looking grass. Bushes and cherry trees lined it, and behind them a wall ran all the way around the edge. The next door led onto a narrow stairway that led upward. She listened for a moment, but she couldn't hear anyone up there. She was beginning to believe that the thieves had gone straight through the temple, into the garden and away into the bustling city, secure in the knowledge that they had shaken off any pursuers, when she came to the next door. Assuming it was another meditation space or suchlike, she stepped into a small, square room and found the two thieves standing in front of a table on which the briefcase sat, open. The contents – several sheets of A4 paper – had been removed and were spread out on the table. The male thief was taking photographs of the papers with his mobile phone.

'Oh, I'm sorry,' she said automatically, 'I thought this was part of the tour.'

'This is private,' the blond man said. He had a rough, raspy voice. He quickly held a mobile to his head, as if he was just about to make a call, or had just completed one.

'Sorry,' Bex said again, and backed away, trying her best to put a polite smile on her face. As she went she tried to take in as many details of the room as possible. A laptop sat on the floor, plugged into some kind of portable charging device and a Wi-Fi router.

'Very clever,' Kieron said in her earpiece. 'Who in a Jain temple is going to complain about intruders? The monks are so polite they'd just smile at them and let them get on with whatever they're doing. It's the perfect cover.'

The blonde woman stared at Bex challengingly. Her hair had been pulled into a high ponytail which made her face look tight and dangerous. 'Hey, I've seen her before,' she said to her companion. 'She was at the Gateway when we got the briefcase.'

'Are you sure?' The man scowled at Bex.

'She was looking at us. Right at us.'

The man's lips twisted into a snarl. 'We've been identified. Get her! I'll secure the case.'

The woman came towards Bex, her hand moving to the small of her back. Whether she was reaching for a knife, a gun or some other weapon, Bex didn't intend hanging around long enough to find out. She turned and ran, all pretence of being a tourist thrown to the wind.

Bex's bare feet slapped against the tiles as she sprinted across the open area of the temple for the main door. Monks looked over to see what was going on, their faces showing the shock they felt at the violation of their tranquil temple. Bex felt an almost irresistible desire to shout, 'I'm sorry!' as she ran, but managed to suppress it. Hens scattered before her in a flurry of feathers and clucking.

She could hear the thud of the woman's shoes as she tried to catch up with Bex. It sounded like she wore boots. No respecter of the temple's customs then.

Bex got to the door, but the wall by her head suddenly

exploded in a cloud of sharp stone fragments. She hadn't heard a shot: the woman must be using a silencer. If she went through the doorway now she'd be a perfect target, outlined in the light from outside for enough time that the woman could put a bullet in her back. Instead she jinked sideways, behind one of the pillars, and sprinted along the colonnade that ran around the outside of the temple space.

She passed another of the life-size statues just as a bullet smashed its forehead open. No point in going into the meditation rooms: she'd be trapped there, and she'd be endangering the lives of the Jains who were in there. She could see the door leading to the stairs across a corner of the open space, half hidden by a column. Should she head for there?

'I've got the plans of the temple up,' Kieron said urgently in her ear. 'Don't go upstairs. There's only one stairway and the windows are too narrow to escape through. You'll be trapped.'

'Thanks,' she muttered, and changed course.

The doorway leading to the garden appeared up ahead. She ran straight for it.

Bex pelted through the doorway and into the garden. A trio of Japanese tourists was heading towards her, along one of the paths. She ran through them, scattering them like the hens earlier. A cherry tree up ahead had branches that extended over the wall. She leaped for the lower branches, pulling herself up and into the foliage and the blossoms.

She heard the sound of boots on the paving slabs. That had to be the woman chasing her. Nobody else in the temple apart from her and her companion would be wearing footwear.

The footsteps slowed to a halt. Bex imagined the woman looking around, holding the gun ready to fire. The leaves and the flowers were shielding her: if she tried to get up to the top branches and over the wall now the woman would hear her. Even if the woman couldn't see her, she could still fire into the leaves and she'd almost certainly hit Bex. Instead, Bex stayed where she was, perched on one branch and holding on to another for stability. She tried to breathe slowly.

More footsteps. It sounded as if the woman with the gun was standing by the tree trunk now.

A cherry blossom beside Bex's nose was giving out a strong scent. She felt a tickling in her nose. She wanted to sneeze. The feeling was building up and building up. It was almost unbearable now. Slowly, Bex bought her free hand up to her face and held her nose tight. Gradually the feeling subsided.

More footsteps, getting quieter as the woman moved away. The sound of the footsteps changed as the woman went back into the temple again.

Bex counted to twenty, just to make sure, then began to scramble up the branches to the top of the tree. She glanced over the wall, seeing a narrow alley with a rivulet of dirty water running down it. A mangy cat prowled, looking for food. Bex clambered onto the wall. Holding onto the brickwork at the top, she gradually let herself down, feet pressed against the wall, until only a drop of a couple of feet separated her from the muddy alley.

The brickwork beneath her fingers crumbled.

She fell the last few feet and landed on her back in the mud. The cat yowled and ran. Although her back hurt, she couldn't afford to relax. She turned over and scrambled to her feet. Somewhere outside the front of the temple her trainers were sitting demurely – assuming they hadn't been stolen by now. She couldn't go back for them: it would be an obvious place for the thieves to wait and set a trap.

She began to squelch her way along the alleyway, away from the temple wall.

'Anything I can do?' Kieron asked uncertainly in her ear.

'Find me a shop where I can get some trainers,' she said tiredly. 'Oh, and a replacement shirt. This one is soaked.'

An hour later she felt much better. She'd bought new trainers, changed her hairstyle and replaced her shirt with something very different in style. She'd dumped the muddy one in a bin on the street. As she walked away from the bin she heard a scuffling sound behind her. Turning her head, she saw three scruffy Indian children pulling the shirt out and fighting over it. They were pulling so hard it looked likely to tear.

Not her problem. At least she'd changed her appearance. If the briefcase thieves were still looking for her, they'd be looking for someone with different hair and a differently coloured shirt. She'd even managed to find some gel insoles in a pharmacy. Slid into the new trainers, they altered the way she walked. Not obviously, but she'd been trained to identify people by the way they walked, and she presumed the briefcase thieves had been given the same kind of training by whoever they were working for. If she had to run anywhere then she might have to take the insoles out and throw them away, but for the moment they were a part of her disguise.

It was a shame she still had to wear the sunglasses. They'd been made to look as anonymous as possible, but if she'd been able to she would have ditched them and replaced them with something with more bling, something that would have changed the look of her face. The trouble was, they were her link back to England, and help. If Kieron could actually be described as 'help'.

Now she sat in a coffee shop, sipping a flat white that had, according to the barista, been made with cardamom added to the ground coffee. It tasted rather good.

Somewhere in her earpiece Kieron was telling her about cardamom. She'd turned the volume down, to give herself time to think. He was still enthusiastic about the technology, like a kid with a Christmas present. The trouble was, she didn't know what to do next.

She suddenly realised that Kieron had gone quiet as if he was waiting for an answer. She touched the earpiece, turning up the volume again. 'Sorry – did you say something?'

'I said: would you rather I kept quiet for a while? You seem distracted.'

'No. Well, yes.' She sighed. 'Look, you've got yourself into a dangerous situation, and I need to get you out of it.'

'OK.' He didn't sound convinced. 'Look, you're in India and I'm in Newcastle. You can't actually do anything to stop me helping you, can you?'

'I can tell my superiors that you've got the agent-handling kit,' she bluffed.

'That would get me into trouble, and I don't think you want to do that.' His tone was reasonable, and he made a good point; she had to give him marks for that. 'And besides, you suspect that one of your superiors is responsible for the thugs that took your friend Bradley. If you tell the wrong person then you're exposing yourself, and putting me in danger.' Another good point.

'I could tell the police.' That one was a gamble, but she couldn't think of anything better in a hurry.

'They'd think you'd made it up. A secret agent operating abroad but being fed information by a teenager in Newcastle? There's no way they'd send anybody round to the flat to impound the kit from me.' He paused momentarily. 'Besides, I'm the one with the information goggles, not you. You don't even know where I live.'

'Fair enough,' she said, and took a sip of her coffee. 'What are my chances of persuading you to just pop the glasses and the earpiece in an envelope and post them somewhere?'

'Zero. I'm having far too much fun, and you need my help. Now – treat me like I'm Bradley. What do we do?'

She sighed. 'OK: we have three problems, if we ignore the fact that highly expensive and top-secret technology has got into the hands of a couple of teenagers.'

'Don't push it,' he said, but he sounded amused.

'The first problem is that Bradley's been taken prisoner or hostage by these "Blood and Soil" right-wing fanatics in Newcastle. They might be hurting him, torturing him for information.' The thought made her queasy.

'But you think one of your bosses is linked to Blood and Soil. I checked that number plate using the glasses. It's linked to a firm that's actually a front for MI6.'

'We've been over that.'

'Yes, but you're missing the point. The traitor inside MI6 would know everything that Bradley knows, wouldn't they?'

Bex would've hit her own forehead, but it would have attracted too much attention in the coffee bar. 'You're right. So – why did they take him?' Before Kieron could reply she came up with the answer herself. 'They needed to disrupt our mission so that the thieves here could steal the briefcase from Fahim.'

'That's right.' Kieron sounded pleased with himself. 'They weren't expecting me to pick up the kit and help you chase the thieves.'

She felt better now. Bradley might not have been safe, but at least he wasn't being tortured. Probably.

'That means,' she went on, making the connections in her mind as fast as she spoke, 'that the briefcase thieves and the thugs who took Bradley are all part of the same plot or organisation.'

'I think we knew that from the way they looked,' Kieron said. 'All blond and clean-cut.'

'So if I can somehow find them here in Mumbai, I can find out what they're doing and perhaps, perhaps, get them to tell me who the traitor is back in MI6. Then we can get the traitor to tell me where Bradley is being held.'

'Good idea.' Kieron sounded smug, as if he'd just received an A on his homework.

Bex felt her mood deflating. 'The problem is they'll have cleared out of the Jain temple, and probably eradicated any clues as to where they might have relocated. I don't know where they might be now.'

'I can help with that,' Kieron said, sounding even smugger.

'How?'

'Firstly, remember the person on the hotel roof – the one with the telescopic rifle who created the distraction that enabled the thieves to take the briefcase? They might have left some clue on the roof that would identify them.'

Bex thought about that for a moment. 'Unlikely,' she mused, 'but possible. It's a long shot though. Do you have anything else?'

'I do. Remember those sheets of paper on the table in the temple?'

Bex cast her mind back. The briefcase had been open, and the papers had been on the table. The male thief was photographing them with his mobile phone. 'Yes, I do, but they'll have been taken away by now.'

'Yes, but I found out how to record stuff through the camera in your glasses. I photographed him photographing the papers.'

'So we can identify him?' Bex was dubious.

'No.' Kieron's levels of smugness were becoming irritating now. 'So I could take the bit of the image where the papers were, enlarge it and read what's on the sheets. I could only see the top few, and they were in some foreign language, but I bet I can get your computer thing to translate them. Hopefully it'll tell us what the thieves are trying to do, and that'll help us locate them.'

'Kieron,' Bex said, 'I take it all back. You're a genius.'

'I know,' he said. 'And there's one more thing.'

She felt a small bud of unease begin to flower in her mind. 'What?'

'Sam and I are going to go and get your friend Bradley back from Blood and Soil.'

CHAPTER FIVE

'I absolutely forbid it,' Bex said in the same tone of voice that Kieron's mum used when she told him he couldn't go into Newcastle city centre at eleven o'clock at night to see his friends.

'Look,' Kieron said, trying to sound adult and reasonable, 'we're here, and Bradley is here, and you're in India.' He threw in a phrase he'd heard on TV, hoping it made him sound like he knew what he was doing. 'We've got "boots on the ground". Who else is going to help get Bradley away from these thugs?' He decided to apply a little bit of pressure. 'Who knows what they're doing to him right now? We're his last, best hope!'

'Kieron, you're just a *kid*. I can't get you and Sam involved – not like that. I mean, at the moment you're just sitting in a room somewhere, talking to me and helping me out, and believe me I appreciate the help. I wouldn't have been able to get this far without it. The trouble is, trying to get Bradley back is *risky*. You'd be putting yourself out there, where Blood and Soil can find you.' Bex sounded genuinely agonised, and Kieron felt a wave of guilt crash over him at the way he was trying to manipulate her.

Kieron opened his mouth to point out that Blood and Soil were already looking for him and Sam, based on the thug they'd seen back in the shopping mall, but he decided not to. That might just make things worse. Bex might stop all contact if he reminded her of that.

'Let me sort it out from here,' she said. 'As soon as I can work out who in MI6 to trust, I'll alert them and they can get Bradley out. Now, I've got things to do. Give me a few hours without any contact, OK?'

'OK.' Reluctantly he pressed the *Disengage* button on the side of the glasses.

'So we're going to do *what*?' Sam asked, eyebrows raised.

Kieron tried not to meet Sam's gaze. 'We're going to expand the image of the briefcase thieves and their pile of papers, and see if we can pick up any evidence that will help us work out what their plan is and where they might have gone,' he said casually. 'That way Bex can complete her mission and everyone lives happily ever after. Except the bad guys, obviously.'

'You know what I mean,' Sam growled. 'The next bit. The bit about rescuing your girlfriend's mate from right-wing extremists.'

'She's not my girlfriend!' Kieron exclaimed, aghast. 'I've never even met her!'

'OK, your virtual big sister, or whatever you want to call her. We're going to rescue her mate?'

'Yes.'

'From right-wing extremists?'

'Again, yes.'

'Even though she clearly just told you not to do that?'

'Still, yes.'

Sam fell silent for a while, staring at Kieron. 'You *have* spotted the flaw in your plan, haven't you?'

Kieron shrugged. 'We're teenagers with no experience of rescue missions, and we can't fight to save our lives?'

'That's the one.'

Kieron sighed. 'Look, we're the only people in the UK apart from the people who took him who know that Bex's friend Bradley has been taken prisoner, right?' He hesitated a moment. 'Well, presumably he knows, but that's kind of irrelevant at the moment. We're the only people in the UK who know and can do anything about it.'

Sam nodded reluctantly. 'Right.'

'And if we tell the police about it, they'll just pat us on the head and tell us to go away, right?'

'Again – right.'

'And we have possession – accidentally – of a powerful set of augmented-reality computing equipment that enables us to access information that's normally only available to spies and secret agents, right?'

Sam winced, and rubbed the bridge of his nose. 'I don't like where this is going, but right.'

'So who else is better placed to find this Bradley bloke and get him out of where he's being held?'

'Your argument impresses me,' Sam said. 'Please subscribe me to your YouTube channel.' He shook his head. 'OK – two things you have to agree to before we go ahead.'

'Go on then.' Kieron felt a wave of affection for his friend. Sam was endlessly practical, and he would always have Kieron's back. Always. Much as he hated to admit it. They'd been friends for as long as he could remember – their mothers had been in adjacent beds in the local hospital when they were pregnant, they'd got into emo music at exactly the same time and Sam hadn't even minded when he found out that Kieron fancied his sister. They were, and always would be, best friends.

'First, we find out where this Bradley bloke is, and then we have a sensible and mature discussion about whether he is, in fact, rescuable by two teenage greebs. Agreed?'

'Agreed.' Kieron couldn't help but smile at the way the tables had turned. A minute ago it had been him listing the elements of an argument and Sam reluctantly agreeing with them. Now it was the other way around.

'Second, when we – or someone else – get this Bradley bloke out of wherever he is, he takes over that augmented-reality computer kit and we walk away.'

That condition made Kieron think for a minute. He didn't want to walk away from all of this, from Bex and her mission in India, but he knew that he was only part of it due to an accidental combination of circumstances. He was probably the last person who ought to be helping a secret agent. He hated sports, and he didn't know anything about politics. There were much better trained people out there – this Bradley being one of them. And if he tried to continue, if he still tried to be a part of this world that he'd inadvertently stumbled into, then he might actually put Bex's life at risk. He couldn't in all conscience do that.

'Agreed,' he said.

Sam nodded. 'All right then – where do we start?'

'The first thing we do is get that information off the image for Bex so she can do her job.' Kieron considered. 'OK, although these glasses have a really good resolution for the augmented-reality images they display, I think we're better off downloading the image and putting it on a bigger screen.' He pointed across to his desk, where his computer sat. It had been a Christmas present from his mother. It was expensive – even if it was second-hand – and he knew in his heart it was partly an unspoken apology for the fact she spent so much time away working and partly also a bribe so he accepted the fact that she would be working hard for the foreseeable future. He knew that she didn't want things to be this way, but he also knew *why* things had to be this way – she was working hard to earn money to keep them going. He also loved the computer so he wasn't going to complain. The keyboard lit up when it was switched on, the keys outlined in green, and there were LEDs inside the case that could be seen through a transparent panel. 'You open it and get a picture editor up while I work out how to email this picture to myself.'

Actually, once he'd located the directory structure where the picture of the two briefcase thieves had been stored, emailing it was just a matter of selecting it, waving his hands until a menu appeared, then selecting the option to email it and typing his email address into the virtual keyboard that appeared in front of him.

'Aren't you afraid of the wrong people getting hold of your email address and finding out who you are?' Sam asked as Kieron's computer pinged to say that an email had arrived.

'It's a Gmail account,' Kieron pointed out. 'I'm emohead257@gmail.com. It's already relatively anonymous, but if there's any sign that people are looking at it I'll just junk it and use another email address. I'm emohead258 and emohead259 as well. Covering the bases.'

Sam nodded approvingly. 'That's neat. And a little bit creepy as well. I didn't realise your paranoia went so far that you have three email addresses. You're worse than me.' He opened Kieron's email program and selected one of the messages that had just arrived. 'Oh, you've got several things here from game companies, and – oh, interesting – you've got a message from Naomi!'

'That's private!' Kieron said quickly. 'Don't open it!'

'Is that Naomi who we see down in the city centre sometimes – the one with the green edges to her hair?'

'She probably just wants to know where we are.' He could feel his heart beating faster. When he saw that Sam had opened up the top message – the one with the graphics file that he'd just sent himself, he relaxed a little and continued: 'I actually have eight email addresses. Only three of them are on Gmail.' He tapped the side of the glasses. 'If you ever doubted that Big Brother was watching you then these things should make you reconsider, mate.'

'Just because Big Brother *can* watch you, it doesn't mean he does.' Sam turned from his typing and grinned at Kieron. 'Besides, in your case it's Big Sister, surely?'

'Yeah, very funny.' Kieron crossed the bedroom and stood over Sam's shoulder. The picture editor he'd installed so he could make memes and stuff for the Internet had opened the graphic file. The picture was exactly the way he remembered the scene: the two blond thieves standing over a table with the stolen briefcase open, and a pile of A4 sheets beside it.

Sam frowned. 'You know what? They look just like those people who march through Newcastle city centre every now and then demanding that all the migrants go back to where they came from.'

'Ignoring the fact that most of the people who work in the corner stores and Indian restaurants come from families that have been here for longer than they have,' Kieron pointed out. 'OK – try zooming in on that pile of papers.'

Sam created a box around the papers and clicked the mouse. The screen instantly refreshed with a close-up of the papers. Several sheets had visible writing on them. The pixelation was hardly noticeable. 'That's a good-quality lens she's got in her glasses,' he observed.

'That writing just looks like squiggles to me,' Kieron said, leaning closer. 'Zoom in further.'

Sam repeated his actions. The paper now filled the screen.

'The reason that writing looks like squiggles,' Sam said after a few seconds of intently staring at it, 'is that it's in a foreign language. It looks like Urdu.'

Kieron stared at him. '"It looks like Urdu,"' he repeated. 'Since when did you recognise Urdu?'

'You know that girl in Mrs Adams's class?' Sam hunched

his shoulders slightly. Kieron knew it was a sign of embarrassment. 'Shahlyla? We kind of made out a couple of times. I saw a lot of Urdu books around her parents' place.'

'You and Shahlyla?'

'Leave it.'

'Are you still seeing her?'

'I said leave it.' Sam shrugged in an offhand manner. 'Turns out she prefers rugby players to greebs. Could've told me that before we kissed rather than afterwards.'

'And you have the cheek to ask me about Naomi. You dog.' Kieron laughed. 'OK – Urdu it is. We should be able to translate it. There's tools on the Internet.'

'Your augmented-reality kit could do it,' Sam pointed out.

'Yeah, but it's quicker doing it here. Let me have a go.' He pushed Sam out of the chair and took over, calling up an Internet browser, using it to find a site that could recognise and translate text in graphic images, then uploading the file to the site and setting it to work.

'You're really not worried about security?' Sam asked from Kieron's bed, to which he had retreated.

'These sites deal with thousands of images a minute,' Kieron pointed out.

'But the NSA's computers can analyse millions of images a second.'

'Besides, I use an anonymising router and my email address can't be traced back to me. Paranoid, remember?'

The computer pinged again, telling Kieron that the website had sent a translation directly to his email account. He opened the email and scanned its contents.

'OK,' he said dubiously, 'that looks like a terrorist's shopping list. The translation isn't perfect – the words are jumbled up and the grammar is all over the place, but I can see "polonium", "neutron", "radiation", "centrifuge" and "plutonium", as well as what looks like a set of map co-ordinates.' He hesitated, trying to work out the sense behind the scrambled text. 'I think what it's saying is that there's a cache of . . .' He trailed off, feeling a sense of unreality sweeping over him. 'Oh boy. I think it's saying that one particular nuclear weapon is stored at a particular location near the border between India and Pakistan. No, hang on, it's saying that the nuclear weapon is being moved from a bunker near the border to a safer location deeper in Pakistan. It's a shipping manifest!'

'It's a film script,' Sam observed darkly, 'that's what it is.'

'No.' Kieron shook his head firmly. 'This is real. It's describing a bunker a few hundred miles south of Islamabad – wherever that is. I think we need to tell Bex about this.'

Kieron turned around to look at Sam, trying to gauge his reaction, but his friend was lying back on his bed with the augmented-reality glasses on. He waved his hands around, obviously accessing menus and the keyboard.

'Hey!' Kieron yelled. 'Leave that alone!'

'What – only you can use it?' Sam snorted. 'It's not your personal property, you know.'

Kieron leaped across the space between the desk and the bed and snatched the glasses off Sam's head. 'That's delicate technology – you can't just use it to play first-person-shooter games.'

'I wasn't,' Sam said, sitting up, He looked peeved. 'Look, if you have to know, I was seeing if I could access the school's server. Just think – if we can get hold of any exam papers before the exam happens we could sell them! Hell, we could just keep them to ourselves and pass all the exams with top marks!'

'Which wouldn't be suspicious at all,' Kieron said, checking the glasses over for any damage. 'Look, we're already thigh-deep in government business. The last thing we want to do is raise any suspicions or draw attention to ourselves. Just – just leave this stuff alone, OK?'

Sam opened his mouth to say something that was probably going to be as cutting and sarcastic as he could manage, based on the expression on his face, but the distant slamming of a door interrupted him.

'Your mum!' he said, a panicked look crossing his face.

'Kieron,' a voice called, 'are you in?'

'I'm in my room!' Kieron called back. He threw the glasses back to Sam. 'Hide them!' he hissed. He moved towards the door, desperate to intercept his mother before she could get to the bedroom, but Sam waved his hands madly.

'Earpiece!' he mouthed.

Kieron nodded. Whipping the earpiece from his ear, he threw it towards his friend.

Outside the bedroom, he closed the door behind him and moved out into the hall. He could hear movement in the kitchen. 'How was work?' he asked.

'Another day, another set of bills paid.' His mum pushed back her hair from her face distractedly, as if she was trying to push the world away. Dishes clattered, and then the door of the fridge opened and closed. 'Look, I've got to go out. The boss wants me to be at a dinner to entertain a client. There's a microwavable spag bol in the fridge. Can you manage?'

'Yeah, we'll be fine.'

'We?' She stepped back from the counter so she could look down the hall at him. She wore her one good work suit, but she'd lost weight and she looked lost inside it, like a girl dressing up as an adult. 'You've got someone here? Is it a girl?' A look of panic crossed her face. 'Not that it matters. A girl, I mean. You're a growing boy – you can have girls in your room if you want.' Kieron didn't think it was possible but his mother's face took on an even more panicked look. 'Or a boy. I'm not judging. If it's a boy in your room that's just as good. Maybe even better – at least a boy can't get pregnant. Not that I think you'd –'

'It's Sam,' he said.

A smile swept across her face. 'Sam Rosenfelt? Oh, lovely. How is he?'

'He's good.'

'Still in his "emo" phase?'

'It's not a phase, Mum,' he said heavily, 'it's a lifestyle choice. He's not an emo: he's a greeb. And so am I, in case you hadn't noticed.'

She stared at him intently, and from her expression it almost seemed as if she was actually seeing him for the first time in a while. 'You're so big now. How did you get to be so big? When did that happen?'

'Gradually,' he said.

She shook her head. 'No, I swear last week you were –' she waved her hand at waist height – 'just up to here. And now you're –' she gestured vaguely towards his head.

'Mum, it's called "growing up".'

'Well, I don't like it. Please stop.' The wistful, almost sad expression on her face disappeared, replaced with a frown. 'Your collar is frayed.' She gave him a quick visual sweep, toes to top of head. 'And I can see your socks. You need new trousers. We'll go out at the weekend and get some.' A pained look crossed her face. 'No, scratch that – I'll order some online, a size up from last time. Maybe two sizes.'

'Skinny jeans,' he warned. 'And black. Not like last time.'

'Skinny jeans make it look like I'm not feeding you properly.' Her face seemed to age ten years in a moment. 'Which I'm not. I'm sorry.'

Kieron stepped forward and hugged her. She hugged him back fiercely.

'It is what it is,' he said softly. 'You're working yourself into the ground to keep us going. I just wish . . .'

'Wish what?' she asked, her voice muffled by his hair.

'That things were different, but they aren't.'

She tightened her grip for a moment, then let go and stepped back. 'I've got to go,' she said. Her voice was practical, but a trace of moisture glittered around her eyes. 'Be good, and if you can't be good then be careful. Make sure you eat something – you and Sam – and don't touch the bottle of wine in the fridge. That's for me, for later.'

'Bye. Have fun.'

'Brush your teeth,' she called back over her shoulder. 'And have a shower!'

Back in his bedroom, Sam was playing around with the augmented-reality goggles again. 'Everything OK?' he asked.

The sound of the flat's front door slamming made Kieron's curtains shiver momentarily.

'Everything's just wonderful,' he said, then: 'Right – your time is up. My go now.'

Sam slipped the glasses off with ill grace and left them lying on the bed as he rolled off. He threw the earpiece next to them. 'All yours. Have at it. What are you going to do now?'

'First,' Kieron answered, 'we need to tell Bex about the documents we translated, and then, while she's deciding what to do about that, we try and track down her friend Bradley.'

'Oh, we do, do we?' Sam said, slumping into the chair next to the computer.

'Don't be like that. You can help.' A thought tugged at Kieron's mind as he slipped the glasses on and put the earpiece in his ear. 'You haven't been . . . talking to Bex, have you?'

Sam shrugged. 'Would that be a bad thing to do? She's not your girlfriend – we already established that. And you can't own an MI6 agent.'

'I think,' Kieron said heavily, 'that in order to avoid confusion Bex needs one person interfacing with her.'

'Ah, we're "interfacing" now, are we?'

'Leave it out.'

Sam shrugged, turned around and started bringing Kieron's computer out of sleep mode. 'Actually,' he said without turning his head, 'I was looking for downloadable DLCs for games. Stuff that hasn't been released yet. Didn't find any.'

Putting the glasses on had activated a Start button that floated in front of Kieron's eyes. He pressed it, and a window opened up, showing him what Bex was doing. For a sudden panicked moment he thought she was in the shower – water cascaded down in front of her – but he realised that he was looking through a window at rain at exactly the same time he realised that nobody wore glasses in the shower. Which made him feel a lot better.

'Where are you?' he asked.

'Oh – you're there. I'm back in my hotel room.'

'The weather doesn't look too good.'

Bex laughed. 'Monsoon season, apparently. We can expect scattered torrential rain, but no let-up in the stifling humidity. It's like living in a small kitchen where a kettle is perpetually boiling.'

As Bex spoke, Kieron realised that he could see her reflection dimly in the window; a ghostly figure overlaid on the waterfall outside. He gazed at her for a moment, interested in this person he'd got to know so well in so little time but never actually seen. He couldn't tell her height – he was effectively looking at her from the level of her own eyes – but she seemed young, like someone who'd left sixth form and gone to college. She had long, brown hair, and she looked . . . normal. Like someone you might see behind a till at a supermarket, or behind the counter at a chemist's.

'How's everything going at your end?' she said, breaking the spell. 'Made any progress?' She turned her head, and Kieron got a view of her hotel room. It was small, but nicely and rather ornately furnished. Compared to his bedroom it was incredibly neat: an open suitcase sat on a table near the door, but no clothes or other possessions were scattered around. Bex seemed to live in a world where she might have to snatch up her case and move at a moment's notice, so she made sure that everything she needed was in there.

'I've got a document to show you,' he said. 'How do I get it onto your glasses?'

'You can't,' she replied. 'Apart from the camera, which is hidden in a hinge, these glasses are just glasses. It's a safety precaution in case anyone behind me spots the pictures being projected on the lenses, or gets suspicious and picks them up off the table if I've stupidly left them lying around, or even snatches them off my head. You're the one who can access all the information, not me.'

'What about the earpiece?' he asked, intrigued. 'Won't people spot that?'

'I've got long hair. The earpiece is hidden behind my ear and it's covered. If anybody does see it and ask about it, I just tell them that my hearing got damaged standing next to the amplifier stack at too many rock concerts when I was younger.'

'Really? They had rock music when you were younger? I thought it was, like, jazz, or classical, or stuff like that.'

She laughed: an attractive rippling sound. 'Yeah, right. Every generation thinks it invented rock music. What kind of stuff do you guys listen to?'

Kieron shrugged, even though she couldn't see him. 'Fatal Insomnia, Bearclaw, things like that. Screamo mostly, with quite a lot of goth added in. What about you?'

'I used to be addicted to Sisters of Mercy. They counted as goth as well, although probably an earlier version of goth than yours. Oh, and Dead Can Dance, although they were more post-rock than goth. I guess you guys are on post-post-rock now. Or even post-post-post-rock.'

'Look,' he said awkwardly, 'I'm sorry about earlier. I just want to help.'

'I know. And thanks.' He heard her take a breath, and her voice became more practical. 'So, what's this thing you want to show me?'

'We enlarged the photo of the documents that were on the table in that temple. We could only translate the top sheet, but it looks as if it mentioned a nuclear device that's being stored at some military base in Pakistan. It's being moved sometime soon. What we saw was some kind of shipping order.'

'A shipping order?' Bex's tone was thoughtful. 'Interesting. Pakistan is one of the seven nations we know have nuclear weapons, and they're paranoid about their neighbours in India. Anything bad that happens in Pakistan is blamed by the government on Indian interference. It's the same in India as well – they blame the Pakistanis for a lot of their problems.' She sighed. 'I hope this doesn't mean that tensions are ratcheting up in the area.'

'Are you going to report this back to your bosses? I mean, even if one of them *is* a traitor, they still gave you a job to do.'

'Yes, but I haven't done the job properly yet. I know what was being handed over, but I don't know who it was being handed over to, or why, or what these Blood and Soil idiots were doing there – if it was them, and not just a coincidence. Look – thanks for the work you've done. Leave it with me and get some sleep.'

'OK. Goodnight.'

'Goodnight, Kieron. And tell Sam goodnight as well.'

He switched off the ARCC equipment. For a moment he just stared at his wall, letting the reality of his room flood back in to replace the distant magic of India.

'Right,' he said, clapping his hands. 'Now we find Bradley, and surprise Bex with the news tomorrow.'

Sam stared at him, eyebrows raised. 'And how exactly are we going to do that?'

'Don't know. Any ideas?'

Sam thought for a moment. 'You've got the licence plate of the van they took this bloke away in, haven't you?'

Kieron displayed the purple Sharpie text on his arm.

'You should get that made into a tattoo,' Sam said. 'You know, so you can remember all this after it's over.'

'Focus.'

'Yeah. OK, there are CCTV cameras on most junction traffic lights these days – have you noticed?'

'Speed cameras?' Kieron asked.

'No, they sense approaching traffic and change the

traffic-light priorities if there's nobody approaching the junction from the left or right, but they also look for people who drive through red lights. That means they have licence-plate recognition.'

'Ah!' Kieron nodded. 'So we use the ARCC kit to search the DVLA records for all licence plates on blue vans that drove away from the shopping mall at about the right time. Simple!'

'Yes,' Sam said. 'Simple. The complicated bit is, what do we do after that?'

CHAPTER SIX

It was night in Mumbai, but the street outside Bex's hotel window was lit in a rainbow spectrum by the yellow streetlights, the various advertising hoardings and numerous neon signs for cafes and restaurants that still seemed to be doing a brisk business. As Bex stared down at the people passing by she felt the muscles in her back and her shoulders spasm. Getting away from the Jain temple had taken its toll. She needed a long, hot bath to ease the pain away, but she suspected that wasn't going to be on the cards for a while. She still had work to do.

Mumbai was four and a half hours ahead of England, so midnight Bex's time was only seven thirty in the evening for Kieron and his friend Sam. Part of her hoped that when she put the glasses on the next morning Kieron wasn't going to be there. Maybe his attention would wander on to something else. Teenagers were like that, she vaguely remembered from her own teenage years, which hadn't been that long ago, but seemed an age away. Maybe his mum would find the ARCC equipment, assume he'd stolen it and confiscate it. Maybe . . .

Oh, who was she kidding? She knew he'd be there, and she knew she needed him there. Being an agent abroad was fraught with difficulties, and having that lifeline back to someone who could access blueprints, databases and any other information she needed was vital. Having a friendly voice in your ear when you were feeling isolated was sometimes the difference between succeeding in a mission or failing. Even if he was just a kid, he was her lifeline.

She shook her head abruptly, trying to shake out the intrusive thoughts about the risk she was putting Kieron and his friend at. Instead she concentrated on what was going on outside her window. The short rainstorm had passed, and she could see what looked like steam hanging over the pavement. Obviously it was just water vapour – the climate in Mumbai wasn't *that* hot – but she knew that the atmosphere down there would still be so humid the sweat would just trickle down her skin and soak her clothes if she went out. When she went out.

Thank heavens for air-conditioning and decent hotel rooms.

She tried to imagine where Kieron was now and what he might be doing. Eating dinner with his mother? Watching YouTube videos? She still didn't know what he looked like, although she suspected he'd caught glimpses of her in windows and mirrors as she'd passed by them. Working with Bradley, she'd quickly developed a set of rules – take the glasses off before going into any bathroom or removing any item of clothing was the most important one. Not chatting was another – it was all too easy to find yourself losing track of where you were and what you were doing, and make the people around you suspicious. But spending time with someone else's voice in your ear and your voice in their ear made you feel close to that person whether you wanted to or not. Bradley was like a brother to her – an older brother. He'd seen her at her lowest moments, and despite the rule about chatting she'd helped him through some emotional issues of his own. The problem was that Kieron was beginning to feel like a younger brother, and she had to break that link before either of them became too reliant on it.

When the mission was over. When Bradley was safe.

She stared down at the street, looking to see if any passers-by lingered too long or paid too much attention to her window. She'd booked into a small hotel – much smaller than the Taj Mahal Palace, outside which she had watched the briefcase being stolen. Smaller, and more anonymous. She was supposed to be on a budget sightseeing tour – that was her cover story. Staying somewhere expensive and billing MI6 for the opulence and the room service was tempting, but hardly qualified as undercover work. And, of course, one of the factors that made MI6 use Bex and Bradley as freelance agents was that they were cheap. Cheap, but very, very good.

She'd left the light in her room off when she'd got back. She didn't want to make an obvious silhouette in the window, even though she had registered in the hotel under a false name and made sure she hadn't been followed there from the coffee shop. Tradecraft, as it was called – the set of habits that an agent either picked up in training or developed on the job – quickly became ingrained. Sometimes those habits stopped you being exposed as an agent, and sometimes they saved your life.

If Kieron did come back online in the morning, she supposed she'd have to teach him some of those habits. He seemed to be a quick learner. At least that was something. It could have been some idiot kid who had picked up the augmented-reality kit.

Even though she'd taken precautions, she'd scanned the room quickly when she entered, looking for signs that anyone might have searched it. The trouble was that it often proved difficult to distinguish between someone suspiciously going through her stuff and hotel maids having a quick look to see if she'd left any loose money lying around. The cliché from the old secret-agent movies she used to watch with her dad on rainy Saturday nights was that you could take a hair from your head and stick it unobtrusively across the corner of a drawer or the gap between your suitcase's body and its lid, using your saliva to secure it, and then see if it was still there later. It always looked good in movies, but in reality the saliva dried up and the hairs dropped off. Thank air-conditioning for that.

Someone she'd worked with once had told her that, when he was searching hotel rooms of suspected foreign agents, he would deliberately pull a couple of hairs off his own head and stick them on a couple of drawers and suitcases. It had been his idea of a joke; something to confuse the foreign agents. If they had been foreign agents. She hadn't been sure whether to believe him or not. After a while, she'd noticed that he wasn't around any more. Maybe he'd played too many jokes. Or finally played one on the wrong person.

Thinking of her dad, and the old movies they'd enjoyed together when she was a kid, had triggered a feeling of sadness inside her. She knew she ought to dismiss it, push it away so she could concentrate on what she was doing, but just for a moment she gave in and thought about her dad, and where he was now. The man who had once been tall and reassuring, with arms that could wrap around her and squeeze all her fears away, was now a shrunken shell of his former self. The staff at the home where he was being looked after were marvellous, but every time she went to see him it took him longer to remember her name. One day he wouldn't remember at all, and that would break her heart. Her mother had died years ago, of a sudden heart attack. That had devastated both Bex and her father at the time, but now her father had forgotten all about it and Bex had come to the conclusion that her mother had been the fortunate one.

She glanced at her watch. Time to go on the hunt.

She'd already decided that it was pointless going back to the Jain temple and searching it for clues. The two briefcase thieves would have cleared out long ago, and they wouldn't have left anything behind. They had struck her as professionals: they wouldn't have dropped anything. No convenient maps or notes that would help her track them down. They might even have set fire to the temple, just to cover their tracks completely, although she hoped not. The Jain monks deserved better than that for their gentle hospitality.

The sniper on the roof of the Taj Mahal Palace hotel was another matter. They had vanished quickly after they had taken their shots. Snipers had their own tradecraft, just like undercover agents. They always collected up the spent shell casings ejected from their rifles, just in case there were any incriminating fingerprints or DNA evidence on them. The problem for this particular sniper was that they had been resting their rifle on the edge of the roof, and with a bit of luck one of the casings might have fallen over the edge. The sniper certainly wouldn't have gone down immediately to collect it – that would have been stupid. The chances were that they would hope it had been lost, and not worth the risk to come back for it later – but thanks to the recording Bex knew roughly where it would have fallen. If she could find one then maybe – maybe – there might be some evidence on it that would enable her to identify the sniper. It was a long shot – she smiled at the pun – but it might just work.

Grabbing a camera for disguise and the ARCC glasses, Bex left her room and set out on her quest.

Her hotel was just a short walk away from the Taj Mahal Palace. Her muscles were still protesting, but she tried not to let it affect the way she walked. Still pretending to be just a tourist, she cast curious glances at a park as she passed its locked gates, and at an impressively large building that had obviously been built in the days when India had been a part of the British Empire but which was now apparently a museum. She had been right about the heat: it was as if all the paving stones and old buildings had absorbed the heat of the day, like a battery storing up electrical charge, and were now radiating it back into the air. The odour of spices and frying meat fought for attention with the smell of the flowers that filled the park.

Bex crossed an intersection where five roads came together and the traffic seemed to be treating the lights as decoration rather than instruction. Bex approached the Taj Mahal Palace hotel. Ignoring the impressive entrance, she diverted around the side of the building. There, at the back of the hotel, was the open space where she had seen the briefcase stolen earlier that day. Ferries were still letting passengers off and taking them on. To one side a small group of musicians with drums and sitars were playing for the tourists.

Bex moved through the crowd – more sparse than it had been previously but still large – to the place where she had been standing earlier, when Kieron had alerted her to the presence of the sniper. Picturing the images that the ARCC equipment had recorded and Kieron had played back to her, she turned and gazed at the impressive facade of the hotel. Yes, if the sniper had been up *there*, then any falling cartridge cases might well have bounced off the ledge *there* and fallen . . . yes, *there*, in a cluster of bushes with glossy green leaves and white flowers.

She moved closer, camera raised as if she was taking photographs of the flowers. She scanned the soil beneath the bushes. No sign of the casing there. She glanced left and right, but still couldn't see anything. Maybe a leaf had been knocked off one of the bushes by the heavy rain, or some passing tourist, and had fallen onto it, hiding it. Maybe the rain had churned the soil up enough that the casing had sunk into the mud. Maybe it just wasn't there at all, and she was looking in completely the wrong place.

A little way away, a tourist took a photograph of her husband standing in front of the Taj Mahal Palace hotel. The camera's flash illuminated the hotel's impressive architecture in stark white light, and Bex suddenly saw a metallic glint beside the stem of one of the bushes. It's just a coin, she thought, or a key, or something normal, but she moved closer to it just in case. Bending down and picking it up would look suspicious, so she fumbled with her camera as if trying to remove the memory card that held the photographs, and deliberately dropped it.

'Oh, stupid!' she said, loudly enough for anyone nearby to hear, and bent down. Her fingers brushed against the glinting metal object half buried in the mud, and she carefully picked it up, holding it by its bottom rim so that she didn't cover up any fingerprints that might be there, as she grabbed at the camera's strap with her other hand.

'Is it OK?' the woman who had taken the photograph of her husband called.

'I think it's fine!' Bex called back. 'Thanks!'

She pretended to examine it, but really she was looking at the thing she had picked out of the mud.

A gleaming brass cartridge case with burnt markings around the crimped hole where the bullet had been held, and a dimpled mark on the flat end where the firing pin had struck it.

Perfect.

Deliberately fumbling to get the camera strap around her neck, she slipped the cartridge case into her pocket. She could worry about how to organise the DNA and fingerprint analysis later; at least she'd got it.

She hung around for a few more minutes, taking photographs of the illuminated Gateway of India, before heading back to her hotel.

Halfway back, she realised she was being followed.

It started as a prickle on the back of her neck, her subconscious telling her that it had spotted someone dawdling a little too long, or staring at her a little too hard. Agents were trained not to ignore feelings like that: the brain often knew things that it didn't know it knew, and it had ways of trying to alert you.

Bex stopped by the gates to the park and pulled the camera strap over her neck. Holding the camera up, she took a photograph of the museum, but as she brought the camera down to her side she deliberately pointed the lens behind her and took another photograph, timing it so that the flash activated at the same time as another group of passing tourists took a whole series of selfies. She set off again, towards her hotel, raising her camera up obviously as she walked so that she could apparently check on the screen how the photograph of the museum had come out, but actually examining the image of the street behind her.

A woman stood about twenty feet away. Not aware that she was being photographed, she was staring directly at Bex, and frowning.

The image of the sniper that the ARCC equipment had recorded had been blurred, but Bex felt pretty sure this was the same person.

It was obvious now what had happened. The sniper had returned to look for the missing casing, and she had seen Bex take it. Now she was following Bex – either to retrieve the casing or to find out why Bex wanted it. Or perhaps both.

Bex wasn't sure if this was a good thing or a bad thing. On the one hand, she'd found the sniper – and with less trouble than she had expected. On the other hand, the sniper had also found her.

She had to find a way to turn the situation to her advantage.

She started walking again, still feeling that prickle at the back of her neck. Her hotel was only a few minutes' walk away. She had to decide what to do quickly, and then put the plan into immediate action.

Bex felt a fluttering in her stomach. She wasn't used to this kind of thing. Her work was usually either long-distance or close-up but undercover. She'd been trained in what to do if someone realised she was undercover, of course – close-up fighting – and that was what had got her through the chase in the Jain temple. This was different. This was her being followed and planning on taking out her follower. Not permanently, but long enough to restrain and question her.

Fluttery feeling or not, when she entered her hotel lobby she walked straight up to the desk.

'I'm in room two oh eight,' she said to the clerk: a small Indian girl in a sari and heavy make-up. She spoke loudly enough that the woman following her, who had come in and was standing by the door looking at her watch, pretending that she was meeting someone who was late, could hear her. 'I want to complain. The people in the room opposite mine were making a lot of noise last night. Could you maybe ask them to keep quiet?'

The girl quickly typed something into her computer, then looked up with a frown. 'The room opposite you is empty at the moment,' she said apologetically. 'Perhaps it was above you?'

'Maybe,' Bex said. 'I could be mistaken.'

'If it happens again, please let us know and we'll find out who it is.'

Bex smiled. 'Thank you. I'd appreciate it.'

Turning away and heading for the lifts, she suppressed a satisfied smile. She'd been fairly sure the room wasn't occupied – the maids hadn't been in, as far as she could tell – but it was worth checking.

When the lift doors opened the corridor was, fortunately, deserted. She sprinted down to her door, then turned to the room opposite instead. Fortunately the hotel was old-fashioned – deliberately so – with metal keys for the rooms attached to big fobs instead of key cards. That made it easier. She slipped a small but efficient crowbar out of her purse, slid it between the door and the jamb and gave it a quick pull. The lock splintered. She pushed the door open and entered the darkened room, then closed the door again. If the door had been secured electronically, with a key card rather than a key lock, she'd have had to think of something else because the electronic lock would have alerted the desk that someone had opened the door of a room that was supposed to be empty.

She pressed up against the door and put her eye to the little peephole. It gave her a fish-eye view of her own door.

Bex waited.

It was probably twenty minutes later that she heard the door to the stairs at the end of the corridor open. The sniper hadn't used the lift. That was clever – lifts were clunky and slow. And, of course, difficult to fight in. Bex remembered one film in particular she'd watched with her dad where two men had tried to have a fight in a lift. It hadn't been easy.

A minute went by, then a dark shape appeared in her field of view. Someone wearing a hoodie and a cap, with the hood pulled up over the cap. It was a woman – the sniper. She looked both ways down the corridor, then took something from her pocket. Probably something that would get her through the door quickly, before Bex could react – except Bex wasn't in the room.

The sniper bought her hand up to face-level, and Bex saw that she'd been wrong. It was an atomiser – a spray bottle with an aerosol button on top. It almost certainly sprayed an instant anaesthetic. She was going to knock on the door, probably say she was from housekeeping – no, more likely she was checking on the room noise that Bex had reported! – and when Bex opened the door she would spray the anaesthetic into Bex's face.

If Bex had been there.

Just as the thoughts were passing through Bex's mind, the sniper raised her left hand to knock on the door.

This was the moment.

Bex pulled open her own door and said, in a flustered voice, 'Oh, I'm sorry – I didn't see you there!' Even as she said the words she moved out into the corridor. The hooded sniper turned her head in a reflex action but, caught halfway between attacking and stopping the attack, she momentarily froze. In that split-second Bex grabbed the hand with the spray, turned it towards the sniper's face and pushed the woman's finger down on the button.

A cloud of mist enveloped the sniper's face. Bex held her breath, and kept her finger on the button. The sniper tried to bring her right hand around to hit Bex, or push her away, but already her legs were buckling. Bex caught her before she fell. The spray can dropped to the ground. Bex fumbled in her pocket for her massive key fob, then opened the door with her right hand while her left arm supported the now-unconscious woman. When the door opened Bex pushed it in, kicked the spray can in, carried the sniper inside then pushed the door shut with her foot.

Five seconds, max. She was proud of herself. Her trainers would have been pleased.

She dumped the sniper on the bed, aware of a smell that reminded her of hospitals, dissipating in the room's air-conditioning.

Bex glanced around the room, looking for something with which she could tie the woman up. She was painfully aware that, had events gone a slightly different way, the sniper might now be doing exactly the same thing, but hey! That was life.

Her gaze fixed on the two lamps, one on each side of the bed, and the electrical flex that ran from them to the unsafe-looking plugs that were half hanging off the wall, but then she remembered the Ethernet cables in the desk drawer. She pulled them out quickly and tied the sniper's ankles together, then turned her over and tied her wrists together before turning her back. The sniper's breathing was heavy, and Bex hadn't heard any changes that made her think she might be waking up. The woman was a professional: she wouldn't use an anaesthetic spray that wore off in a couple of minutes.

The sniper wasn't secured to the bed, but Bex had the anaesthetic spray. That should be enough to stop the woman from struggling.

She checked her watch quickly. Two o'clock in the morning, so, nine thirty at night in England. Teenagers being teenagers, Kieron was probably still awake, and she needed his help. She pressed the small button on the side of her glasses that activated a visual alarm in the ARCC glasses and a repeated *ping* in the earpiece.

A few moments later, Kieron said, 'Oh, hi!' He sounded flustered. 'I thought you didn't want to talk until tomorrow.'

Bex thought she heard an engine revving in the background. 'Sorry – are you driving?'

'No. Well, yes. Sam is.'

'Sam can drive?'

'Of course Sam can drive!' Kieron sounded offended on his friend's behalf.

'No, I mean: is Sam allowed to drive?'

A long silence was interrupted by Kieron saying, casually, 'So, what's up with you then?'

She sighed. 'Long story short, I've found the sniper.' She glanced at the bed so that Kieron could see.

'Oh. Yes.' A pause. 'And what are you going to do – torture her for information?'

Bex felt offended. 'Certainly not.'

'OK – you want me to locate a pharmacy in Mumbai that can sell you a truth drug.' A moment's pause. 'Apparently scopolamine is recommended, but it's tricky to use.'

'No, not that.' She sighed again. 'Actually, I haven't really thought this through. It all went pear-shaped a bit quickly. Can you suggest something? And by that I mean something that doesn't involve pain.' She had to swallow, to get rid of a lump in her throat. 'I don't think I could do that.'

'Let me think.' Bex heard Kieron mutter something to Sam. The next thing she heard was a squeal of brakes.

'Are you two all right?'

'We're fine.' Another pause. 'Actually, I think I've got something. Give me a high-definition of that woman's face.'

Bex moved in closer and pulled the sniper's hoodie down. She made sure she didn't put her hand anywhere near the woman's mouth, just in case she was faking and decided to take a sudden bite. Best to be sure.

'Right, hold still for a sec. Yes, the ARCC system has identified her. Apparently she's in the MI6 database. Her name is Emma Sprue, and . . . oh, she's a freelance assassin responsible for around twenty known assassinations. You know, we're in the wrong business. Based on what she charges, she's seriously rich.'

'That's lovely for her,' Bex said. She thought she could see a quiver in the sniper's right eyelid. 'I hope she's got a good pension plan as well. How does that help us, apart from motivating us with jealousy as well as loyalty to the Crown?'

'Actually,' Kieron said, 'I've got an idea . . .'

CHAPTER SEVEN

A cold wind blew off the River Tyne, bringing with it a complex and nasty smell that seemed to blend dead fish, industrial effluent and rotting vegetation into some toxic mix that made Kieron's nose itch. He turned his collar up against the chill and tried to ignore the smell. It was hard, but then this was Newcastle and he was an emo teen. Everything was hard.

Why couldn't he live somewhere interesting, like New York or London?

Why couldn't his mum and dad still be together?

He'd read something once where a person said, 'If wishes were fishes then we'd all have a feast!' He supposed that was a way of saying that everyone wished for lots of things all the time. He'd also read somewhere that if you wanted something badly enough, and worked hard enough, then you'd get it. But life had taught him that sayings like that were just sayings, designed to make people feel slightly better. They weren't actually true.

He and Sam stood in the shadow of a large building with metal walls that creaked occasionally as the wind gusted. The metal panels were fastened together with rivets, and each rivet had streaks of rust running down from it. Somewhere around the side a panel had come loose and whenever the wind was particularly harsh it banged against the metal scaffolding to which the panels were attached. The building had probably looked wonderful when it was first built, but now, Kieron reflected, it just looked sad and tired and broken.

Nothing lasted. He was beginning to realise that, and it made him feel strangely grown-up in a way that he didn't want. Buildings rusted and fell down; neatly mown parks became overgrown with weeds; hills and cliffs crumbled; and childhood just melted away when you weren't looking. He had a vague feeling that it was something called entropy – he'd learned about that in physics lessons – but knowing that something happened and it had a name didn't really explain why it happened. It just did.

'We might be at the wrong place,' Sam muttered. He looked cold as well: hands stuck in pockets and feet stamping on the ground to keep himself warm. His breath rose in front of him like steam.

Kieron gestured towards the sign on the warehouse across the other side of the tarmac parking area from where they were standing. A sign attached to the wall read: Horowitz Automotive.

'The CCTV images of the van that took Bex's friend showed it stopping at a place called Horowitz Automotive,' he pointed out. 'According to Google, there's only one Horowitz Automotive in the whole of Newcastle and

Gateshead, and this is it. The van stopped here somewhere. We just have to find it.'

'Where is there another Horowitz Automotive?' Sam asked.

'Manchester. Why?'

Sam shrugged. 'They might have gone there, not here.'

'OK, two things,' Kieron pointed out irritably. 'First: the CCTV images had timestamps, and they couldn't have driven to Manchester from here before the picture was taken. Second: we haven't got time and can't afford to get to Manchester today, so if they're not here we have a problem. So they'd better be here.'

'All right. I was just saying.' He glanced at Kieron's face. 'Your cheeks have gone white.'

'I'm cold.' He indicated the thin black knee-length coat he was wearing. 'That's the problem with being a greeb in winter – we're not really dressed for it.'

'Just be thankful we're lads, not girls,' Sam pointed out. 'At least we're wearing trousers instead of tights with holes in them.' He glanced down at his ripped jeans. 'Well, you know what I mean. At least the material is thicker.'

Kieron looked around. When they'd first arrived, having caught a bus into the centre of Newcastle and another bus out again, the industrial park had been filled with cars and vans, but come five o'clock everyone had left, and by five twenty the place was almost deserted. Somewhere in the distance it sounded like someone was rehearsing a mediocre pub band in one of the warehouse units, or maybe they were just playing the radio loudly, but the relative silence just emphasised the noise. The song was an old one Kieron's dad used to play badly on his electric guitar – 'House of the Rising Sun'. Just hearing it again made Kieron feel sad.

'I think the last people have left,' Sam said, 'and if we don't move then my feet will freeze to the tarmac.'

Kieron looked around. A central spine road led off the main road, with metal warehouses clustered around short side roads that ran off like ribs. The signs on the buildings indicated a mixture of car mechanics, sign-makers and computer repairers, with one picture framer and one provider of solar panels in evidence.

'OK,' he said, 'I'll take the right, you take the left. Call my mobile if you find a dark blue Delica van. I'll do the same.'

'I'm out of credit,' Sam said. 'I can receive calls, but I can't make them.'

Kieron sighed. 'OK. If I find anything I'll call you. If you find anything, then come back to the road and wait for me. If you haven't seen me and I haven't called by the time you've checked your side to the end then we'll meet back here. Say, half an hour.'

'You've got enough battery power?'

Kieron pulled his mobile out of his pocket and checked. The little battery bar icon indicated that he was pretty low. He glanced back at Sam and shrugged. Sam delved in his pocket and pulled out a small bright purple cube from which a short micro-USB cable dangled. 'Extra power,' he said. 'You have it; I've got enough.'

Taking it, Kieron nodded his thanks.

They split up: Sam running across to the other side of

the spine road and, keeping close to the buildings, heading off in one direction while Kieron stayed on his side and did the same. Off in the distance, 'House of the Rising Sun' started up again, the opening ripple of notes sounding as if someone was painfully searching for each string on the guitar and each fret on the neck.

The first road was empty of cars. Instead of coming all the way back to the spine road, Kieron found that he could slip along the side of the last warehouse, along a path between the metal walls and a wooden fence taller than him. The ground was covered with weeds and grass, but a faint bare trail existed all the way along. Probably left by foxes, Kieron thought. The next side road had several company vans parked in it, left overnight presumably, and he checked that the dark blue Delica wasn't hidden between them before he moved on.

When he got back to the spine road Sam had just arrived. His dark clothes hid him well against the warehouse walls. He waved, and Kieron waved back.

They moved on, in opposite directions. The third side road of Kieron's had a large lorry parked in one of the bays, sticking out so far it was almost across to the other side, and Kieron had to squeeze past it before he could check the three cars that were hidden there. Still no Delica. At the end he did the same thing he had done before – slip along the rough path between the warehouse and the fence. This time a bush grew right in the middle, and he had to squeeze past it. A small pile of cigarette butts had gathered beneath the bush, probably shepherded by the wind.

The fourth side road had a dark blue van parked halfway along. Kieron felt his heart beating faster as he cautiously crept forward. While he was still six feet away he realised that it was the wrong shape. The licence plate confirmed that it wasn't the Delica.

When he got back to the spine road again he halted, waiting for Sam to appear.

Sam didn't appear.

Kieron skulked in the shadow of the last warehouse on his side, waiting for Sam. Surely his friend couldn't have got ahead of him? Kieron had only stopped briefly to look at the licence plate on the van, so it wasn't likely that Sam had already got to his end of the road and moved on. Even if Sam wasn't using the path on the far side of his warehouses, he still would have covered the same distance as Kieron, almost certainly in the same time – give or take.

Maybe Sam had found something.

Kieron waited for a few minutes, arms folded to try to conserve some heat, but Sam didn't appear. In the end, he looked left and right to check that nobody else was around and then crossed to Sam's side.

Two cars with flat tyres and a motorcycle that looked like it had been abandoned occupied that stretch of tarmac. When he got to the end, Kieron turned around and looked back towards the junction. Still no sign of Sam. He felt slightly stupid, knowing that it was more likely than not that his friend had somehow got ahead of him, but a growing bud of worry expanded in his chest.

Maybe something had found Sam.

Taking a deep breath, he headed down the side of the warehouse, between its wall and the fence, back towards the side road he'd last seen Sam heading along.

Just before he got to the corner his foot caught an exposed root. It pulled him back with a jolt.

'Is he the only one?' The voice was male, and harsh.

It came from just around the corner. If Kieron's foot hadn't been caught by the root he would have walked right into the person who had spoken.

'Only one I've seen.' Another man's voice.

'Take a look around – quietly. Kids are like rats: they travel in packs. Fortunately, unlike rats you can break their necks quite easily. With rats you have to put a lot of effort into twisting.'

Freeing his foot, Kieron moved quietly towards the corner of the warehouse. He knew there was a risk that the second man might suddenly appear, but Kieron was too far away from the other corner to have got back there in time. Not quietly, anyway. Besides, it was more likely the second man would go along the side road and look up and down the spine road.

He heard footsteps heading away. They sounded heavy, as if the man wore boots.

He thought the men in the shopping centre, the ones who had taken Bex's friend Bradley, had been wearing boots.

'I hate kids,' the first man said. Kieron heard a scuff of rubber on tarmac as he turned around, and then footsteps as he headed away. The footsteps suddenly became a lot quieter, as if he had gone into a building. Into the warehouse, probably.

Kieron took a risk and peered around the corner. A new, highly polished BMW sat on the tarmac, and beyond it he saw a man walking away from him: short blond hair and a puffy waterproof jacket. The sun was behind the warehouses now, heading for the horizon, and the sky was dim and overcast. The man was almost, but not quite, just a silhouette against the light. As Kieron watched he got to the spine road, looked in both directions, then turned left and disappeared from sight.

Dim light spilled out of an opening a few feet away from Kieron. Taking a deep breath, he slipped along the few feet of metal that separated the corner from the door and peered around the edge.

The opening was a door in a larger garage door that could lift up so that a car or small van could drive into the space. A van sat inside: a dark blue Mitsubishi Delica. Kieron didn't have to check the licence plate, but he did anyway. It was the van he'd seen back in the car park of the shopping centre.

A doorway at the back of the garage area, half hidden by the van, led into the depths of the warehouse. Kieron heard the first man's voice echoing from it, saying, 'Got any friends out there, have you? Any more little rats like you?'

'I called the police,' Sam's voice said. 'They'll be here soon. You'd better let me go before they arrive.'

'I've got your mobile right here,' the first man said. 'You ought to put a security code on it, by the way. Anyone could just look at it and see there's been no calls made today.' Something hard suddenly hit concrete, followed by the sound of a boot heel coming down on something that cracked under the pressure. 'There you go – problem solved. No need for a security code now.'

'You're going to pay for that,' Sam snarled. Kieron could tell from his voice that he was scared, but Sam's immediate reaction when someone pushed him was to push back harder.

The first man sounded amused. 'Pretty soon,' he said, 'you're going to be as broken as that mobile. The only choice you get is how fast it happens. A few seconds if you tell me where your friends are; a few hours if you don't. I'm not playing a game here, son. I need to know.'

'I'm by myself,' Sam said. Kieron felt a little glow of appreciation for his friend's bravery.

'On an industrial estate? After everyone's gone home? I doubt it.'

'It's something I do – exploring places when there's nobody around.'

Kieron slipped along the side of the van, past a metal table with a toolbox and a set of car keys sitting on it, to a point where he could see through the doorway into the rest of the warehouse. The door opened into the garage area, and he could see heavy shelving on both sides of the warehouse. The space itself was dark and shadowed, full of stacked crates and lit only by occasional lights high up in the metal rafters. There were tables and chairs in there, and a large plasma TV screen, but they weren't what immediately grabbed Kieron's attention. Sam had been secured to a metal chair near the doorway using plastic zip ties. And beside him, secured in the same way, sat Bradley. Unlike Sam, he looked like he was in a bad way: head low on his chest. There might have been dried bloodstains on his shirt.

Kieron's mind raced: possible courses of action appearing almost fully formed and then vanishing again when he realised they were flawed. If he phoned the police, they wouldn't believe him. If he went to release Sam and Bradley he'd be caught. If he did nothing, his friend was going to be hurt, possibly killed. What was left? What option was he missing?

He could create a diversion. Maybe, if both the men were lured away, he'd have time to rescue them both.

But what kind of diversion?

It had to be outside, and far enough away that the men would go to investigate it. He supposed he could set fire to something, but there was a good chance the fire would spread out of control. He wondered if he could make some kind of noise – banging a heavy spanner from the toolbox against the metal walls of a nearby warehouse – but he quickly realised that would leave him outside and at the same place where the two thugs would be heading.

The two thugs. He turned his head, suddenly convinced that the second man – the one who had gone searching for him – was standing right behind him. There was nobody in the garage space. As his heartbeat returned to merely the panicked rate it had previously been at he started to breathe again.

'Look,' the first man said in a reasonable tone from inside the cavernous interior of the warehouse, 'let's be sensible. I don't want to spend too much time hurting you, and you don't want to be hurt. It's in both our interests to co-operate on this. There's a garage out there where I can pick up anything from a pair of pliers to a blowtorch. If I really wanted to be unpleasant, I'd get a car battery and a set of jump leads and wire you up. Believe me, when you see your skin start to smoke you'll tell me everything you know. Let's save me the trouble and you the pain.'

'Is that what you did to him?' He could hear a tremor in Sam's voice as he nodded his head towards the unconscious Bradley.

The first man shrugged. 'That sort of thing. He's been trained to resist interrogation. You haven't. Cracking you will be easier than cracking an egg with a hammer. And talking about hammers, how fond are you of your kneecaps?'

Kieron looked around wildly, trying to find anything that might help. His gaze snagged on the car keys, which had a BMW key fob on them, and a plan formed in his mind so quickly it was as if it had always been there and a spotlight had suddenly been shone on it.

He snatched the keys up and quickly moved to the far side of the Delica. The keys had two buttons for remotely locking and unlocking the car outside. If they were anything like his mum's car keys then pressing the 'lock' button twice would set off the car alarm.

So he pressed the 'lock' button twice.

Outside, the BMW's horn started to blare. Flashing lights illuminated the night.

'What the –'

As Kieron hid, the first man ran out of the warehouse, through the garage area past the van, and outside to see what had set off the alarm.

Kieron dropped the car keys, snatched a knife and a handful of plastic cable ties from the toolbox and ran into the warehouse, pulling the door shut behind him and engaging the lock. He moved quickly to Sam's side and sliced through the cable ties that were securing him to the chair.

'I thought you were still searching,' Sam breathed. 'I thought I was finished!'

'Never,' Kieron said. He handed the knife to Sam. 'Cut Bradley free. I've got to do something.'

Outside, the BMW's alarm abruptly stopped. Kieron cursed himself. He should have kept the keys.

While Sam moved across to the other chair, Kieron quickly strung together the extra plastic zip ties into a chain about six feet long.

The door to the garage area rattled: first slightly, then heavily. Seconds later the entire wall shook as someone wrenched at the handle.

Kieron knelt down and, working fast, passed the chain he'd made through the struts of the metal shelving on either side of the door. He made sure the ties were tight, and set at about ankle height. Standing up, he saw that Sam had pulled Bradley from his chair. The man appeared woozy, but he seemed to understand what was going on.

'Go into the shadows, round the back of the crates,' Kieron said hurriedly to Sam. 'Get out of sight.'

As Sam helped Bradley away, Kieron grabbed the two

chairs, dragged them to the doorway and turned them over so that their metal legs pointed upward, and towards the door. Once he felt happy with the placement, he checked that Sam and Bradley couldn't be seen and followed them.

He'd only just got to the nearest crates when the door to the garage area burst open. The second man had obviously returned, and the two of them had used the metal table to smash the door. They threw the table behind them and came through the doorway together. They were holding guns. Kieron caught his breath in shock. They were actually holding guns.

The first man, the one who had menaced Sam, hit the stretched cable ties first. His feet stopped while the rest of his body kept moving. His face contorted in surprise as he toppled forward. His friend was only a moment behind him. He stumbled over the first man, rather than the cable ties, but they both fell into the warehouse.

And into the upturned chairs.

Grunts of surprise turned to cries of pain as the metal legs hit their faces, their shoulders and their ribs like so many blunt spears. They tried rolling out of the way, but their arms and legs got tangled together and the chairs rolled with them, ending up in a confused mess of men and furniture. Both of them managed to hold on to their guns, however, which made Kieron curse. He'd been hoping to grab one of them at least.

He sensed Sam behind him. 'Have you got the knife?' he whispered.

'Not much use against guns,' Sam whispered back.

'Depends how you use it.' Kieron reached a hand backwards and felt the handle of the knife being pressed into his palm. He waited while the two men disengaged themselves from the chairs with a lot of swearing and climbed unsteadily to their feet. The first man had a long line of blood beneath his left eye. The second man held his right arm as if the shoulder was damaged. They both looked very, very angry. Actually, they both looked like they were going seriously insane with rage.

'Get them!' the first man snarled. 'I really want to hurt them, and then I really want to kill them.'

Kieron reached his arm backwards and threw the knife across to the other side of the warehouse. It spun through the darkness, arcing above the concrete floor and hitting a pile of crates with a clatter.

'Over there!' the second man said, pointing.

Both men hobbled, rather than ran, away from Kieron, Sam and Bradley, towards the place where the knife had hit the crates. They vanished into the shadows of an aisle between the rows.

'Right,' Kieron whispered. 'Let's go.'

With him under one of Bradley's shoulders and Sam under the other they scooted across the ground, with Bradley sometimes helping and sometimes allowing himself to be dragged. They got to the door into the garage area without being spotted. The door was wrecked, so unfortunately Kieron couldn't close it behind them. He hoped it would take the thugs a while to realise they'd gone, but he wasn't holding out much hope.

'What now?' Sam hissed as they got to the blue van.

'I hadn't thought that far ahead,' Kieron admitted. 'Maybe we could steal the BMW outside.'

'Have you got the keys?'

'No,' he admitted sheepishly. 'You can hot-wire a car, can't you? You used to hot-wire teachers' cars and move them to different parts of the school car park. You almost got expelled for that.'

'Not the ones with a security chip in the key and an engine-management system,' Sam replied urgently. 'Didn't you learn anything in motor mechanics?'

'No.'

Between them, Bradley tried to struggle upright. For the first time since the shopping centre Kieron saw his face clearly, and he was shocked by the bloody cuts and dark bruises.

'The van,' Bradley said through bruised lips.

'What?' Kieron asked stupidly.

'The van,' he mumbled. 'No security chip. Just keys.'

Kieron reached out and tugged at the sliding side door of the van. It moved smoothly backwards, along the van's length, on oiled runners. Quickly he and Sam helped Bradley get in, joined him and slid the door shut.

They both hung back, each waiting for the other to get into the driver's seat.

'Look,' Kieron admitted, 'I can't drive. You'll have to do it.'

Sam shook his head. 'How do you ever intend getting a girlfriend?' he asked.

Kieron shrugged. 'My whimsical sense of humour?'

While Sam squirmed his way into the driver's seat, Kieron leaned over Bradley.

'We're friends,' he said. 'We're helping Bex.'

'Shouldn't be risking your lives,' Bradley murmured.

'Try not to talk. We're going to get you to somewhere safe.'

Shouts from outside were followed by the two thugs running into the garage area, having figured out what had happened. Fortunately they ran past the van and outside, through the open door and into the gathering darkness.

Sam turned and flashed an anxious glance at Kieron. Kieron tried to look as confident as possible, and nodded firmly.

Sam reached beneath the dashboard, grabbed a set of hidden wires and pulled them into view. Selecting two, he pulled hard until they broke, then touched the bare metal of the wires together.

The van's engine started with a roar.

Outside, the two thugs turned around. Sam flicked the headlights on – main beam. The thugs staggered backwards, shielding their eyes.

Sam slammed the gearstick into 'drive', yanked the handbrake off and pressed his foot on the accelerator. The van leaped forward, heading for a doorway about a third its size. The bull bar on the front hit the much larger, and closed, main door to the garage – the one that folded up into the ceiling to let cars in and out. For a stomach-churning second Kieron thought the van was just going to bounce back and its engine stutter to a halt, but instead it ripped the main door out of its frame and carried it forward.

Right into the two thugs.

Kieron didn't see where they fell, but the van kept going. One side of the door hit the rear corner of the BMW. The door spun around and fell onto the car, leaving Sam to jerkily drive the van past it and out onto the tarmac.

Kieron expected his friend to turn and head out onto the spine road, and away to safety, but he didn't.

Sam braked.

Before Kieron could ask him what the hell he thought he was doing, Sam slammed the van into reverse, turned the wheel hard and accelerated backwards at an angle, right into the bonnet of the BMW.

Kieron couldn't see what had happened, but he heard an almighty smashing of glass and crumpling of metal. As Sam put the van into 'drive' again and pulled away with squealing tyres, he scuttled to the rear door and glanced out of the window. Behind them, getting smaller as the van raced away in a cloud of blue exhaust fumes, the BWM was canted to one side, its bonnet rucked up and the nearest wheel leaning at an odd angle. Kieron hadn't learned much in motor mechanics, but he didn't think it was drivable.

The two thugs suddenly appeared from behind the car, where they must have taken refuge. The first one – the one who had threatened Sam – raised his hand and pointed his gun at the van. The van's engine was racing too loudly for Kieron to hear anything, but a hole suddenly appeared in the glass, surrounded by a halo of white cracks. Then the figures disappeared as the van careered round the corner.

'Good work!' Bradley said weakly from where he lay on the floor.

'Any idea where we're going?' Sam yelled over his shoulder.

CHAPTER EIGHT

The sniper – Emma Sprue, if that was her real name – stared darkly up at Bex from the hotel bed. Bex could see that she was surreptitiously testing the Ethernet cables that Bex had used to tie her up – flexing her muscles to see if there might be any give in the wires. There wasn't. Bex had been very careful: the last thing you wanted to do when tying up a certified killer was give them a chance to get away. She excelled at tying knots: it was funny how outward bound from school kept coming in useful in her work. They ought to rename them Secret Agent Preparation lessons, she thought. That would get attendance numbers up.

Enough, Bex thought. She was just delaying the inevitable.

'So,' she said brightly. 'Where do we start?'

Sprue just stared back at her.

Bex felt nervous. She'd never had to do this before, and she wasn't sure how it would go. This woman was a seasoned professional assassin who had managed to evade capture by, presumably, most of the intelligence agencies of the world. Bex was a young undercover operative working under contract to MI6, whose expertise was based on her ability to listen to a voice in her ear and act on the information it gave her while pretending that she couldn't hear anything. One of her bosses in MI6 had once said, and while she was in earshot as well, that any newsreader who could look at an autocue and read out the news headlines with a smile could do the job Bex did. It had been a cruel, and not entirely fair, comparison. Newsreaders didn't normally have to read out the headlines as if they'd only just thought them while knowing at the same time that the person they were talking to probably had a gun in their pocket. However, Bex usually had the comfort of knowing she was acting, playing a part, and the lines were being fed into her ear by Bradley. Now it was her, alone and unscripted, facing a true professional.

Except . . . except that she was still playing a part, wasn't she? It was a bit like being in a school play where someone else had forgotten their lines and she had to improvise in character. And Kieron was there, listening and feeding her information. He wasn't Bradley, but he wasn't doing too badly.

'Let's summarise, shall we?' she went on. 'Your name is Emma Sprue, and you're a professional assassin. My name is – well, let's not worry about that – and I'm an agent for – well, let's not worry about that either. The important point is that you have information I want, and I intend to get it out of you.'

Sprue was still staring blankly, emotionlessly, but Bex thought she could detect a hint of amusement in her eyes. At least she was listening, even if she wasn't actually believing. Not yet, anyway.

'You probably think that I'm going to hurt you until you tell me what I want to know,' Bex said after a few moments. 'After all, that's what *you* would do, and that's what the people who usually *hire* you would do. And you've killed many people that we know of, and almost certainly many more that we don't, so I have no illusions about your ability to inflict suffering. I'm sure you don't have a conscience. Maybe I do, or maybe I just can't be bothered with the mess it would cause to this hotel room, but I'm not going to hurt you.'

The amused expression in Sprue's eyes had shifted to one of wariness now.

'Also, there's no *point* hurting you. I have a feeling your threshold of pain is quite high. You'd pass out, or have a heart attack and die, before I could cause you enough pain to make you talk. That would be a waste of time. I almost wish, at times like these, that I *was* a practised and trained torturer, because that way I could probably keep you conscious and alive for much longer, but I'm glad I'm not. If I was, I'd probably have had to trade my conscience for that ability, and that's a trade I wouldn't want to make. Not ever. I'd rather continue to be one of the good guys.'

Sprue's upper lip had begun to curl slightly in what looked like might be contempt. She was accidentally letting her guard down, letting some emotions come through. She was underestimating Bex, and that was exactly what Bex wanted. It would make the coming shock all the more, well, shocking.

'So I'm going to try a different approach.' Bex smiled cheerily. 'And no, it won't be truth drugs. Even if I could get hold of some – and I don't carry them around in my wash-bag just in case I might need them – they are unreliable and, in inexperienced hands like mine, potentially dangerous. So, the drugs are out.' She tilted her head sideways a little bit and stared at Sprue like a teacher looking at a child who'd done something bad but won't admit it. 'I'm not going to appeal to your better nature either, by the way. I'm pretty sure you don't have one of those.'

Curiosity now? A faint but noticeable lift of the right eyebrow. Keep going, she thought. You're doing well.

'I'm not going to offer you money to get you to talk either. You are, by definition, someone who will do the worst things for money, but I don't think paying you is the way to go. For a start, it would be bad for your reputation if you accepted money from one group of people to undertake an illegal mission and then you accepted money from another group of people to blab about it. Business would suffer. It would also set a bad precedent. Just as my – well, let's say my "employers" – don't pay ransoms to hostage-takers to release their hostages, they don't pay mercenaries for information. After all, if they did that then they'd have rats like you lining up to sell them all kinds of tittle-tattle.'

Yes: definitely curiosity, and perhaps a tinge of concern as to where this was all heading.

Bex looked around the hotel room. 'You can also see from the quality of the accommodation I'm staying in that the budget of my employers is not very impressive. Every government is suffering budget cutbacks. It's the world economy, apparently. I'm sure you're doing very well for yourself, however, and I'm also sure that you're staying in a much better standard of hotel than I am. Perhaps even the Taj Mahal Palace. I guess it would be nice to be staying just a few yards away from where you're working, although probably not very professional. It looked very impressive from outside. I can see you there, in a suite of rooms perhaps. Not under your own name, of course. Or maybe you're staying somewhere else. Wherever it is, I'm sure it's five-star. I mean, what's the point of going away on business as often as you do and earning as much as you do each time if you can't indulge in a little luxury? And travel – first-class flights, I presume. I mean, you need to arrive rested and ready for action, and who wants to mix with the commoners like me back in economy?' Bex leaned forward and put her hands together. 'The question is: do you want that situation to continue?'

She left a long pause, long enough that eventually the tip of Sprue's tongue appeared at the corner of her mouth and she licked her lips: an involuntary gesture that told Bex she might be getting nervous. That was good. That was better than good.

'You see, you probably thought that I've been talking so much because I'm nervous, but I think you've realised that's not the case. So you'll be wondering: why *am* I talking so much? And you'll also have realised – just a few seconds ago, I think – that I'm buying time while a colleague of mine is finding stuff out for me.'

A flicker. A definite flicker.

Bex touched her glasses. 'You might have heard of

ARCC – Augmented Reality Computer Capability. It's the next big thing in assisting agents under cover. Through these glasses and –' she touched her hair – 'the earpiece here I can communicate with a colleague back in, well, my country of origin. He doesn't work undercover like I do. He works in coffee shops, restaurants, cafes and all kinds of places. He works on trains and aircraft, and in the passenger seats of cars. And what he does is: mainly he accesses databases. You know what a database is: it's a big collection of information in electronic form, held on a computer server somewhere. Often this information is meant to be secure, but it's not. It's really not. Take bank records, for example. They should be protected by all kinds of uncrackable security, but banks are just businesses like anyone else, and if they think they can get away with installing some cut-price stuff and relying on you choosing a decent password, well, that's more money for them, isn't it? Now you'd think that your bank, which I believe is –'

'The Bank of Commerce and Credit International,' Kieron murmured in her ear.

'The Bank of Commerce and Credit International,' she repeated as if she already knew the words.

'Based in Zurich,' Kieron went on.

'Based in Zurich, of course, would install the most up-to-date firewalls and suchlike, and you know what? They do. At least, they do if you're a hacker trying to get in and steal some money. The trouble is that the resources that, oh, let's say my country can bring to bear on a cryptography problem far outstrip what even the best hacker can do. Not only can we afford better hackers, we can afford quantum supercomputers that can break any security, anywhere, instantly. Which brings us neatly back to you, and your bank account, which is currently sitting at –'

'Eighty-nine point five eight seven million dollars,' Kieron said, sounding seriously impressed.

'Eighty-nine million, five hundred and eighty-seven thousand and a few odd hundred dollars, plus some loose cents. Let's not worry about the exact amount. Let's worry instead about what happens if we remove, say, a hundred thousand dollars from your account and move it to a charity looking after premature babies in neonatal intensive-care units. Let's face it, they could probably do with the money. Have you ever had a relative or a friend who has given birth to a premature baby? The worry and the stress are horrible. Anything that can be done to alleviate that is a good thing, I think.'

'And . . . done,' Kieron said. 'Great Ormond Street Hospital in London is now one hundred thousand dollars better off than it was ten seconds ago.'

Sprue had developed a very subtle twitch in her left eyelid.

'Now I know what you're thinking,' Bex went on calmly. 'You're thinking that I'm just making this up. Bluffing. "Having you on", as they say where I was bought up. You probably want me to provide some proof that my colleague currently has his electronic fingers inside your most private account, waving them around and causing all kinds of damage. That's a reasonable request, and I'm happy to comply. I presume you know your own account number, which is –'

Bex thought she could hear Kieron making clicking noises with his tongue as he worked. 'Eight one zero, seven five nine, two three nine four eight.'

'Eight one zero, seven five nine, two three nine four eight. Now we might have been able to access that number without accessing the account, of course, so I'll throw in the fact that your personal password is –'

'Alysheba1987.'

'Alysheba1987.' Bex couldn't help smiling at the way Sprue's eyes had suddenly widened in shock.

'Oh, apparently it's the name of the horse she used to own, and the year she got it. It was a birthday present from her father.'

'Which is the name of the horse you loved so much and the year your father bought it for you. How lovely that you still remember. I think that's very sweet.' She paused for effect. 'Another hundred thousand dollars, I think. What would you say to donating it to a charity that funds research on innovative diabetes treatments? Diabetes is a huge problem in the developed world these days.'

'Done,' Kieron said. 'I like this game.'

'It's not a game,' Bex said, and suddenly realised she'd replied to Kieron without thinking. Quickly she added: 'It's serious, and it's your money. How much can you afford to lose? One hundred thousand dollars a minute is a million dollars every ten minutes, or your entire retirement fund in, oh, an hour and a half. And it's not like I have anything else to do this evening. If I get hungry I'll just order room service.' She gestured towards the window. 'Or there's any number of restaurants just a phone call away who will deliver.'

'What do you want to know?' Sprue's voice sounded harsh, with a trace of an American accent.

'I want to know who hired you, what they hired you to do and where I can find them.'

She shook her head firmly. 'I can't do that. You said it yourself – if I give that kind of information up, my reputation is shot. I'll never be hired again.'

'I understand.' Bex nodded, trying to put a reasonable expression on her face, like a mother negotiating bedtime with a child who wanted to stay up later, even though she felt twitchy and part of her just wanted to punch Sprue in the face. 'Let's see what kind of safeguards we can offer. Oh, and while we do, I think another hundred-thousand-dollar donation would be in order. Any preferences? What about a charity that specialises in rescuing horses from distressing situations? You like horses, don't you? Just think how happy Alysheba would be, if she knew.'

'How about,' Kieron mused, 'the Global Horse Welfare Fund? They have a really impressive website. Lots of good work.'

'I think that would be perfect,' Bex said, as much to Sprue as to Kieron.

'OK!' Sprue was beginning to sweat now. 'How can you guarantee my anonymity if I talk?'

'We'll spread the word that whoever hired you has a traitor in their organisation who told us what we needed to know. We'll even transfer money into someone's account, just to provide evidence.' Bex put a shocked expression on her face. 'Not from your account, of course. That would defeat the whole object, if it was ever traced. From someone else's account.'

'OK. That'll work.' Bex noticed that Sprue's breath came faster and shallower than before. That was good. She was rattled. Funny how someone could resist pain but would crumble if you started taking their money away. 'But how do I know you'll let me go after you've finished . . . finished questioning me?'

'Good question.' And actually, it *was* a good question. 'Well, I suppose I could point out that I'm one of the good guys, so I don't go around killing people – even bad guys – if I can possibly help it. I could also point out that although I know you're responsible for at least twenty murders, I haven't got enough evidence to satisfy a court if you went to trial. I could *also* point out that I have a job to do that doesn't involve you, and I'm keen to get on with that job. I'm more than happy to leave you here for the maid to find tomorrow morning. Now – I thought maybe a music-education charity. They do such good work with kids from deprived areas. Maybe, if I gave them a quarter of a million dollars, they could even name a rehearsal studio after you. The Emma Sprue Rehearsal Space. I think it has a nice ring to it. Not very good for your professional anonymity, but I suspect that's increasingly irrelevant to you at the moment.'

A sigh. 'OK. Yes. I'll tell you. I'll tell you everything. Just – just stop.'

'Who, why and where? That's what I want to know.'

Sprue closed her eyes, composing her thoughts.

'That went a lot easier than I thought,' Kieron said in her ear. Bex wondered where he was. She'd heard engine noises earlier, but they seemed to have stopped. Wherever he happened to be, it sounded like somewhere with fewer distractions. She had a feeling that something might be going on he wasn't telling her about, but it could wait. It wasn't as if she could question him on it now.

'I was hired by some fascist nuts in the UK called Blood and Soil,' Sprue said eventually. She glared at Bex. 'The UK – that's where your employers are based, isn't it?'

'Come on – you know the rules. Keep talking.'

'They're linked with a whole lot of American neo-Nazi survivalist groups in some kind of loose association. They told me to come here to Mumbai and be somewhere overlooking the Gateway of India at a particular time with a sniper rifle. Apparently two guys were having a meeting there.'

Bex couldn't help interrupting. 'But they didn't want you to kill anyone?'

'That's right.' Sprue snorted. 'Easiest money I ever earned. My job was to cause a distraction so they could rush in and steal a briefcase.'

'Why you? Why not one of their own people? I'm sure most of them know how to fire a gun.'

'Not from that range.' It was funny how, now Sprue had opened up to Bex, her entire personality had shifted. She almost seemed to be boasting now. 'They didn't want either of the guys at the meeting killed, because that would attract

140

attention from the police and the security services here in India, and someone would start to wonder what was in the briefcase that was so important it was worth someone being killed for. They just wanted a distraction, and the problem is, with the humidity and the rain here in this godforsaken country, getting an accurate shot from a distance takes a lot of skill. If they'd used one of their own people, they might have ended up killing one of the guys at the meeting by accident. So, they hired an expert.'

Bex tried to make the next question sound casual. 'And what was in the briefcase that was so special?'

Sprue shrugged. 'I don't know. I didn't need to know.' She frowned, and glanced at Bex questioningly. 'You were there. I remember seeing you, just before I fired. You were watching the two guys meeting, but you turned to look at me on top of the hotel.'

'Don't worry about me. Just tell me where I can find the person who hired you.'

'I did some investigation into Blood and Soil. I always do, just so I know that I can trust the people I'm working for to pay me – or so I know where to find them if they don't. There are lots of small Blood and Soil groups that meet to talk about the terrible state the world's got into, but they're really just decoration so you don't see the people behind the scenes. The real person in charge is a man named Darius Trethewey. He's the man who funds most of the behind-the-scenes activities, and he's the man who signed off my payment.'

'You've been very helpful,' Bex said, clapping her hands

and standing up. 'Thank you.' She theatrically slapped her forehead, as if she'd forgotten something. 'Oh, hang on! Wait a second! I think another hundred thousand dollars to a research facility somewhere looking to reverse the effects of Alzheimer's disease and other forms of dementia. After all, it's a problem that's going to affect us all in the end, isn't it?' She smiled at Sprue. 'Well, those people you haven't killed, anyway.'

Sprue had a shocked expression on her face. 'But you *promised*!' she protested like a small child denied a treat.

'Yes, but you know more than you're telling me, don't you? You're holding something back.'

The sniper seemed to crumble, closing her eyes and almost shrinking. 'Yes, yes, OK. The two people who were meeting in that public space: I was given enough information that I'd be able to recognise them. Obviously these Blood and Soil idiots didn't want me disrupting some perfectly innocent meeting.'

'Obviously,' Bex agreed.

'So I got photographs.'

'And you investigated the photographs, because you're curious that way.'

Sprue shrugged: a snake-like motion of her body considering the fact that she was tied up. 'Always useful to know what's going on and who's dealing with who.' She took a deep breath. 'One of them works for the Pakistani Atomic Energy Authority. His name is Fahim Mahmoud.'

'Really?' Bex said, trying to sound intrigued. After all, it never hurt to keep your opponent ignorant of what you already knew and what you didn't. 'And what about the other one?'

'He's a gopher, working for a man named Agni Patel. Patel is a billionaire – made his money in telecommunications. The funny thing is, I've dealt with him before. He's used me as a bodyguard for some difficult deals he's been making over the past year or so.'

Bex felt suddenly intrigued. 'What kind of difficult deals?'

'I don't know. I mean, honestly, I don't know. Take as much money as you want from my account and distribute it to loser groups around the world and it won't change the fact that I just don't have that information.'

'OK. I'll ask an easier question: what's in the briefcase? I know you said you didn't know, but I think you probably do. You're a very organised assassin.'

A pause, as Sprue closed her eyes and sighed.

'Look,' Bex went on, 'I know you think that information is worth something to you. I know you think you can use it for blackmail purposes, or pass it on to someone else for cold, hard cash. Just think of it this way, if it helps – you're selling the information to *me* instead. Admittedly I'm paying you with your own money, by not removing it from your account, but the principle is the same, isn't it?'

A terse nod. 'It's the location of a Pakistani neutron bomb.'

'A neutron bomb?' Bex wasn't familiar with the term.

'It's a kind of nuclear bomb invented and built during the Cold War. Unlike normal nuclear weapons, which destroy everything, neutron bombs just kill people. Well, people and animals. They flood an area with a pulse of neutron radiation, which leaves the buildings entirely intact. The idea was, why destroy an enemy's cities when you could occupy them yourself? Or why destroy cities an enemy had occupied if you could just return them to the original inhabitants afterwards?'

'Very clever.' Bex put her best kindly smile on her face. 'Thank you very much for that. I'm going to pack my bags now and leave. The maid will find you in the morning, I'm sure. I won't even hang the Do Not Disturb sign on the doorknob. By the time you get free I'll be long gone and you'll still have *some* of the money you made by killing people. Just be aware that if you try to come after me, I'll have the rest of your money transferred out to a charity looking after disabled cats or something. And if you try to move your money, we'll move it first. Let's both go our separate ways, and hope we never meet again.' She paused. 'Oh, you don't mind if I leave you with the room bill, do you? It's not like you don't have the money to pay it.'

Collecting up her rucksack and shoulder bag, Bex headed for the door. She turned and waved a hand at Sprue, who had settled back on the bed with a resigned expression on her face, and left. She didn't know where she was going yet, but obviously that particular hotel room had been compromised as a base of operations. She'd have to book into somewhere else, talk to Kieron and figure out what their next step might be.

Their next step. She would have laughed, but the situation seemed to be getting more and more critical.

Finding a hotel after midnight in Mumbai might be a challenge, but she felt sure she was up to it.

As she shut the door behind her she checked left and right with professional glances. The corridor to her left was deserted, but to her right two Indian men were coming towards her. Something about them triggered an alarm in her mind. They were both holding rucksacks, but swinging them loosely by the straps rather than carrying them on their shoulders. They were wearing good, well-cut suits, which was in itself odd compared with the relative casualness of the rucksacks. They were also not looking at her. Sheer curiosity would suggest that they might at least give her a glance, but they were studiously avoiding her by staring at the walls and the carpet respectively.

The alarm in her mind started blaring. It was a trap.

She turned to sprint along the unoccupied stretch of corridor, but it wasn't unoccupied any more. Another Indian man in a suit had emerged from a room on the opposite side. He also held a rucksack.

Two in one direction; one in the other; a sniper and murderer tied up in her room. She didn't have many options here.

Before the thought fully formed in her head she found herself running towards the lone man. If she could just get to him before he pulled out whatever weapon he was carrying, then she might have a chance.

She couldn't. He let the rucksack drop to the carpet, revealing that he had a weapon she didn't recognise in his right hand. It was a design she had never seen before: a thick black tube, more like a grenade launcher than a pistol, with a chunky handle set right at the back of the tube and a smaller grip pointing sideways about halfway down. As Bex desperately tried to speed up and get to him before he could do something serious and potentially lethal, he hefted the tube up by the handle, grabbed the grip with his left hand and pointed at her.

The air itself seemed to ripple between the weapon and her, and Bex suddenly found herself surrounded by a bubble of silence that, paradoxically, was almost deafening. Everything seemed to undulate around her. After that: darkness.

CHAPTER NINE

'Right – let's get him over there.'

Kieron pointed at the sofa. Funny, he thought as he and Sam manoeuvred Bradley across the room, how having a stranger in your flat suddenly made you aware of the fact that it could do with a vacuum and some tidying up. Oh, and maybe a fresh coat of paint on the walls – and not magnolia this time. It worked even if the stranger was semi-conscious.

'What about your mum?' Sam asked.

'She'll be out for a while yet. These business meals go on and on, and then there's cocktails afterwards, and then the clients always want to go clubbing. Middle-aged men and women pretending they're teenagers again – it's disgusting.'

'We're teenagers,' Sam pointed out. He lifted Bradley's left eyelid and checked the size of his pupil. 'And we don't go clubbing.'

'That's because we're already pre-grown-up.' He indicated Bradley. 'How is he?'

'I think he might be concussed. We might need to get him to a hospital, or get an ambulance out, or something.'

Kieron pulled his mobile phone from his pocket. 'I'll ask

Bex what she thinks, but I'll call mum first, just to check she's not heading home early. While I do that, you think of a cover story for Bradley here.'

Sam gazed at Bradley critically. 'He's a burglar? He's my cousin? He just wandered in from the street?'

'Yeah, something like that.' Kieron pressed the redial button for his mum. 'Maybe he was delivering pizzas, but he tripped and fell on the step outside.'

'Ooh.' Sam's expression brightened. 'Pizzas.'

The mobile rang briefly, then he heard his mum laughing as if she'd been caught in the middle of a conversation when she answered. The sound suddenly and unexpectedly made him feel shivery; like a kid again. It had been a long time since he'd heard her laugh like that.

'Sorry, I've got to – yes? Kieron? Is everything OK?'

'Everything's fine,' he said reassuringly. 'I just wanted to check you were all right.'

'I'm good,' she said. 'Look, I can't stay on the line: I have to –'

'I know, you go and have fun. You deserve it.'

He thought he heard her suddenly take a breath, then: 'I love you: you know that?'

'I know.'

'You should be having fun too.'

Kieron glanced at Bradley, slumped on the sofa, then thought back to the events at the industrial estate and the terrifying drive back – terrifying not because they were being chased but because Sam was still a bit ropey on the whole driving thing and because they were worried that at any second they were going to be pulled over by a police car with flashing blue lights. 'Actually,' he said, 'I am having fun.'

'Good. Don't wait up for me.'

'I won't.'

He cut the call off. 'How's Bradley?' he asked, crouching down in front of Bex's friend.

'He's –' Sam started to say, but Bradley raised a hand to interrupt him.

'I'm fine,' he said. His voice was deeper than Kieron had remembered, even though he sounded like he'd been in bed with flu for a week. 'Don't worry about me.' He frowned. 'I should get going. Things to – things to see and people to do. Or something like that.' He tried to lift himself off the sofa, but Kieron gently pushed him back.

'You're not going anywhere.' He glanced at Sam. 'A cup of tea, I think. And some paracetamol.'

Sam looked from Kieron to Bradley and back. 'Yeah, but what about him?'

'They *are* for him, idiot.'

As Sam left the living room, heading for the kitchen, Kieron tapped Bradley on the leg. 'Look, I need to get you caught up with what's been happening. Can you understand what I'm saying?'

'Yeah.' Bradley waved a weak hand. 'Go on.'

'You were abducted from the food court at the shopping centre. Do you remember that?'

Bradley opened his eyes and stared at Kieron. He looked woozy, and his eyes were bloodshot, but there was a sharp intelligence somewhere there, fighting to get through the pain. 'You were at the next table. I remember.'

'I picked up your glasses and your earpiece. I've been using them to talk to Bex.'

Bradley abruptly tried to lever himself out of the sofa. 'Bex! I need to –!' A spasm of pain crossed his face and he fell backwards into the cushions. 'I should –!'

'Bex is fine. I've been talking to her.'

'You've been talking to her?'

'Well, she needed help and you'd been taken prisoner. What else was I supposed to do?'

Bradley nodded. 'OK,' he whispered, eyes closed. 'It is what it is. Go on.'

'The briefcase got stolen by two people – a man and a woman. They looked like the people who took you: neat blond hair and paramilitary clothes. I managed to use the ARCC equipment to identify one of the men who took you as belonging to a right-wing paramilitary organisation called . . .' he thought for a moment, trying to remember, 'Blood and Soil.'

'I've heard of them,' Bradley said. 'They're like a more extreme and more unpleasant version of the British National Party. They're in contact with various right-wing American and European groups who are preparing for a race war. They want the world to be run by blond, blue-eyed people just like themselves. Funny thing is that most of them are bottle-blondes, and their blue eyes come courtesy of contact lenses.' He frowned. 'What would they want with –' He stopped himself from saying any more.

'Nuclear weapons?' Kieron said it for him. 'That's what's worrying Bex.'

'I'm not surprised.' He paused. 'There were leaflets and stuff scattered around the warehouse – propaganda, I think. The kind of thing they hand out in shopping precincts and at rallies.' He laughed bitterly. 'They even had their own Blood and Soil TV channel, which they watched on their laptop like it was *Strictly Come Dancing* or something. Only on for a couple of hours a day, apparently, which annoyed them.' He frowned. 'But why me? Why did they take me?'

'Bex thinks they wanted to stop you and her from disrupting their theft of the briefcase in Mumbai with the nuclear papers inside or seeing who took it. They didn't know Bex's identity, because she was undercover in the crowd, but they knew who you were, so they took you. Without you on the end of the ARCC kit, Bex would have been almost powerless.'

'They underestimated her then,' Bradley said. He opened his eyes and gazed at Kieron. 'And you, apparently.'

Sam chose that moment to come back in with three mugs of tea held in both hands and a packet of paracetamol tucked under his chin. 'You and Bex going out then?' he asked cheerily.

Bradley looked scandalised. 'No! Why are you asking me that? What's she been saying?'

'Nothing.' Sam put the teas down on a table by the side of the sofa and passed one to Kieron. 'It's just that Kieron's mum hasn't got a boyfriend, and I wondered if you were up for it.'

151

Kieron and Bradley just stared at Sam for a long moment in stunned silence.

'Who are you again?' Bradley asked.

'I'm Sam,' Sam said, passing Bradley a mug.

Bradley nodded. 'And you're Kieron,' he said, turning to Kieron. He looked around. 'And this is your flat. Your mum's out, I guess, otherwise she'd be making the tea.' He sipped from the mug experimentally. 'Which might have been a better idea. I once had tea in Ulan Bator made with yak's butter. It tasted better than this.'

'Make the next one yourself,' Sam muttered.

'Ulan Bator is in Mongolia.' Bradley took another sip, and grimaced.

'So – you and Bex then?' Sam said. 'Just friends, yes?'

Bradley raised an eyebrow. 'She's not my type, mate, but thanks anyway.'

'What do your friends think you do?'

'I've told them the truth,' he said defensively. 'That I'm a subcontractor working in IT support for a government department.'

'It sounds really boring when you put it like that,' Kieron said. He sipped at his tea. The liquid burned his mouth, but it tasted like the milk had gone off. 'Did you check the date on this?' he asked Sam.

His friend shrugged. 'They always shave a few days off those dates for health-and-safety reasons.'

Kieron turned back to ask Bradley how he felt, but Bex's friend and handler was holding his mug as if it was providing him with much-needed body heat, and he was frowning.

'If the guys who took me were from Blood and Soil, and if the people who took that briefcase in Mumbai were also from Blood and Soil, then who told them where to find me?' he asked. The words came out slowly, as if he was still working his way through the logic. 'I mean, they're a group of fringe extremists and nutters. They shouldn't have any way of knowing where a subcontractor working for . . . for a government department –'

'MI6,' Sam said brightly.

Bradley's frown morphed into a momentary scowl. 'For a secretive government department would be based. Unless –'

He stopped abruptly, mouth suddenly clamped shut as if he was biting down on the words.

'Unless someone in that secretive government department –'

'MI6!' Sam insisted.

'Had told them.' Kieron caught Bradley's eye. 'Bex thought the same thing. I managed to trace the licence plate of the van they were using, which we've parked a few streets away. It's registered to a company called Three Cornered Square Communications. Apparently that's –'

'A front for MI6.' Bradley nodded. His eyes were beginning to close, Kieron noticed. 'We've got a Blood and Soil sympathiser working right in the department.' He slurred his words. 'I need to talk to Bex, urgently. But first there's something you need to do.'

'What?' Kieron asked.

'Take this mug of tea away.'

Kieron reached out and took it from Bradley's hands.

'It's not that bad,' Sam muttered.

'It's not the taste,' Bradley said quietly; 'it's that I think I'm going to pass out again.' His eyes closed completely, and he slid sideways on the sofa, hitting the cushions with a soft thud.

Kieron and Sam shared a glance.

'Hospital?' Kieron asked.

Sam shook his head. 'I've been thinking about that. It's the first place those nutters from Blood and Soil will look for him, and he'll be vulnerable. We need to keep him safe.'

'What do you suggest?'

'My sister,' Sam said. 'She's a nurse at Newcastle General. She's worked in Accident and Emergency before, but she's on obstetrics now. She's got a flat about fifteen minutes' drive away. If we can get Bradley to her, then she can, you know, evaluate him and stuff. She'll know how to look after him.'

Kieron wasn't sure about the wisdom of this. 'Won't she, like, tell someone? I mean, doesn't she have to?'

Sam shook his head. 'She owes me. When she lived at home before she moved out, I caught her sneaking her boyfriend out of her bedroom window early one morning. I didn't tell Mum.'

'But that was years ago. She's grown up now.'

Sam seemed to shiver. 'You know my mum. Even now, if she found out –'

Kieron nodded decisively. 'All right. Do you want to ring her, make sure she's not got a lodger in, or having a dinner party, or whatever grown-ups do?'

'OK,' Sam said, putting his mobile away, 'I've texted Courtney. She's at the flat now, cos she's on early shifts. She says we can bring Bradley round and she'll take a look at him.' He glanced over to where Bradley was slumped on the sofa. 'You know what – she's not got a boyfriend at the moment either. I wonder if –'

'Mate, just leave it.' Kieron shook his head. Sam was incorrigible. 'All right, how are we going to do this?'

'I'll go get the van. You try to wake your man here up and get him to the door.'

It took ten minutes for Sam to get the van from where they'd left it and bring it to the flat. In that time, Kieron had moved Bradley about halfway to the door. The man was heavier than he seemed, and he kept sliding in and out of consciousness. For a crazy few moments Kieron thought about letting him pass out on a rug and pulling him across the wooden floor, but the thought just made him giggle uncontrollably, and he realised that he might be on the verge of hysteria. He closed his eyes and took several deep breaths until the feeling subsided.

Eventually Sam arrived back in the van and they managed to get Bradley in, and drove the short distance to Courtney's flat. She was already waiting outside – and she had a fold-up wheelchair.

'Your sister is amazing,' Kieron said as they drew up alongside her. It had been a year or so since he'd seen her, but she hadn't changed: red-headed, freckled and vivacious. The nurse's uniform she wore made her look very grown-up, and made him rather uncomfortable.

'You used to fancy her, didn't you?' Sam observed as he switched the engine off.

'Used to,' Kieron said, but he felt himself blushing. Fortunately Sam wasn't looking his way.

'Hi, Kieron,' Courtney said as they got out and slid the side door back. She looked at Bradley with professional interest. 'What happened? He looks like he got into a fight.'

'That is pretty much what happened,' Kieron said. 'Oh, and hi, Courtney.'

She smiled at him. Her eyes were green, and brighter than he remembered. 'And he doesn't want the police involved, I suppose?'

'He was helping a girl,' Kieron explained, using the story he and Sam had agreed during the drive. 'She was being harassed by some bloke, and Bradley stepped in. The trouble is, he hit the bloke and he doesn't want to risk being prosecuted for assault. You know the way people can twist things.'

'He's a hero then. Good for him.'

'It wasn't his girlfriend he was protecting,' Sam pointed out. 'He hasn't got a girlfriend.'

Kieron growled at him. Sam just smiled back cheerfully.

They loaded Bradley into the wheelchair and took him inside Courtney's block. It was only five storeys high, but fortunately it had a lift and fortunately the lift actually worked for once.

Once they were inside Courtney gave Bradley a check-up while he was still in the wheelchair. She even had an electronic blood-pressure monitor.

While she worked, Kieron looked around her flat. It was

156

incredibly tidy, smelled of fruit tea and had blocky prints on the wall that reminded Kieron of art-appreciation lessons at school. In the living room, where most people would have a shelf of DVDs or books, Courtney had a glass-fronted cabinet filled with sharp-bladed or blunt-ended tools made out of gleaming stainless steel. He looked at them with a mixture of fascination and unease. They looked like something from a horror film.

'Medical instruments,' Sam said, moving up behind him. 'She collects them. Homework, she calls it. Weird, I call it.'

Eventually Courtney straightened up and turned to Kieron and Bradley.

'Right, I need to ask you some questions.'

Here it comes, Kieron thought. She's smelled a rat!

'Obviously he's slipping in and out of consciousness, but has he shown any signs of mental confusion, such as forgetting who or where he is?'

Relieved, Kieron shook his head. 'When he's awake he seems quite lucid.'

'Any problems understanding or speaking?'

'Not that I could spot.'

'Any loss of balance or problems walking?'

'It was difficult getting him to the van.'

'OK.' She thought for a moment. 'Any problems with eyesight?'

'Not that we could tell.'

'Any vomiting, fits or seizures?'

'Definitely not.'

No bleeding from his ears?'

'No.'

'OK. The bad news is, he's almost certainly concussed. The good news is that as far as I can tell he's not *badly* concussed, although he'll need to be watched. He'll recover in a few days if he's allowed to rest, and given plenty of fluids.'

'Courtney . . . ?'

She raised a perfectly shaped eyebrow. 'Yes, Kieron?'

'Could he stay here?' He tried to make his face look pleading without looking too pathetic or needy.

He obviously didn't manage too well, because she only kept a straight face for a couple of seconds before bursting into laughter.

'Is he safe?' she asked as the laughter subsided.

'He's perfectly safe.'

'And is that other bloke, the one he had the fight with – is he going to come looking for your friend?'

'No. He's learned his lesson.'

She sighed, and nodded. 'Yes – he can stay here. I'm actually off tomorrow, so I can keep an eye on him. But I have to tell you: if he starts showing evidence of bigger problems I'll call an ambulance. Regardless of whether he wants me to or not.'

'Understood.'

'Right. I'd better get the spare room sorted out. You stay with him. Oh, and I'll need your help getting him into the bed. He's cute, but we've not been properly introduced yet.'

As soon as she vanished from sight, Kieron crouched down by Bradley's side. 'Bradley – are you awake?'

'Just about,' he murmured.

'Do you know what's going on?'

'I'm in a flat belonging to the highly attractive sister of one of the kids I only just met, and she's going to look after me until my head stops hurting and the world stops spinning. Is that right or am I hallucinating?'

'You've got it exactly.'

Bradley reached out and grabbed Kieron's sleeve. 'Bex! What's going to happen to Bex?'

'We're looking after her.'

'I wish I could – you know?'

'We know. That's the problem – you can't.'

'Don't put yourself in any danger.'

Sounds of a duvet being shaken to get it evenly into every corner of its cover drifted from the spare room. While they had a few minutes, and while Bradley seemed relatively alert, Kieron wanted to ask a couple of questions that had been bothering him.

'When you were in the warehouse with those two Blood and Soil goons, did they say anything that might help us work out what they're doing, or intending to do?'

Bradley shook his head, and winced. 'Is it bright in here?' he asked, squinting. 'It seems bright. Sorry – you were asking about those goons. No, I can't remember them saying very much about their plans. It would have been nice if they had. Mostly they either watched that stupid Blood and Soil satellite TV channel or they talked about how hungry they were, and what the chances were of getting a takeaway to deliver to the industrial estate.'

'Did they own that unit? Is that their base?'

'No. From what little they did say, I gathered that they'd broken in. It's used as a storage place by a kitchen and bathroom installation company. Nobody actually works there, and nobody goes there unless they have an order that needs to be filled.' He paused. 'Actually, I think one of them said that a supporter of Blood and Soil works in the company's orders department and would alert them if anyone was going to turn up to collect a bath or a cooker.'

'I think we can assume that they'll have cleared out by now,' Sam added.

The sounds of pillows being punched to plump them up had replaced the sounds of Sam's sister in hand-to-hand combat with a duvet. Kieron looked at Sam and raised an eyebrow. 'She's pulling out all the stops, isn't she?' he said darkly.

Sam grinned. 'She's not allowed pets in the flat,' he said. He jerked his thumb towards Bradley. 'I think she's going to adopt him.'

'Suits me,' Bradley murmured.

'When they were beating you up,' Kieron asked, turning back to the man in the wheelchair, 'what were they asking you?'

Bradley laughed bitterly. 'They weren't really asking me anything. I think they just hit me because they were bored and they had nothing else to do.' He frowned. 'Actually they did ask me whether MI6 was watching Blood and Soil or monitoring their communications. I think they were just being paranoid. I told them Blood and Soil were so trivial and pathetic that we only kept an eye on them for the comedy value.' He winced. 'They hit me harder after that. Fascists: no sense of humour. It's a key indicator.'

Kieron sighed. 'So it looks like they really were just taking you to stop Bex from disrupting their attempt to steal that briefcase, and we still don't know *why* they stole the briefcase.'

'You're lucky they didn't kill you outright,' Sam pointed out.

'Actually,' Bradley said thoughtfully, as they heard the sound of curtains being pulled and windows being opened in the spare room, 'they talked about that. Those two thugs wanted to kill me, but I remember they made a phone call to someone, and whoever it was told them *not* to kill me. I've only just remembered that. They were pretty angry about it as well. That made them hit me harder too. Pretty much any time they got irritated, they hit me harder. Another key indicator of fascism.'

'I wonder who that was,' Kieron mused. 'Their boss, maybe?'

'No.' Bradley's voice was getting weaker, Kieron noticed. His energy levels were flagging. 'They mentioned their boss to whoever was on the phone. This person was important, but it wasn't the person who normally gave them their orders. Except in this case, whoever it was did give them instructions and threatened to call their boss directly.' He clenched his hand into a fist and hit the arm of the wheelchair in frustration. 'Damn my memory. All that being knocked around has scrambled everything. I've just remembered something else – they organised a meeting with this person. They wanted them to explain to their faces why they couldn't kill me.'

'Do you remember where?' Kieron asked urgently.

'I think so.' He hit his leg again. 'It's just on the edge of my brain. It's like I can see it, but I can't reach it. Oh! Yes – it was going to be somewhere public. Newcastle train station! Eight o'clock tomorrow morning!'

Kieron was about to ask another question when Courtney came out of the spare room, looking flushed.

'Right,' she said briskly. 'Well done for keeping Bradley awake and alert, but I'm going to take over now. Time for him to rest. I'll make him a cup of tea. You two, skedaddle. Check in again tomorrow and I'll tell you how he is. If there's any change overnight I'll let you know straight away.'

She took the handles of the wheelchair and steered it towards the spare room.

Bradley twisted his head and tried to catch Kieron's eye. 'Don't even think about spying on that meeting,' he called weakly. 'Too dangerous.'

'Quiet,' Courtney said firmly, then turned to stare at her brother. 'What meeting?'

'Nothing,' Sam said.

She glared at Sam suspiciously for a moment, then turned and pushed the wheelchair away.

Bradley looked up at her. 'Any chance of a bed bath?' he asked hopefully.

Sam and Kieron headed for the front door.

'We're going to spy on that meeting, aren't we?' Sam asked when they were outside.

'Wouldn't miss it for the world,' Kieron responded.

'Is it because you want to find out who it is that's giving them instructions but isn't their boss?'

'It's more than that. We already know there's a traitor in the MI6 organisation – someone who sympathises with Blood and Soil and gave Bex's location away to them so they could disrupt her and Bradley's operation by taking Bradley. I'm guessing that the person coming to this meeting is the traitor in MI6. They've got qualms about Bradley or Bex being killed, and they want to make sure the Blood and Soil pit bulls are kept under control. If we can spy on that meeting we can take photographs of whoever turns up and show them to Bex and Bradley. Hopefully they can identify the traitor and expose them.'

'So we get medals?' Sam asked.

'What?'

'Medals? For exposing a traitor in MI6?'

Kieron shook his head firmly. 'We are not getting medals. We are not even going to *suggest* getting medals. We're just going to help Bex and Bradley.' And maybe, just maybe, he thought, get a job out of this.

They headed back to Kieron's mum's flat.

She still hadn't returned, which wasn't much of a surprise, so Kieron made them cheese and ham sandwiches and poured a couple of glasses of cola from a bottle in the fridge.

'You want to stay tonight?' he asked Sam as he took the food into his bedroom. 'I've got a spare sleeping bag from when we went away for outdoor ed.'

'I think the dog ate mine,' Sam replied. 'Yeah, I don't fancy walking back home now, and I'm not going to drive that van by myself.' He thought for a moment. 'You know what – we could sell the van! That would definitely get us enough money for those gig tickets we were talking about this morning!'

That morning. Kieron felt a suddenly wave of surprise wash over him. Just that morning his life had been a lot simpler. And, to be fair, a lot more boring. But so much had happened in just twelve hours.

'Let's worry about that when things have calmed down,' he said eventually. 'But it's not a bad idea.'

Sam bit into the sandwich. 'Why do you think Blood and Soil are called that?' he asked through a mouthful of food, then frowned. 'What did you say this sandwich was?'

'Cheese and ham.'

'Don't taste like any cheese and ham I'm familiar with.'

Kieron sighed. 'Mum's got this thing about not just buying "basic" foods, even though they're cheaper, so she sometimes buys what she calls "treats" – the cheese is emmenthal and the ham is Serrano. She says it makes her feel like we're not living on the breadline.'

'Yeah,' Sam said, 'about this bread . . .'

'Don't get me started.' Kieron signed. 'OK, Blood and Soil. I've got a feeling that a lot of fascist and Nazi groups have this thing about land, and blood, and belonging. The people in charge motivate the grunts at the bottom of the food chain by appealing to their basic instincts. Everyone wants to belong to something.'

'We don't,' Sam observed. 'We're greebs!'

Kieron stared at him for a few seconds. 'You just don't see the irony, do you?'

'I failed irony at school.' Sam shrugged. 'Good marks

in sarcasm and flippancy though.' He indicated the glasses Kieron was still wearing. 'Anything from your friend in Mumbai?'

'No – I suspect she's asleep now. Which, by the way, is what we should be doing. We've got a meeting between a traitorous secret service agent and a bunch of mad fascists to spy on tomorrow.'

'Can you do me a favour?' Sam said quietly. 'Can you rephrase that comment so it doesn't suddenly sound like a really bad idea?'

'Do you want to check in with her anyway?' Sam asked. 'These secret agents don't work normal office hours, you know?'

Nodding his agreement, Kieron activated the ARCC glasses.

They connected immediately with Bex's glasses, passing him the image they showed: a carpet and a wall, tilted, as if they were lying on their side, abandoned.

CHAPTER TEN

When Bex woke up her immediate reaction was to do nothing: just lie there with her eyes closed using her other senses to determine what might be going on around her. There was no point in letting her abductors know that she had regained consciousness. If she wanted some kind of advantage, then she had to gather as much information as possible as quickly as possible.

She was lying on her back, and it was daytime. She could see sunlight shining through her eyelids and feel it on her skin. The temperature was warm but not uncomfortable, which meant air-conditioning. That, or she wasn't in India any more, but there was something about the faint smell of spice and flowers in the air that suggested she hadn't been moved out of the country. Besides which, her own body-clock told her that she hadn't been unconscious for more than a few hours.

She could feel thick cotton sheets beneath her fingers. They seemed to be good quality as well – decently woven with a high thread-count. Maybe a hotel, or possibly a private hospital?

She deliberately made a moaning noise and turned over onto her side, not because she was uncomfortable but because she wanted to see if she might be connected to any medical equipment: intravenous drips, heart-rate monitors, blood-pressure monitors, any of those machines that made regular and annoying *bing* or *beep* sounds. Nothing tugged at her arms, so she was probably free of any medical impediments that would hold her back if she suddenly decided to leap out of the bed and make a run for it. She was also unrestrained as well: nothing tying her arms or legs to each other or to the bed.

So far, so good. If it hadn't been for the distinct memory of being shot by some strange device in the hotel corridor then she might just have lain there for a while, soaking up the luxury.

Yes, that strange device. Something like a grenade launcher – muzzle the size of a drainpipe – but she didn't feel like she'd been injured at all.

Something creaked nearby. It sounded like a person shifting position in a chair. She listened more closely, but apart from a distant whoosh that she assumed was the air-conditioning, she couldn't hear any other noise.

She breathed in through her nose, and detected another scent apart from the flowers and the hint of spice. If she wasn't mistaken, it was aftershave. Quite strong aftershave, but very pleasant. Not your bog-standard Saturday night nightclub smell. This one was floral, with hints of lime and sandalwood. Daniel Hechter, maybe.

'You're safe,' a voice said. A very mellifluous voice:

smooth and dark, like coffee. 'You're also awake, I think. Your breathing abruptly changed about two minutes ago, as did the movement of your eyes behind your eyelids. Don't worry – you have nothing to fear.'

If the game was up then the game was up. No point pretending any more. Bex opened her eyes and sat up.

She was wearing the same clothes she'd been in the night before, and she was in a pleasant bedroom. To her left a window showed a view of blue sky and a hillside. To her right a man sat stiffly in a large leather armchair. He was Indian, probably in his fifties, with white hair swept back from his forehead, and wearing a suit of very expensive cut and materials. The collar of the suit, and the white shirt beneath, were round, in the style that she thought was called 'Nehru'. A pendant hung around his neck, looking more like a piece of technology than ornamentation. His eyes were brown, and seemed devoid of any malice or anger – although that didn't necessarily mean he wasn't a threat. His hands were laid rigidly on the arms of the chair. Ahead of her a huge LCD TV screen hung on the wall.

She quickly scanned her body for injuries, wounds, bandages – anything that might have indicated she had been shot. Nothing. Whatever that weapon had been it hadn't even left her with a headache, let alone anything that needed medical treatment. Intriguing.

The man gestured, rather clumsily Bex thought, towards an open door to his left. Strangely, she thought she heard a high-pitched whine, like a nearby mosquito, as he moved. 'If you wish to leave then you can leave,' he said. 'You are on an island a few miles off the Indian coast. There is a jetty about ten minutes' walk away, downhill. A boat is waiting there that will take you back to Mumbai. Nothing will obstruct you.'

Bex raised an eyebrow. She wasn't going to enter into conversation with him if she could help it: all interrogations started with the interrogator attempting to engage in discussion with their victim. Once the talking started then it was only a matter of time before something was given away.

'My name is Agni Patel,' the man said, lowering his arm, again very deliberately and slowly. 'You won't have heard of me. You can look me up on the Internet if you wish, but you won't find very much information other than the fact that I have patented several designs for quantum computing chips that use room-temperature superconducting to keep themselves cool. That is how I made my money.'

Agni Patel. The sniper – Emma Sprue – had mentioned that name. She'd said that the man who had turned up to the meeting with Fahim Mahmoud had worked for someone called Agni Patel, and that Patel was some kind of telecommunications billionaire. Well, so far Sprue's information had turned out to be accurate. Bex wasn't sure how much of a help that might be, but it was a start.

The thought started a whole cascade of thoughts in her head about methods of checking Patel out, all of which ended with the ARCC kit and Kieron. She casually raised her hand up to her face, brushing a lock of hair from in front of her eyes while checking whether she was wearing the glasses. She wasn't. When she scratched her ear, she couldn't feel the earpiece. Damn!

She glanced at the door. What were the chances that Patel was telling the truth? Could she actually just walk out of there unhindered and get a boat back to Mumbai? What would happen if she tried?

'You are wondering two things,' Patel said calmly. 'The first is: am I telling the truth about you being able to walk out of here whenever you want? The proof, as you English say, is in the pudding. It's a misunderstood phrase, by the way. One is not proving that the pudding is actually a pudding; the word "proof" used to mean "test", so one is testing the pudding to check that it is edible, by eating it. It is the same sense of the word as is used when we talk about "proofing" weapons.' He waved a hand as if brushing away a fly – and again it was a clumsy motion, and she could hear the whining sound. 'My apologies – one of the problems about having a lot of money and being surrounded by people who work for you is that nobody ever says, "You talk too much, old man. Shut up."'

He left the sentence hanging. Bex knew he was waiting to see if she took the bait and actually said: 'You talk too much, old man; shut up.' That would have initiated a discussion, which was what he wanted, so she said nothing.

'My point being,' he went on eventually, 'that if you want to leave, leave. Take the boat to the port. If you then decide you want to come back and find out the answer to the second question in your mind, then you can. That question, by the way, is: what is it that I actually want of you? Why are you here?'

Again, he left a gap for her to ask the question. She just smiled at him.

'There is a third question which will occur to you at some stage, but has not yet. That question is: what kind of weapon did my people use that left no injuries and incapacitated you so quickly at long range – not like that rather clumsy anaesthetic spray my people found in your shoulder bag. The answers to those last two questions are connected, by the way, and they also relate to my name.'

He was wrong about that. Thoughts about that strange weapon *had* already occurred to her.

Patel raised his left hand from the arm of the chair. He held what she thought at first was a mobile phone, but which she quickly realised was a remote-control unit. He pressed a button, and he began to stand up from the chair, supporting himself with his right hand on the chair's arm. It wasn't the chair lifting him up, Bex saw: it was a lightweight metal structure, like an exoskeleton, into which his body had been strapped. Each joint had a small motor arrangement on it. On his chest and arms the exoskeleton had been hidden by his suit jacket – which, she now saw, was draped over a body that seemed thinner than she had previously thought. On his legs it was over the suit trousers but it had been hidden by the way he had been sitting in the bulky chair.

Standing, Patel pressed a series of buttons, and the exoskeleton walked him over to the window. He stopped and stared out.

'"Agni",' he said, 'is the ancient Hindu fire god. He is usually depicted as being red-skinned, with three legs, seven arms, and two faces. I've always thought it a pity, by the way, that your Christian god is invisible and unknowable. Hindu gods are so much more . . . theatrical.' He pressed a button, and his head turned to face her. 'At least say something, my dear, just so I know you're mentally aware and alert.'

'I'm not a Christian,' she said. She probably couldn't go forever without saying anything, and she was beginning to think that Patel might not be a threat – or, at least, not as much of a threat as Blood and Soil appeared to be.

'That's OK.' He smiled, and at least he could do that without a machine. 'I'm not a Hindu. Or at least not a practising one. I do appreciate the theatricality though. Hindu gods are more like strange alien creatures than supernatural beings, I've always thought.'

'Illness, or injury?' Bex asked, indicating the exoskeleton.

'Illness,' he said. Pressing a single button caused the exoskeleton to turn him so that he was facing her – probably a pre-programmed instruction, often used. He had the light behind him now, meaning that his face was in shadow. It was a tactically advantageous position: it made it much harder for her to read his expression like that. Maybe it was accidental, but she doubted it. Bex had already decided that nothing this man did was accidental. 'I was, for many years, involved in helping my country develop nuclear weapons,' he went on. 'It's difficult for a country to get taken seriously in a political or military sense unless they have nuclear weapons, and any country that does have nuclear weapons tries their best to stop anyone else from getting them. The nuclear "club" is very exclusive.' He smiled, but there was little humour in the expression. 'Ironically, we Indians found the same thing when you British were running our country and setting up your own social clubs: we weren't allowed in except as waiters, maids or cooks. History has an unfortunate habit of repeating itself at different scales and in different ways.'

Nuclear weapons. The casual use of the phrase chilled Bex. This was the connection with the Pakistani official selling Pakistan's nuclear secrets, but what did it all mean?

'Go on,' she said calmly.

'In March 1992 I was part of a secret Indian military mission to Russia's Sosnovyi Bor nuclear facility. We were looking at making a deal with them to use some of their reprocessing technology.' He paused. The memory was obviously difficult. 'An accident occurred. Radioactive iodine leaked into the atmosphere from a ruptured pipe. I became exposed, along with several of my colleagues. I breathed it in. It burned, so much.' A brief expression flickered across his face: regret and sadness combined. 'Most of my colleagues are dead now. I am still alive, but at a cost. A literal and physical cost – it takes a lot of money to keep the sickness at bay and allow me to move.'

Bex couldn't help herself. And, she thought, provocation was a good interrogation technique, and it did seem that she was now interrogating him rather than the other way around. 'And yet that doesn't stop you playing around with neutron bombs. Surely when a child gets burned it stops playing with fire?'

He nodded: a weak movement, unaided by electronics or mechanics. 'One of the benefits of having money is that you can collect things. Some billionaires collect expensive sports cars; some collect sports teams; I collect weapons of mass destruction.'

'I think I've seen this film,' Bex said. 'It doesn't end well.'

'I'm not some supervillain hell-bent on blackmailing the world,' Patel said. He seemed offended. 'I collect them so I can destroy them.'

'Seriously?'

'Seriously. There are too many nuclear weapons in the world. Current estimates put the number at around fifteen thousand. Do you know how many it would take to render the world uninhabitable?'

Bex opened her mouth to answer, but Patel kept talking.

'A hundred. Only one hundred. A regional war of a hundred nuclear detonations would produce five billion kilograms of dust and debris that would rise up to the Earth's stratosphere and block sunlight. This would produce a sudden drop in global temperatures that could last longer than twenty-five years and temporarily destroy much of the Earth's protective ozone layer. This could also cause as much as an eighty per cent increase in UV radiation on the Earth's surface and destroy both land- and sea-based ecosystems, potentially leading to global nuclear famine. And we could do that a hundred and fifty times over, with the number of weapons we have stored away in remote bunkers.'

'Once would be enough.' Bex shivered. 'Agni – the Hindu god of fire.'

'Indeed. Most of these weapons are held by America and Russia, of course, but some are orphans, left over from failed

174

military regimes, while some have been stolen by, or even are being built by, terrorists. And as the world's governments have shown no real will to get to grips with the problem, a small group of wealthy individuals have decided to step in. We take the weapons – or steal them, if we have to – and we store them safely and securely, under heavy guard, while we develop the technology to disassemble them and sequester the nuclear fuel somewhere. One of my billionaire friends – you'd recognise the name if I mentioned it – thinks we should build rockets to fire the fuel into the sun where it would burn up without trace. Another thinks we should inject it into the molten core of the planet. Either option would require more money than any government has, but not more money than we have.'

'Very altruistic,' Bex conceded.

'You're making fun of me, but I am sincere. And then, of course, there are the biological weapons – mutated versions of smallpox, cholera or anthrax, not to mention diseases that have never existed in nature but which have been created in a laboratory purely to kill people. Although they have been outlawed by the Biological Weapons Convention, they are still being worked on by many countries, and nobody knows how many biological weapons currently exist. I collect those as well – collect them and destroy them.'

Bex remembered the weapon fired at her in the corridor of the hotel. 'Your people were using non-lethal weapons. That probably indicates that you are telling the truth.'

He nodded. A grimace of pain crossed his face, and he pressed a series of buttons on the remote-control device. 'If you don't mind,' he said as he started walking back to the chair, 'I will sit down again. The harness into which I am strapped is tight, and begins to hurt after a while. I shall need to make some design changes, I think.' As the exoskeleton lowered him back into the chunky leather chair, he went on: 'Yes, the vortex ring guns. They use explosive charges to generate small self-sustaining vortices of air, like little smoke-rings. These vortices have enough force to knock a person over, but they also induce sudden pressure changes that can cause unconsciousness. I find them much more humane than crude devices that use explosions to propel chunks of metal into people's flesh.'

'I agree with that,' Bex said in a heartfelt manner. Patel's words were convincing, but he hadn't offered her anything more than words. No evidence. Part of her wanted to stay and hear more, see more, but part of her wanted to get back in contact with Kieron and find out what was going on. She raised a hand to her face. 'Oh, by the way,' she said casually, 'I think my glasses got knocked off. There's an earpiece as well – I have bad hearing in my right ear. Is there any chance your men scooped them up when they scooped me up?'

'I will check. If not, I will send a man back to your hotel to find them.' He initiated a movement with his left hand, and his right hand reached up to his throat. He touched the large pendant that hung around his neck and murmured something in Urdu. The pendant was obviously some kind of communications device. Looking back at Bex, he raised an eyebrow. 'Would you like us to bring back the sniper you left in your hotel room, or shall we leave her where she is? I ask because she has worked for me before, and I find her . . . useful.'

'But she does kill people,' Bex pointed out. 'Doesn't that go against your pacifist tendencies?'

He smiled. 'I'm not a complete pacifist. There are times when some people must die so that more may live. It's the indiscriminate nature of weapons of mass destruction that offends me. Ms Sprue kills people one at a time – and she doesn't kill people when she is working for me.' Patel looked offended. 'I wouldn't pay her if she did. I use her for her marksmanship abilities, not her murderous ones.'

'Nice to know you make a distinction.' Bex stared at him. He stared back. 'You still haven't got around to answering that second question: why am I here?'

He nodded. 'You are a British Secret Service agent, and you were at the Gateway of India when my attempt to intercept and rescue a Pakistani neutron bomb was prevented. I strongly suspect that the people who stole that documentation want to intercept the neutron bomb and use it for their own purposes. I want to stop them.'

'Yes, so do I.' Bex thought for a moment. 'Look, I want to help – I really do – but only if you're telling me the truth. How do I know? Can you show me the facility you're using to take these weapons apart? Can I actually see it happening?'

'The facility is on a remote island,' Patel said. 'I wouldn't do something that dangerous so close to one of the world's most populated cities. But yes – I could take you there. You'll be able to see that I'm not just hanging these things on a wall and treating them like works of art. I'm afraid it would take some arranging however. I do not travel well, I'm afraid.' He paused for a moment. 'There is an alternative possibility, if you'll allow me.'

Again he touched the medallion around his neck and murmured a few words. Moments later the door opened and a woman in a sari entered, carrying what looked like a large computer tablet. She bowed to Patel, then smiled at Bex and handed the tablet to her and left. Bex glanced at the screen. It showed what appeared to be a picture from a webcam somewhere: a rocky wall, a section of metal piping and a table with some papers on it. She looked back at Patel and shrugged. 'What am I looking at?'

'Sometimes,' he said, 'when I want to remind myself that I am actually accomplishing something, I take a virtual tour of the island where this work is being carried out. The tablet you hold shows the view from a drone fitted with a high-definition camera. You can make the drone take off, and you can steer it anywhere you like, look at what it shows you. This isn't virtual reality, or some kind of simulation. This is a real facility with real people.' He nodded at the tablet. 'Go ahead. Play with it.'

Bex held the tablet with her left hand while she experimented with touching the screen with her right index finger. Sliding her finger up the screen launched the drone smoothly into the air. The table dropped away, and all she could see was rock wall and more piping. Drawing a circle made the drone rotate, and suddenly she was looking along a corridor carved out of rock, big enough for two London buses to drive through side by side. People moved along the corridor and crossed it. Some wore white coats; others blue jumpsuits and white hard hats. Far in the distance there appeared to be a massive pair of doors, but between the drone and that distant exit, all along the length of the corridor, the rock gave way every now and then to a huge window. It reminded Bex strangely of an aquarium.

'Tap the bottom of the screen and the drone will start flying,' Patel said. 'One tap for slow, more taps if you want it to go faster. Tap the top of the screen and it will slow down.'

Bex tapped the screen and the drone, wherever it was, started moving forward. It made her feel like she was fifteen feet tall, and striding down the rocky tunnel. She glanced at Patel. He watched her intently. She slowed the drone and turned it so that she could see through the first of the vast windows.

She was looking at a laboratory tiled entirely in white. On a bench in the centre sat a conical device about the size of a Labrador. It lay on its side, with the sharp end pointed at a wall. Robotic arms attached to a rotating hub on the ceiling were removing screws so that another arm ending in a sucker could pull a hatch away. Bex couldn't see anyone in the room, but on the other side of the laboratory, through another large window, she could see more people in white coats looking at computer screens.

A movement drew her attention back to the conical device – a nuclear warhead, she assumed. The arm with the sucker at the end was lifting the hatch away, revealing a mass of circuitry and two metallic spheres connected by a short black tube. More robotic arms – these ones fitted with cameras – gathered around to peer inside.

'Impressive,' she said, and meant it.

'It always reminds me of that kids' game,' Patel said. 'What is it called? Operation? Why don't you check the next laboratory?'

'Why don't I head down to the far end and take a look there?' Bex challenged. She wanted to see Patel's reaction: if he had set up a tour for her, showing her particular things in a particular order, then she was determined to do something unexpected. Maybe it would reveal something, some clue that this had all been set up to impress and convince her – unlikely as that sounded.

'Whatever you wish,' he said. 'This drone is yours to command.'

Bex sent the drone flying down the rocky tunnel, over the heads of workers who barely even registered that the thing was there. She intended going as far as the huge doors, just to see what was there, but as the drone moved she realised that there were doorways in the rock, between the windows, and when one of the doorways slid open as she passed by she quickly diverted the drone sideways and through the opening, surprising a woman in a blue jumpsuit who had to fling herself against the doorframe to avoid being hit.

Bex glanced at Patel's face. He seemed unconcerned. He was even smiling slightly.

At the end of a rocky corridor, another door slid open as the drone approached. More corridors stretched out left and right. Bex chose the left-hand branch. A few metres along it, on the left-hand side, a third door was being held open by two people, a man and a woman, who were standing chatting. Bex flew between them, into the equivalent of the control room she'd seen earlier, on the other side of the nuclear warhead. Computers lined up on white tables were being operated by more of the white-coated personnel. They glanced up at the drone, briefly interested, then looked back at their screens.

The far wall was entirely made of glass. Bex flew the drone close, to see what was in the laboratory on the other side.

Another warhead on another table, except that this one had curved sides rather than straight ones, and several hatches had already been removed by the robotic arms to reveal a cluster of silvery spheres all crammed into the cavity. As Bex watched, another robot arm ending in five elongated fingers gently removed one of the spheres from its nest, moved it to a side table and placed it in a foam rubber cradle. While the 'hand' held the sphere steady, a new arm approached. This one was swathed in plastic tubes and ended in a whirring drill bit, but the bit emerged from a rubber sleeve. As the drill came close to the curved metal surface it retreated into the sleeve, which the robot arm then pressed against the ball to form an airtight seal. Bex couldn't hear anything, but she assumed that inside the rubber tube the drill bit was biting into the sphere.

'The trick, obviously,' Patel said quietly, 'is to be able to drill into the sphere and drain the contents without releasing them into the atmosphere.'

'Chemical weapons?' Bex guessed.

'More likely biological. Genetically enhanced anthrax

perhaps. We will know more when my people have conducted their analysis. Would you like to see more? You can go anywhere you like.'

Bex put the tablet down on her pillow, slid off the bed and walked over to the window. She found herself looking down onto a harbour: rolling brown waves with a distant dark lump on the horizon that might have been the Indian mainland seen through a haze of woodsmoke and industrial pollutants. True to Patel's words, a jetty projected from the harbour into the water, and an expensive-looking speedboat bobbed alongside, waiting. Between the harbour and the room where she stood a steep hillside dropped away, covered with green leaves and bright red and orange flowers. 'I can't see how you could have faked all that,' she said, 'but then, I'm not an expert in computer simulation. And even if it's real, the fact that you're taking apart weapons of mass destruction doesn't mean you're not doing something bad with the stuff you take out.'

'There is someone I think might be able to convince you further,' Patel said – 'a friend, and fellow entrepreneur.' He took a remote control out of his pocket and pressed some buttons. A sudden noise – a mobile ringtone, but louder, attracted Bex's attention away from the window. She turned to see that the LCD TV screen had sprung into life. A holding screen cleared to show a picture generated probably from a camera on a laptop or PC, judging by the angle. A man was just leaning back from having pressed a key on the keyboard to answer the call. His face was instantly familiar to Bex. She had seen him in newspapers and on TV news reports. He had never given an interview, but his fame had spread all across the world for the computing and engineering empire he had built up, for his charitable works and for his efforts to design and invent the shape of the future for the human race. And Agni Patel had got straight through to him.

'Agni,' the man said, smiling. 'Good to see your face.'

'And you, my friend.'

'How are you keeping?'

'Life goes on,' Patel replied philosophically. 'We flow wherever the current takes us.'

'My engineers have just about perfected some motors for your exoskeleton. They're smaller and lighter than the ones you already use. I'll have them shipped across by drone within the next day or two. Your people can just slot them in. You should see a major improvement in speed, stability and battery life.'

'Many thanks.' Patel pressed a button on the remote in his left hand, and his head bowed, then straightened up again. 'I wouldn't disturb your valued peace and quiet, but I need you to vouch for me to an agent from the British Secret Service.'

The billionaire on the other end of the line pursed his lips. 'Sensible?' he asked.

'Necessary.'

'Then I'll trust you. Let me know the story some time.' The man refocused his gaze towards Bex. 'You know who I am, young lady?'

'Everyone knows who you are,' she breathed, unexpectedly star-struck.

'Don't worry – I still put on my pants one leg at a time, just like everyone else. If it means anything, I am aware of everything that Agni is doing, I am involved to the extent that my fame allows me to be, and I think that together we are making the world a safer place. Agni is on the side of the angels that he doesn't believe in. Does that work for you?'

'It works for me,' she said. 'Thank you.'

'Agni,' the man said, switching his gaze back, 'we'll talk. Oh, and Miranda says you should fly over for dinner some time. She's perfected a recipe for Malabar Mealworms she wants to try out on you.'

The screen went dark as the man leaned forward to press a key. Bex turned to Patel.

'Mealworms?'

He shrugged: a difficult movement for him. 'The world is running out of food. Eating insects is one of the potential solutions. The problem is: they're not very palatable. Cooking them with spices is a workable solution and, I must say, the Malabar Coast is famed for its fine cuisine. However, duckweed is my preferred option: it grows indiscriminately in waterways around the world, it contains twenty-five per cent more protein than soya beans and it does not have the "euch!" factor that insects have and so doesn't need as much disguising. My apologies – I am talking too much again. So – do you believe me now?'

'For now. Temporarily. To be rescinded the moment something happens which goes against the story you've told me.'

'Good enough. Let us get down to basics: have you discovered who took the briefcase with the information on the location of the Pakistani neutron bomb?'

'It was a group of home-grown fascists and racists in Britain called Blood and Soil.'

'And what do they want it for?'

'That we don't know, although it will apparently lead to hundreds of thousands, if not millions, of deaths.'

'Of people they dislike or disapprove of,' Patel said grimly. 'Like me.'

'And me,' Bex said, surprising herself. 'My grandmother was Jewish. I'm sure that's enough to condemn me in their eyes.'

'Quite possibly.' He thought for a moment. 'My intention was to discover where the neutron bomb was being stored and intercept it while the Pakistani Army moved it to its new location. Obviously these Blood and Soil people want to do exactly the same thing, but whereas I intend dismantling the bomb and rendering it inactive, they intend a much more violent use.'

'Then we need to stop them getting hold of that bomb,' Bex said.

Patel shook his head. 'The information about its location and route were in that briefcase, and we do not have the briefcase.'

'But we do have a photograph of the top sheets of paper inside,' Bex pointed out. 'One of those sheets does tell us the location. If we move fast, we can get there before Blood and Soil.'

'Take the weapon and stop them using it.' Patel nodded. 'That seems feasible.'

Bex was about to elaborate on the plan when she heard a soft knock on the open door. Looking up, she saw a man standing there. He was a Sikh, with an impressive white turban, white robes and a black beard that extended down his chest. He held something in his hands. Bowing, he raised his hands to show Patel that he held Bex's ARCC glasses and earpiece. Patel nodded towards Bex, and the man crossed the room to hand them to her. Quickly she put them both on.

As the Sikh servant left, he leant over Patel and muttered something in his ear.

'Augmented-reality technology,' Patel said as the man left. 'Intriguing. I presume you can use them to access help from some contact or handler back in Mumbai.' He thought for a moment. 'Why Mumbai? Why not England? The world is getting smaller and smaller these days.'

Bex indicated the ARCC equipment. 'May I?' she asked. It was a test. If Patel objected, or tried to stop her, then she would know his story was suspect and she wasn't free to leave, or even communicate with anyone. On the other hand, he had made sure they were given straight back to her.

'Go ahead,' he said. 'My only request is that you do not expose to the world in general what I am doing here. The world needs saving, but I'm not sure it wants to be saved. Not yet, anyway.'

Bex initiated contact with Kieron. Almost immediately she heard his voice in her ear. 'Oh, thank God for that! I thought something bad had happened to you!'

'Not yet,' she said, 'but things have moved on. I need to bring you up to date, and then we need to find that neutron bomb and stop Blood and Soil from stealing it.'

'There may not be any point,' Kieron said. He sounded scared. 'We've discovered that they already have four neutron bombs they've got hold of from other places. This one would be the fifth and last. Whatever they're planning, it's going to be big and it's going to be soon.'

CHAPTER ELEVEN

The concourse of Newcastle station was a bustling mass of people heading in all directions. The crowd was surrounded by coffee bars and fast-food outlets where still more people stood quietly, absorbed in their own thoughts or making desultory conversation with their companions. Pigeons walked through what to them must have been a moving mass of columns, each of which could break their spines and ribs. It was, thought Kieron from his position on a balcony overlooking the organised chaos below, almost as if the entire thing had been painstakingly choreographed. At any second, if a waltz broke out over the public address system, he could imagine people just grabbing the person nearest to them and dancing gracefully until the music stopped and they all continued on their way again.

The balcony he and Sam were standing on was home to a number of shops which sold strange things people only seemed to buy in stations: expensive notebooks with leather covers in which the buyers were supposed to record their thoughts; ties with pictures of Disney characters; shirts with those double-cuffs that you needed separate cufflinks for;

balls of chalky coloured stuff that dissolved in the bath leaving behind an oil that smelled of flowers. Oh, and socks. Lots of socks. Did any commuter, he wondered, ever get to the station and think: 'Oh, hang on, I forgot my socks – I wonder if there's a shop here that might help?'

'Sheep,' Sam observed morosely. 'Just sheep, moving from one pen to another, unaware that they'll eventually be walking into the slaughterhouse.'

'Ooh, deep,' Kieron said.

'You can laugh, but I'll never be one of them. I'll never have a steady nine-to-five job sitting at a desk. I want to get out and see things. I want to make an impact.'

Kieron peered over the edge of the balcony. 'If you jump now, I'd say you'd make a pretty big impact.'

'Funny. At least you've got a career in MI6 to look forward to, if you play your cards right. What have I got? My mum wants me to get an apprenticeship in a garage. Imagine me with a spanner.'

Prompted by Sam's mention of MI6, Kieron reached up and pressed the connect button on the ARCC glasses. It was probably the twentieth time he'd tried it. The first ten times he'd just got that same view of the carpet in the Mumbai hotel. The next nine times the glasses had been dark. Maybe the battery had died; maybe the glasses had shut down automatically to conserve power. Or maybe someone had picked them up and put them in a box.

'Nothing?' Sam asked.

'Nothing.' If possible, Kieron's mood slipped even lower. He knew that Bex must be in trouble, but she was thousands of miles away and he couldn't help. She'd have to get out of this situation, whatever it happened to be, herself, and find the glasses again if she wanted to get back in touch. And the trouble was, he had so much to tell her about getting Bradley back from Blood and Soil and discovering that this meeting between them and probably their MI6 contact was taking place at Newcastle station.

Thinking of Bradley diverted Kieron into wondering how he was getting on. 'Have you heard anything from Courtney?' he asked Sam.

'Just that she's cooked Bradley a huge breakfast of bacon, eggs and mushrooms, and he's wolfed it all down.'

'Sounds like he's better.'

'Kind of, but she's worried about his eyes. Apparently he's still got blurred vision. She thinks it might just sort itself out, but she's keeping an eye on it.' He sniggered. 'As it were.'

Kieron let his gaze scan across the crowd, looking for anyone with the distinctive blond hair of the Blood and Soil thugs. So far, nothing. The morning crowd was comprised largely of commuters heading from the trains into the city with a mixture of shoppers doing the same. Later, in the evening, he knew the tide would turn, with the commuters and shoppers heading home, and then turn again when people came into the city for an evening out at the cinema, the theatre, a bar or a restaurant.

He looked beyond the crowd, past the barriers and as far as he could into the area where the trains arrived and left: unloading their human cargoes and then loading up again before pulling out. No sign of anyone who might be coming in for a meeting with Blood and Soil, although he had a feeling that whoever turned up would be wearing a neutral suit and tie, just like the majority of the commuters. Nondescript. Anonymous.

He glanced up at the destination boards that rippled with orange dots as the display changed: Aberdeen, Edinburgh and Glasgow were all north-east of the city; York, Leicester and London were all south. As far as he was concerned they were all magical places on a par with Narnia or Hogwarts. He had no idea what they were like, but he longed to visit them, even to live there. They had to be better than Newcastle, surely.

It seemed that Sam was having the same thoughts. 'We should move to London some time,' he said. 'When we're older, like. We could share a flat, get jobs doing bar work, maybe make some money streaming gaming sessions on YouTube when we're not at work. We'd need money from the bar work to get the latest games – nobody wants to see a streaming session dedicated to something that came out seven months ago but which we just got for our birthdays. That's old news.'

'People livestream classic games,' Kieron pointed out.

'Yeah, but a game has to be at least twenty years old before it becomes a classic.'

'I don't think that –'

'Wait. Look.' Sam indicated with a nod of his head a position near an expensive juice bar. 'Isn't that the two blokes who beat up Bradley?'

Kieron looked casually in that direction and reached up to press a virtual button on the display of the ARCC glasses, making it look as if he was waving at someone down near the ticket office. The glasses obligingly took a still photograph of the area he'd been looking at and displayed it in a corner of his vision. Looking away now, so he didn't arouse their suspicions by staring directly at them, Kieron examined the photograph.

'It certainly looks like them,' he said.

The two men were scanning the crowd with ill-disguised impatience. If, as Kieron suspected, the person they were waiting for was an expert intelligence operative, then these two were untrained morons. They radiated suspicion.

'Can you see who they're waiting for?' Kieron asked.

Sam shook his head. 'No, but it's interesting how a clear space opens up around them. Either people are subconsciously scared of getting too close, or they haven't had a bath for a while.'

'Actually, that van did whiff a bit,' Kieron observed.

The two Blood and Soil thugs were looking at everyone who went past, scowling. Usually Newcastle station saw people looking and dressing like them only on a Saturday and only when the local team were playing at home.

A person suddenly diverted from the crowd and walked up to them. It was a boy: young – younger than Kieron or Sam. He handed one of the thugs an envelope before vanishing again as fast as he could.

The thug ripped the envelope open and pulled out a sheet of paper. He looked at it, then showed it to his companion.

'Maybe they can't read,' Sam muttered. 'We could go down and offer to help.'

'They've seen us, remember? They'll recognise us.'

'Only me,' Sam responded. 'You could go.'

The two thugs conferred for a moment, then started to walk off.

'The meeting's off,' Sam said darkly. 'We've wasted our time.'

'I don't think so.' Kieron stepped back, so that he wasn't visible from the concourse, and accessed a set of the virtual menu options by waving his hands and making pressing gestures. He called up a screen showing a recording of the momentary handover, then highlighted the figure of the young boy with an arrow. He then instructed the recording to scroll backwards, but always keeping the arrow over the head of the boy.

'Are you conducting Mozart?' Sam asked. 'It's Mozart, isn't it?'

'Just because Mozart is the only composer you've heard of,' Kieron murmured, 'you don't need to bring him out any time you want to make a classical music reference.'

'I've heard of Beethoven too,' Sam said defensively. 'Metallica worked with him on a video. It's on YouTube.'

'I don't think they actually worked with him.' Kieron watched as the video played in reverse, people walking backwards with assurance, not bumping into each other. 'He died before anyone in Metallica was born.' The arrow pointing to the kid's head moved across the concourse in a weaving line, finishing up on the far side near the ticket barriers. There the kid met with a woman wearing smart casual clothes – jacket, slacks and a silk blouse.

He handed her the envelope and a five-pound note, and they split up.

Kieron set the video to play normally, and watched as the well-dressed woman stopped the boy as he walked past her, said something and pointed towards where the two thugs were standing. He nodded, and she gave him the envelope and a five-pound note. He smiled, nodded, and set off across the concourse again.

'The meeting's been moved, I think,' he said to Sam. 'There's a woman there who sent that kid over with the envelope. I think she's told them to go somewhere else and wait for her. She's probably looking to see if they were followed.'

'Maybe she's just cancelled the meeting.'

'Then why travel all this way just to have the envelope handed to them? No, it has to be a change of location.'

'We should follow them,' Sam said, pushing himself away from the railings.

'No,' Kieron said. 'She's going to be looking for someone following them, and if she sees us then the meeting is off. We have to follow her.'

He watched the woman as she watched the two thugs go. Her gaze swept across the station, looking for anyone else who seemed to be heading in the same direction, then she started walking away, towards a different exit.

'Quick,' he said; 'down the escalators and head left at the bottom.'

He'd made a mental note of the colour of the woman's jacket – black – and her silk blouse – turquoise. Once he and

Sam got to the bottom of the escalators he glanced around, trying to locate her. She was just leaving through an arched exit. He grabbed hold of Sam's shirt and dragged his friend in that direction.

While they were moving, Kieron quickly accessed the ARCC glasses, trying to get them to identify the woman, but all that happened was that a red box appeared with the text: 'Identity Restricted: Refer to Supervisor'. That, he thought, wasn't much help, except that it did indicate she might be something to do with MI6.

The woman crossed the brick-tiled area outside the station and turned right, heading along Neville Street. She walked fast, and both Kieron and Sam had to almost run to keep up. She crossed under the dual carriageway and then turned right on Milk Market. Every now and then she paused to look in a shop window or gaze into the massive glass frontage of an office block. Kieron assumed she was checking to see if she was being followed, but probably more out of habit than anything else. She had no reason to believe that she'd been spotted at the station. And besides, even if she saw Kieron and Sam, who would suspect two greeb kids?

'Heading for the Quayside Market?' Sam asked breathlessly.

'More likely the Millennium Bridge,' Kieron replied.

She was indeed heading for the Gateshead Millennium Bridge: the structure of arched white metal that curved from the Newcastle-Upon-Tyne Quayside to the Gateshead Quay arts quarter across the glittering blue waters of the Tyne. People still referred to it as 'the new bridge', although it had been built before Kieron was born. They also called it 'that hideous eyesore', but he rather liked its tilted, asymmetrical charm.

The bridge was down, which meant they could follow the woman around the curve of its length to the other side. There she turned left and strode down Shore Road, along the bank of the Tyne.

'Unless she's heading for a hotel,' Kieron said, 'I think she's going to the Baltic Centre.'

The woman was, indeed, heading for the Baltic Centre for Contemporary Art, as the ARCC glasses insisted on telling Kieron. He waved away the box of information that tried to inform him that the Baltic Centre had originally been built in the 1950s as a flour mill and a store for animal feed before being converted into an arts centre in 2002. Fascinating but useless information, Kieron thought as he pushed it away, although he did find himself wondering how many arts centres had been converted from flour mills. Not that many, he suspected.

The woman headed straight for the blocky yellow-and-red brick building. Posters outside the main glass doors advertised an exhibition of artwork by someone Kieron had never heard of.

Once inside, the two boys found themselves in a large hall whose walls were painted entirely in white, with a floor made from narrow wooden planks. Stairs and lifts led up to other levels, and the space was filled with artworks made out of metal shapes that seemed to melt and flow into differently coloured blocks of ceramic without any obvious boundary or join. Kieron felt as if he wanted to spend more time looking, but not right now. They had work to do.

'There's a couple of restaurants in here,' Sam muttered. 'If she goes to one of them for this meeting then we're screwed. We'd stand out like a mouse in a loaf of bread, and besides, I haven't got any money.'

'It's OK,' Kieron replied. He'd just seen the two Blood and Soil thugs. They were standing over by a particular sculpture and looking at it in bemusement. The woman was heading their way but via a circuitous route that took her past several other sculptures. Kieron suspected she wasn't so much appreciating the art as looking for anyone following her, or them.

'Like you said, they've seen you up close, in the industrial unit,' he murmured to Sam. 'You can't get too close. Let me do this.'

Reluctantly, Sam held back as Kieron moved towards the point where the woman was walking up to the two thugs. A group of young people stood nearby, staring at another sculpture while a teacher tried to get them to tell him how it made them feel. Fortunately they were sixth formers, all dressed in their own clothes rather than a school uniform. Kieron latched on to the outskirts of the group in a position where he could stare past the sculpture at the meeting. He zoomed a window on his ARCC glasses in to focus on the thugs, and suddenly noticed an option on the menu that said: 'Highly Directional Microphone'. He activated it with a flick of his fingers, and suddenly the din of voices in the huge exhibition hall faded, and he was listening to the two men as if he were standing beside them.

'I dunno much about art,' one of them said as the woman joined them, 'but the welding is crap.'

'I'm not used to being summoned,' the woman interrupted. 'Especially north of Watford. This had better be good.'

'How do we know who you are?' one of the blond thugs – the one named Kyle Renner who had tried to find Kieron and Sam in the shopping mall – said belligerently.

'Because you asked me to be here, and I'm here. Who else would I be?'

'All right – how do you know we're who we say we are?'

'Because I've got files on both of you, with photographs and everything. I'd be tempted to say I know more about you than your mothers do, but they've changed your nappies and I haven't, which means there are some things only they know about. So – don't waste any more of my time than you have to. Tell me what's so important.'

'You need to know that someone's been interfering with our operations,' Renner said. 'When we took that bloke from the shopping centre, he dropped those glasses and earpiece you wanted. I went back for them, but someone else had picked them up. I was told it was a couple of kids, so I didn't worry too much – I just reckoned I could pick the kit up later from the nearest second-hand electricals place, but then something happened.' He scowled, making his face look like some kind of fright mask, and looked away. 'These two kids somehow found out where we were holding that bloke, and they rescued him.'

'They rescued him,' the woman repeated. It wasn't a

question, as far as Kieron could tell; it was her attempt to come to terms with the stupidity of their actions. 'A couple of kids. This is what I get for working with idiots.'

'Oi,' the second man said. Kieron quickly accessed the ARCC equipment and asked it to identify him. It came back: David Allen Crisp. British citizen; aged twenty-five. Convictions for theft. Linked to right-wing group Blood and Soil. 'You don't get to talk to us like that!'

'Not only do I talk to you any way I want, I also tell Darius Trethewey how incompetent you are. If you ever want to amount to anything in Blood and Soil then you need your boss on your side, and he's a very good friend of mine.' She thought for a moment. 'All right, I suppose the fact that you've told me what's happened counts in your favour. You could have pretended that everything was OK. Do what you can – I need that man and those kids found.'

'And hidden away until you can talk to them,' Renner said.

'And killed, I think. I was hoping not to go that far, but needs must when the devil drives. Kill all three of them and dispose of the bodies.' She sniffed. 'Of course, this is Newcastle. You could probably leave them out in the street and nobody would notice.' She glanced at Renner. 'Do not leave them in the street. Understand?'

He nodded. 'Yeah.'

The second thug, Crisp, thrust his chin forward aggressively. 'The plan's still goin' ahead, yeah? You ain't goin' to stop it?'

The woman looked at him as if she'd just found him on the sole of her shoe. 'You don't know anything about the plan. You're too stupid. And by that I mean you're too stupid to understand it, but you're also too stupid to be told, because you'd blab to people in the pub when you get drunk, and that would be the end of the plan.'

Crisp looked like he was about to hit her. The woman just stared him down. Eventually Renner took Crisp's arm and said, 'Just go over to the window and watch the boats for a while. Go on.'

Crisp left, still fuming. When he moved out of earshot, the woman said, 'That man is a liability. Get rid of him. If you don't, I'll tell Trethewey to get rid of both of you.'

'No need for threats.' Renner lifted his head momentarily, acknowledging her point. 'I'd already worked out that he's a security risk. I asked Darius for permission to deal with him. Give it a day and he won't be a problem for anyone apart from those blokes who get paid to keep the canal clear of rubbish.'

The woman stared at Renner as if she was evaluating him for the first time. 'You're a lot cleverer than you look, and than he actually is. How much do you know?'

'About the plan?' Renner paused for a moment, and looked around. 'Some things that you don't. For instance, I heard from one of our sisters out in India. She's part of the team trying to get hold of the fifth device. She said someone tried to interfere with their operation. It was the girl, the one whose partner we took prisoner.'

'And lost again,' the woman pointed out.

'Yes, and lost again. Regardless, the point is that we might not get that fifth device if someone's in the way.'

'You know what the devices are for?' the woman challenged.

'You want me to name the targets?' he shot back. 'Here? In public?'

'Just name five cities in the Middle East and the Indian subcontinent. Any five that come to mind. Nobody can say that's giving anything away. Five cities you've heard of in the news recently.'

'Tehran, Baghdad, Riyadh, Islamabad and Tel Aviv,' Renner said without blinking.

'Quite right. Four Muslim, and one Jewish, just to throw some confusion into the mix,' she said, nodding. 'A good spread across five different countries – Iraq, Iran, Saudi Arabia, Pakistan and Israel. Nothing in Egypt or Turkey, because we Brits like going there on holiday, and they can be dealt with diplomatically. And there's lots of Muslims in those cities. Over thirty million of them, plus 400,000 Jews in Tel Aviv. If we only had, say, four devices to play with then we'd remove a city from the list – probably Riyadh. After all, Saudi Arabia is supposed to be our friend, even if the Wahabi regime there is supporting Muslim extremists with huge amounts of their oil money. You see what I'm saying? Four devices isn't as good as five, but we can absorb the loss. And besides; we don't know for sure that the fifth device is unavailable. Let's wait and see how all this pans out.'

Renner's expression had changed from challenging to something almost worshipful. 'I can't believe we're going to wipe them out.'

'Careful. Let's not say too much out loud. At the moment it's all deniable.'

He frowned. 'Why take Riyadh off the list, if we only end up with four devices? Surely the point is to –' he caught himself – 'deal with as many Muslims as possible?'

'The point isn't to deal with Muslims, much as that might surprise you. Most Muslims are lovely people, with a wonderful set of different cuisines and some magnificent architecture. The point is to deal with the main trouble-making population areas, the ones that are providing the extremist terrorists or are supporting them financially. So why keep Tel Aviv on the list, you ask? Because if thirty million Muslims suddenly die, a lot of fingers will be pointed at Israel. The Jews hate the Arabs, after all. The last thing we want is a messy and destructive war, but if Israel is provoked militarily then they might respond with their own nuclear weapons, and there's no controlling that. But if 400,000 Jews die as well then nobody will know who to blame. There will be accusations and counteraccusations, but eventually people will be glad that these hotbeds of fanatics and funds for fanatics have been removed – and with no nasty radiation to deal with after that first blast.'

Renner looked as if all his Christmases had come at once. 'They'll take us seriously then,' he said.

Kieron felt sick. He knew that he'd fallen into something big, just because of the mention of neutron bombs, but this? Killing millions of people in some misguided attempt to make the world safer for white British people? Not every one of those people would be a terrorist, or a terrorist funder.

202

'Is there anything else?' the woman asked.

Renner shook his head.

'OK then. Thank you for the information about losing your prisoner and his equipment. Get them back and get rid of them. Get rid of your friend as well. Oh, and thank you also for the information about the operation in India. I will talk to Trethewey about that. Now, go.'

Renner nodded, turned and walked away. As he passed Crisp he grabbed the man's jacket and pulled him along. Crisp looked like he was arguing, but Kieron couldn't hear what he said. Kieron felt vaguely sorry for the man – he wasn't going to survive the night, if Kieron understood the implications of the previous conversation.

'Hey,' a voice said. 'Aren't you a little young to be a sixth former?'

He turned and saw one of the group of teens staring at him challengingly.

Kieron smiled. 'Special permission,' he said. 'Our school was allowed to send a few of us along to join you.'

The kid sneered, and looked at Kieron's New Rock boots. 'Nice footwear,' he said.

'Think of them as a work of art.' Kieron turned away, and scanned the crowd for the woman. It took him a few moments to realise that she hadn't moved. She had taken a pair of glasses from her bag, and as Kieron watched she slipped them on. She touched the right-hand side of the glasses and looked around. She frowned. Raising a hand, she started to make gestures in the air. To anyone passing by, it might look as if she was mirroring the shape of the sculpture she stood beside in some kind of artistic appreciation, but Kieron knew what she was really doing.

She was using ARCC glasses.

She opened her mouth and murmured something. For a second Kieron thought she was talking to her own agent handler somewhere – another rogue MI6 agent who had allied themselves with Blood and Soil – but then he heard a burst of static in his earpiece and her voice saying: 'I don't know about you, but I find that the arms on these things begin to rub on the top of the ear after a while. What with that and the earpiece, it's really quite uncomfortable. Millions of pounds of development funding, and they can't make them fit nicely. It's a scandal.'

He felt as if his heart had momentarily stopped and then restarted with a heavy thump. Was she talking to him?

'I know you're out there,' she went on. 'For security reasons any set of ARCC kit won't identify the location of another set – it would be too easy for an enemy to take advantage of that – but I can tell that someone is accessing the same receive-and-transmit bandwidth. It has to be the person who took Bradley Marshall's ARCC kit. Am I right? I'm right, aren't I?'

She spoke very reasonably, very calmly, but Kieron had just heard her order the deaths of him, Sam, Bradley and the Blood and Soil thug Crisp in the same tone of voice.

She was looking around now, scanning the crowd. Kieron moved back behind one of the sixth formers, hoping desperately they weren't going to move on in a hurry.

'I'm guessing that you're just some ordinary member of

the public who had picked the equipment up and doesn't really understand what they've got themselves into,' she went on. 'My advice to you would be: put it all in the nearest rubbish bin and walk away. This is too risky for you.'

Again she left a silence, but he didn't say anything. She wanted him to respond, probably so she could find out more about him, but he wasn't going to fall into that trap.

'If you don't, I will throw the entire weight of MI6 behind finding out who you are, where you live, what your family situation is and even how many pets you have. And I will kill you, your family and your pets. Do you understand?'

Kieron felt a wave of emotion wash over him. It was mainly anger that she could so calmly threaten his family, but beneath that he could feel an undertow of fear. It was the anger, however, that made him say: 'You can't use the full weight of MI6. You're a traitor working with neo-Nazis, and you're planning mass murder. Someone has to stop you.'

'And that person is you?' She sounded amused. 'Little man, the world of international politics is very murky. Maybe I'm operating outside the boundaries of my job, but I'm trying to make the world safe for people like you – and your family, and even your pets. Are you willing to risk all of them?'

'We know who you are,' Kieron bluffed. 'We can expose you. If you threaten my family, we *will* expose you.'

'I don't think you do know who I am. I'm not in any database you can access. However –' she paused, and raised another hand to caress the air – 'just in case you *are* here, and you have my photograph, let me show you what I can do to ARCC equipment using Administrator privileges.'

Static obscured Kieron's vision. He pulled the glasses off his face, feeling suddenly like he was trapped in a tiny box. Looking down at the lenses in his hand he could see a line of tiny red text: 'Unexpected reset has occurred. All recorded data will be lost. System rebooting.' In his earpiece he heard her voice say, 'Remember your family, little man. Because if you continue on this path that's all you'll be able to do – remember them.'

By the time Kieron dared to look out from behind the school group he was using for cover, she had gone.

He felt as if he might throw up. This had become more than just a fun game. This was *real*.

CHAPTER TWELVE

Bex felt an icy hand clutch at her heart. 'What do you mean, *four* other neutron bombs?' she asked.

She could hear the strain in Kieron's voice, even over the ARCC earpiece and the several thousand miles between them. 'A lot of stuff has happened that you need to know about,' he said, 'but the really important thing is that Sam and I overheard a conversation between the traitor in MI6 and the Blood and Soil thugs. A meeting took place that we found out about while we were getting Bradley back.'

Agni Patel frowned at her from across the room, obviously worried at the fact that she'd unexpectedly mentioned four more bombs, not just the one. She raised a hand, trying to get him to wait until the information hurricane she currently found herself standing inside had subsided somewhat and she could tell him what was happening. Her mind snagged on one of the facts fluttering past: not directly related to neutron bombs, but important to her none the less. 'You got Bradley back? Is he OK?'

'He's concussed, but Sam's sister is looking after him.'

'Sam's sister?' No, leave that. 'Right – back up a bit. You

found out about a meeting between the MI6 traitor and Blood and Soil? Where did this meeting take place?'

'Newcastle station, then the Baltic Centre. It's a kind of art gallery thing.'

'OK. You saw the traitor? You've got photographs?' She felt a wave of euphoria sweep over her. This nightmare might be over soon!

'Yes and no. Yes, we saw the traitor, but no, we didn't get any photographs. She reset our ARCC equipment and flushed the memory. By the time it had rebooted she'd gone.'

'She?' A woman. How many women did Bex know in the SIS-TERR team that she worked for? Six? Eight including the admin staff. 'What did she look like?'

'Old. Blonde. Well-dressed: like a school inspector.'

'*How* old?' she said, hearing the anger and frustration in her voice and hating herself for it.

'I don't know!' Kieron was feeling the pressure too. 'Older than me and Sam! Maybe younger than my mum! Look, we're teenagers – everyone over twenty looks old to us!'

'Doesn't matter.' Bex waved her hand dismissively, even though Kieron couldn't see her. 'She was probably wearing a wig anyway, and she was probably made up to look older than her actual age. Nobody in MI6 goes out in public without some kind of disguise.'

'I know,' Kieron said. 'There's this thing on YouTube – it's an interview that one of your guys did for the BBC. He was wearing a fake moustache as a disguise, but under the heat of the studio lights the glue softened and the moustache started to slide off his upper lip. It was brilliant.'

'Yeah – moving on. At least we've narrowed the field down a bit.' She took a deep breath, trying to calm herself. 'OK, you overheard her saying something about there being more bombs? Tell me everything.'

'Yeah. There's five bombs in total. The one in Pakistan is the last one. The rest are already in place.'

The wave of euphoria she'd felt when she had thought that the identity of the traitor was out in the open had ebbed away now, like a retreating tide, leaving a sick feeling behind it. 'Kieron, this is important. Where are those bombs right now?'

'They're located in –' he hesitated for a moment, 'Tehran, Baghdad, Riyadh and Islamabad,' he recited. 'The fifth one – the one that's being stolen in Pakistan – is going to be flown to Tel Aviv. Bex – once those bombs are all in position, they're going to be blown up! Millions of people will die!'

'Yes, I know,' she said grimly. This all felt so unreal. 'Where exactly are these bombs in those cities?'

'She didn't say.'

'Hold on a moment.' She turned to Agni Patel, who looked concerned. 'Five bombs in total, including the one you were trying to buy,' she said hurriedly. 'All controlled by a fascist group who want to cause massive loss of life. Four are already in place in Saudi Arabia, Pakistan, Iraq and Iran. We've got to do something!'

'Who are you talking to?' Kieron asked on the ARCC link.

'A friend. I think a friend.'

Agni's expression seemed trapped somewhere between concern and thoughtfulness. 'For the most devastating results,' he said, 'the bombs would have to be triggered in mid-air, over the cities. Let's assume this fascist group intends triggering them all at the same time, for best psychological effect. If it were me I would use large remote-controlled drones to carry the bombs as high as I could, and then send the triggering signal to all of them at the same time. That would require some kind of global satellite coverage.' He saw the expression on Bex's face and shrugged. 'If it were me, which it is not. I am thinking hypothetically, but if we get to the *last* bomb then we can prevent all the bombs being triggered. Or at least delay the moment so we can do something.' The fingers on his right hand clenched spasmodically, as if he wanted to hit his fist against his leg but didn't have the strength. 'Ah, no! If they know we have the fifth bomb then they might just trigger the other four anyway!'

'We should alert –' Bex started to say, but Agni interrupted her.

'Alert who? The intelligence services of four separate and antagonistic countries who don't have any real channel of communication between them? It's an impossible task. What if you notify MI6, in the UK? That's where the signal will be sent from, surely?'

'Yes, but where in the UK?' Bex clenched her fists in angry frustration. 'And the traitor in MI6 will just tie everything up in delays and confusion. It's up to us!'

Bex heard a throat-clearing sound over the ARCC link. 'Actually,' Kieron said, almost apologetically, 'I think I might have an idea.'

Across the room, Agni had pressed the device hanging

around his neck. He muttered instructions to someone on his staff.

'Go on,' Bex said to Kieron. 'At the moment we're all out of ideas.'

'According to this conversation we overheard, some bloke called Darius Trethewey is in charge of Blood and Soil.'

'Yes, I know that,' Bex said impatiently, remembering what the sniper, Emma Sprue, had told her. 'It doesn't help.'

'It might do. He's going to be there in Pakistan when his people steal the fifth neutron bomb! He wants to make sure that the whole thing goes according to plan. Apparently he's very hands-on – doesn't trust his own people.'

A second wave of euphoria swept over Bex, leaving her shivering. This constant rollercoaster of emotions was exhausting her. 'So if we can get to him –'

'Then we can stop him ordering the detonation of the bombs!'

'And hope he hasn't left instructions that if he's somehow incapacitated then the bombs should be set off anyway.' She thought for a moment. 'We can always threaten him. Say we'll kill him if he tries to detonate the bombs. Hell, we could fly him to one of those cities and keep him there. He wouldn't order the detonation if it was going to kill him as well. These guys are cowards to the core.'

Kieron's voice sounded hushed. 'Would we? I mean, would you?'

'Don't know,' Bex admitted, remembering her reluctance to inflict pain on Emma Sprue. 'Let's hope he plays ball and we never have to find out.'

The door to the room opened and the turbaned Sikh servant she'd seen before entered. He crossed to Agni, bent down and whispered something in his ear.

'Wait a moment,' she said to Kieron.

Agni nodded, then turned to her. 'I have a task force ready to go,' he said. 'There's a helicopter waiting outside. It's about four hundred miles to the border with Pakistan, which means that you'll be there within two hours. You're in charge. If there's a language problem then Anoup here will translate your orders. He's also been told to protect your life with his own.'

The Sikh man – Anoup – bowed. Straightening, he smiled, revealing gleaming white teeth. 'My responsibility, my duty and my pleasure,' he said.

'Well,' she said, taken aback, 'let's hope it doesn't come to that.'

'The main task is to secure the neutron bomb,' Agni added, 'but I gather from the conversation with your distant friend that there is a secondary task, to take this man – Darius Trethewey – prisoner. Am I right?'

She stared at the painfully thin Indian man, trying to evaluate him. She'd only known him for an hour or so, but here she was, entrusting her life and potentially the lives of millions of people to him. This was surely madness, but what choice did she have? Circumstances had been pushing her towards this room and this moment, perhaps for longer than she knew.

He smiled a gentle smile. 'Sometimes,' he said as if he knew exactly what she was thinking, 'we just have to release ourselves and trust to the current of life to deposit us on whatever shore it chooses.'

'Thank you,' she said. 'Whichever shore we end up on, thank you for trusting me, and for helping me.'

'I only wish I could go with you,' he said, with a slight and awkward shrug. 'But I would only hold you back.'

Nodding, she turned to the door, aware that Anoup had moved to stand at her shoulder. 'Kieron – we're on a mission to save, well, not the world, but a measurable part of it. Are you with me?'

'Did we ever get to talk about a salary?' Kieron asked. He sounded scared. He had every right to be, Bex thought. 'Or just a payment. Enough so that Sam and I can go to this concert next week – that's all we want.'

'If this all works out,' Bex said, 'I'll guarantee you front-row seats.'

'Then I'm with you.'

'That's all I wanted to know. Talk later.'

She headed out of the room, Anoup beside her. He pointed right. 'That way, miss.'

Down the corridor and a flight of stairs, Bex found herself walking along a tiled hall towards a large doorway. From outside she heard the regular *thap-thap-thap* of a helicopter's rotor blades. Emerging from the doorway, she saw ahead of her a grassy lawn. The building she had just left was a palatial residence of white stone, and in front of her a helicopter hovered, skids just touching the grass. Its whirling rotors were just a blur against the blue sky. For a few seconds her mind just froze, stunned by the speed of events, but she took a deep breath and trusted the current to take her where she needed to go.

'Russian helicopter,' Anoup shouted. 'Mi-24, NATO designation HIND. 1970s technology, but still perfectly workable. We acquired many of them after the Russians left Afghanistan.'

Bex stared at the hovering craft. It looked like someone had tried to make a helicopter disguised as an insect; maybe a mosquito. The colour scheme was nondescript sand, and the front section, where the pilot sat, was made of bubbles of armoured glass set low, near the ground. Rods that might have been radio aerials, sensors, machine guns or air-speed indicators projected forward from the transparent bubbles like antennae. Behind the rounded 'head' the high cargo section and higher engines gave it a hunched appearance. It had wings as well; short, stubby wings with missiles hanging from them.

Anoup led her towards the helicopter. They had to keep low, not because there was any risk of the rotors taking the top of their heads off – they were too high up for that – but because the pressure of the air being forced down and sideways meant that even crouching they had to scrunch their eyes up and push against the tornado-force wind towards the open cargo door. Once inside Bex saw that there were seven Indian men strapped into seats, each wearing anonymous grey coveralls and each holding one of the stubby black weapons that she'd seen – and fallen victim to – back at her hotel. 'Vortex ring guns' Agni had called them – non-lethal weapons that used explosively driven rings of compressed air to knock people over, or knock them out. She glanced at the stubby wings through the narrowing gap as Anoup slid the armoured door closed. They seemed to droop under the weight of the missiles suspended from them. She wondered if they were non-lethal too. Probably not.

The helicopter lurched into the air, and she strapped herself into a spare seat before she fell over. The rest of the team were looking at her expectantly. She glanced at them, at Anoup, and then back at them again.

'Thank you all for being here,' she said, uncertainly at first but then with increasing confidence. She had to raise her voice almost to a shout in order to make herself heard over the throbbing of the rotors. 'We know where we're going, but we're not sure exactly what we will find when we get there. A dangerous weapon is either being transported or being hijacked. Our job is to grab it and bring it back, and in doing so make the world a safer place. There's a man likely to be there, hijacking the weapon, and I want to bring him back as well.' She hesitated, aware that she wasn't sure what Darius Trethewey looked like and wondering how she was going to be able to identify him, but before her silence became uncomfortable Anoup pulled a pile of tablets out from underneath a seat. They had been put in ruggedised shells to protect against damage. He handed them out.

'On here you will find satellite pictures of the location, which is in Pakistan, fifty miles over the border,' he said in his deep and strangely reassuring voice. 'Familiarise yourselves with the geography. You will also find photographs of this man, Trethewey. Familiarise yourselves with him as well.' As the men started checking out the tablets he turned to

Bex, handing one to her as well. 'Updated a few moments ago from Mr Patel's command centre,' he said more quietly. 'You should take a look.'

Bex took it with a smile. She touched the ARCC glasses, perched on her nose. 'I have my own information source,' she said, 'but thanks.'

Glancing out of the armoured window in the middle of the sliding door, she saw the Indian countryside flashing past beneath them: a mottled patchwork of brown and green, with occasional pools of blue-green water. A regular vibration shook everything in the bay where they were sitting; she could feel it in her bones, her teeth and in the pit of her stomach. Every now and then the helicopter lurched, dropping down a few feet or suddenly rising upward, and she could tell that they were swinging left and right as well, like a cabin suspended from a big wheel at a funfair. She desperately hoped she wasn't going to be sick. That really wouldn't impress the team she was meant to be leading.

'I'm getting nauseous just looking at the pictures,' Kieron's voice said in her ear. 'I hate to think what it's like for you.'

'No worse than flying into Hong Kong in a thunderstorm,' she said. 'Did you hear the stuff about the mission briefing on the tablets?'

'Yeah, and your friend Agni Patel also sent it through to my ARCC kit. I don't know how he found me, but I'm looking at it now, and comparing it with what I've found out. We can talk it through, if you like.'

For the next twenty minutes, as the HIND helicopter swung and shifted, and as the deep vibration set up a gradual ache at the base of her spine, Kieron and Bex compared notes on the visuals they both had. The location in Pakistan where the neutron bomb was being kept was a collection of concrete bunkers set into dusty brown hills where the only vegetation was the occasional spindly bush or tree and the only access for traffic a straight dirt road that, sixty miles away, joined up with one of the highways crossing Pakistan. The site was surrounded by three separate electrified fences, and guarded by a regiment of Pakistani Army troops. Ground-to-air missile emplacements around the perimeter were supposed to protect the site against attack from above, but that only worked if the neutron bomb was actually inside the fences. If it was being moved then it was vulnerable, protected only by the troops accompanying it and by its anonymity, and that was almost certainly where Blood and Soil intended to hijack it – not in the base but on the road.

'The documents that Blood and Soil snatched in Mumbai said that the neutron bomb is being moved today,' Kieron said. 'Right now it's being loaded onto a lorry which is part of a convoy. In one hour it will leave the base and head out along the road to the main highway. Once it gets there it will make its way to the main Army base near Peshawar, which is where it's going to be stored more securely.' He paused, then went on. 'I've got to say, the Pakistani government seem quite casual about the way they treat their weapons. If this was Britain or America security would be much tighter.'

'Back when I was in the Army,' Bex said, 'before Bradley persuaded me to leave and go freelance with him, working for MI6 and SIS-TERR, I had a friend who spent a month at a Pakistani Army base training the troops in bomb-disposal techniques. At the time they were having a lot of problems with terrorists. He told me that when he arrived the colonel who was looking after him showed him all the explosives they'd obtained in raids on terrorist hideouts. It was all stacked up by the side of the road for him to see, and there were soldiers guarding it who were smoking. Actually smoking. Next to containers of explosives. And, just to make it worse, there was a school on the other side of the road for the kids of the officers. He said that he learned very quickly that the Pakistanis have a different attitude towards risk than we do. It's all in Allah's hands, apparently, and if something is going to go wrong then it will go wrong.'

They spent the remainder of the flight going over possible attack strategies, using the tablets that Anoup had handed out. With the satellite photographs of the location of the nuclear storage bunker as a background, he used a special pen to draw on his screen, and the resulting pictures instantly appeared on everyone else's device. He set up a series of possibilities, such as: the convoy with the bomb was just leaving the bunker; the convoy with the bomb was already en route on the access road; the convoy with the bomb was ahead of schedule and on the main road to Islamabad; there were three separate convoys, two of which were decoys while the other one was real, and they were all going in different directions at different speeds; the Blood and Soil team were attacking the convoy; and the Blood and Soil team hadn't arrived yet. He then indicated with an 'X' where the helicopter would set down in each case and drew arrows to show which directions he wanted everyone to go. In a different colour he also showed where he expected the Blood and Soil people to be, if they were already there, and he made sure that some of his people were tasked to keep them engaged while the others took the neutron bomb. Very quickly and concisely he covered all the potential options, giving them code names based on Gujarati numbers. The only option he didn't cover, as far as Bex could see, was the one where Blood and Soil had got there early and already taken the bomb themselves. That one would require a whole different set of tactical options.

What impressed Bex the most was that Anoup kept checking with her to make sure she was happy with the instructions he gave: glancing up, making eye contact and waiting for her nod. She was pretty sure he could have led the whole operation himself with no problems, but he was going along with Agni's order that she was in charge, and he wanted the team to know it.

She didn't feel as if she was in charge. The swinging motion of the helicopter made her feel sick, and the sticky, oppressive heat didn't help. And, of course, there was the tension of knowing she was heading into a firefight where she might be responsible for people's deaths.

Anoup put his hand up to the headphones he wore, pressing them tighter to his head to block out the heavy noise of the engine and the rotor blades. He nodded, then turned to Bex.

'We have just crossed into Pakistani airspace,' he shouted.

She looked out of the window in the door. The ground below seemed not to have changed: it was still dusty brown earth punctuated by the occasional bush and tree that appeared to be struggling to survive.

'We are flying low,' he went on, 'to make sure we stay underneath the Pakistani Air Force's air defence radar, but we are now breaking international treaties. Technically we have just invaded another nation.' He smiled, showing his gleaming, perfect teeth. 'But at least it's in a good cause, eh?'

She nodded, feeling a flutter of panic in her stomach. 'One less nuclear bomb in the world means a safer world,' she said.

'That's why Mr Patel does what he does. He makes the world a safer place, one device at a time.'

The helicopter banked left, and Bex had to reach up and catch hold of a rail to stop herself sliding off her bench.

She slipped the ARCC glasses from the pocket where she had stowed them, put them on and pressed the hidden button that would send a message to the set back in Newcastle, telling Kieron that she was back online. A few seconds later she heard his voice say: 'It's incredibly noisy there.'

'It would be. I'm in a helicopter, flying into Pakistan.'

'So your essay on "What I did For My Holidays" is going to be fun then.'

She laughed. 'It's like being in a National Express coach, except there's no toilet at the back.'

'Actually,' he said, 'I'm just checking the specifications of that helicopter now. According to these glasses, one of the seats lifts up and there's a toilet underneath.'

'Oh,' she said, trying to imagine what that would be like to use. 'Great.'

'Do you need anything?'

'No,' she said, and swallowed, her mouth suddenly dry. 'I just wanted to say – well, this could be dangerous. I wanted to say thanks. And if you don't hear from me again, destroy the ARCC kit and . . . and . . . forget all about it.'

'I'll destroy it,' he said sombrely, 'but I'll never forget.'

'Signing off now. Talk later, with luck.'

'Yes,' he repeated. 'Talk later.'

She felt like she was a teenager again, on the phone to someone and not wanting to be the one to hang up. Eventually she just removed the glasses and switched them off.

Something flashed on the screen of Anoup's tablet.

'We are approaching the target point,' he announced. 'According to the latest satellite reconnaissance, there is one convoy and it is halfway along the access road. There is no sign of Blood and Soil yet. Attack Pattern *Chah*.'

The helicopter banked right, and the sound made by the engine and the rotors changed in some subtle way. Bex could tell from the way her stomach seemed to rise up that they were descending.

Agni's men checked their vortex ring guns. Their faces were grim.

Through the window, the ground was approaching fast.

Anoup waved one hand urgently, the other hand holding the padded earpiece of his headphones to his ear. 'Update from the pilot!' he shouted. 'Direct observation of the landing site indicates a fight is going on. Switch to Attack Pattern *Paanch*!'

The helicopter suddenly seemed to shudder, and jerk to the left. Hands clutched for support.

Several bangs shook the airframe.

'We're taking fire,' Anoup shouted to Bex. 'I think we're in the right place.'

'Who's firing at us?' she yelled back. 'The Pakistani military, or Blood and Soil?'

'Apparently both,' he said.

The helicopter landed with a bone-shaking jolt. The door slid back, and suddenly the men she was supposed to be in charge of all scrambled out, weapons held ready.

'They know what they're doing,' Anoup said, grabbing her arm and pulling her towards the door. 'Our job is to find that man – Darius Trethewey.'

Bex and Anoup jumped out of the helicopter together. The downdraught from the still-whirling rotor flattened Bex's hair across her eyes and she brushed it away. The air smelled dry and old, and the helicopter's rotors were pushing clouds of dust away from them, giving them some cover but making it difficult to see what was going on. She quickly scanned left to right, doing her best to match the apparent chaos of what she could see to Anoup's precise diagrams.

They had landed on top of a low hill: one of a number that erupted from the terrain like boils. Rocks ranging from the size of a cricket ball to the size of a car littered the hillsides as if thrown there by some gigantic, careless hand. Down below, in a dip between the hills, she could see the curve of a dusty road that seemed to wind its way across the lowest point in the ground, like a river. A large lorry, painted in military green, had stopped in the road. Two Land Rovers were stationary in front of it; two more behind. Pakistani

Army troops in green uniforms and caps were sheltered behind the vehicles, firing at men dressed in anonymous black clothes who were heading over the top of, and around the sides of, the hill on the other side of the vehicles to Bex, using the rocks for cover. The men in black were firing down at the Pakistani Army personnel, who were in turn firing upward. The appearance of Agni's helicopter and fighters had thrown everything into apparent confusion. The men in black were holding back hesitantly, not sure which side Agni's men were there to support, and some of the Pakistani Army soldiers were trying to slide beneath their vehicles, having assumed they were now under attack from both sides.

Gunfire echoed between and around the rocks, the cracks sounding disconcertingly like fireworks. Small plumes of dust erupted from the ground where they hit. Every now and then Bex heard a metallic *ching* as a bullet hit one of the vehicles.

Something whizzed past Bex's ear. She flinched reflexively, only realising after a few seconds that it had been a bullet, not an insect. The men in black were firing at them.

Agni's men started to climb down the hill, using the rocks as cover in the same way as the black-clad attackers. They started firing their vortex ring guns at the Blood and Soil troops, sending little ripples of air flowing across the gap between the hills. Each shot made a sound strangely like a suppressed cough. Having been on the business end of one of those bullets of air, Bex knew how it felt for the several black-clad men who dropped to the ground, unconscious.

The black-clad men intensified their fire at the troops with whom Bex had shared the flight. One of them got hit in the chest, his armour absorbing the impact. He staggered, then kept moving. Another man wasn't so lucky. A bullet hit him in the hip, where he had no protection. He fell to the ground, crying out in pain. Another man moved to help him.

Bex glanced back at the helicopter. More particularly, she gazed wistfully at the twin machine guns that stuck out from the front bubble canopy like mandible jaws. They would make short work of the Blood and Soil men, but Agni wanted to minimise loss of life.

She glanced up at the top of the hill that the Blood and Soil troops were descending. Their own transport – maybe a helicopter, maybe ground transport – would be over the other side. As would Darius Trethewey, she guessed.

Something moved in the sky above her, attracting her attention. She glanced up, expecting to see a hawk gliding over, looking for food, but instead saw a remote-control drone with five rotors and a professional-looking video camera hanging below it, focused on the action. That must be how Trethewey was keeping track of what was going on.

She grabbed Anoup's shoulder and directed his attention to the drone. He nodded.

'Other side of the hill,' she mouthed over the sound of gunfire and air-projectiles. 'We go round.'

Instead of heading towards the vehicles, Bex led Anoup sideways, down the side of the hill. When they got to the lowest point, she could see, across the road, a similar valley from which the hill that the Blood and Soil team were using for cover rose. She led the way across the road, glancing right to where the vehicles and the soldiers were under attack. The soldiers seemed to have accepted that Agni's men were on their side: they were standing side-by-side in some cases: one firing lethal bullets, the other firing non-lethal slugs of compressed air.

Five Pakistani Army men lay in the dust; bloodstains almost black against the green material. Two of Agni's men had joined them: colleagues in death or injury.

Bex's head turned back to look where she was going, just as a black-clad, blond-haired fighter came into sight around the curve of the hill. He was almost certainly a guard, and almost certainly furious at being kept out of the action. He saw Bex at the same time as she saw him, and raised his gun eagerly. He wasn't going to ask any questions: just shoot.

Bex brought her own weapon up at the same time as Anoup. They fired together. Bex felt a strong kick-back from the weapon as it slammed into her shoulder, sending a sudden spike of pain through her. The air between them and the Blood and Soil guard seemed to ripple like a duvet cover being shaken. He suddenly flew backwards, a surprised expression on his face. The expression changed to shock as he impacted a rock, and then unconsciousness as he slid down it to the ground.

'I like these,' Bex said, hefting the gun.

'It's like vaping,' Anoup said with a flash of his teeth, 'all of the effect, but none of the danger.'

She ran forward, putting the bulk of the hill between them and the action centred on the vehicles. She could still hear the sounds of gunfire and air-slugs being exchanged

225

however. After a few moments two other vehicles came into sight: strange things that looked like a cross between a dune buggy and an armoured car. Each one had six huge tyres with treads so large you could fit a football into the gaps between them. Darius Trethewey's men had obviously travelled across the country to intercept the convoy: probably from some convenient country that had a right-wing group that shared allegiances with Blood and Soil. From Turkey, through Afghanistan, at a guess.

Five men wearing black stood around the two vehicles. One of them was obviously Darius Trethewey. He had black hair rather than blond for a start, and he had a beard. He also wore a pinstriped three-piece suit that seemed wildly out of place for the location, but his natural charisma had the strange effect of making everyone *else* look like they were wrongly dressed. He also held a tablet with which he was apparently controlling his reconnaissance drone and accessing the information from it.

And Bex recognised him. It took a moment, but she knew she'd seen him before. He had been at the Gateway of India, outside the Taj Mahal Palace hotel, when the briefcase containing the location and travel plans for the Pakistani neutron bomb had been stolen. She'd thought he'd been a tourist or a businessman or something, but he must have been there to oversee the snatch, to make sure that his people didn't screw it up. Obviously a man who didn't trust the people he delegated to.

And he'd looked at her. She remembered that: the blackness of his eyes, and the force of his personality.

Trethewey was engrossed in the information from his drone, but his bodyguards saw Bex and Anoup instantly. They swung their guns around and started firing. Three of them had automatic handguns, but the other two had Kalashnikov semi-automatic rifles. A spray of bullets zoomed towards Bex and Anoup. They ducked sideways: Bex going left and Anoup going right, both seeking sanctuary behind a large rock, but not before one bullet smashed into Bex's chest with an impact like being hit by a cricket ball. Her entire chest seemed to radiate pain, and she couldn't catch her breath. For a moment she thought she might be dead, but then she remembered the ceramic plates. The armour had protected her, but the impact had still been crippling.

She heard a voice from near the two intruding vehicles. 'Don't bother going round after them, you fools! Use grenades!'

Trethewey.

'And check the remains for identification,' he added loudly. 'I don't know who these interfering morons are, but I'd like to find out.'

Bex flashed a glance across the ground between her rock and Anoup's. The Blood and Soil thugs were going to throw grenades over the rocks! What could they do?

Anoup grinned. He pulled something from his belt: an object the size of a tin can, but black and with a rubberised coating. He drew his arm back, looking strangely like a cricketer about to bowl, then threw the object over the rock towards where Trethewey and his bodyguards stood. As soon as the object had left his hands he shoved his fingers in his ears, and nodded towards Bex. Taking his cue, she did the same. He screwed his eyes closed, and so did she.

From where the two Blood and Soil vehicles were parked there came a tightly compressed *bang!* so loud that the ground shook beneath her feet, and a flash of light so bright she could see it through her eyelids. It left an amorphous floating shape in her vision: green against red. Even when she opened her eyes again and blinked she could still see it.

Non-lethal grenades, designed to incapacitate through temporary blindness and deafness. What a great idea!

She glanced over at Anoup. He stared at her, waiting for her signal.

'Go!' she mouthed, pointing towards the vehicles.

They ran out together, weapons raised in case of trouble, but there wasn't any. The six men were lying on the ground. Some had their hands over their ears or their eyes, but all of them were curled up as if they were in extreme discomfort.

Anoup fired his vortex ring gun at the four bodyguards, rendering them unconscious. He nodded his head towards Trethewey. 'Would you like me to carry him back to the helicopter?'

'Please.' She turned her head, listening for the sounds of gunfire, but the battle on the other side of the hill seemed to have ended. 'Did we win?' she asked.

Anoup turned and whistled: a complex series of notes. Moments later a similar whistle floated back over the brow of the hill.

'We won,' he confirmed.

'Good stuff. I'll tie this lot up. There's bound to be some rope in their vehicles.'

While Anoup carried Trethewey away over his shoulder, as if he was a sack of potatoes, Bex secured the unconscious Blood and Soil personnel. When she trekked back around the hill to the site of the battle she found her people and the Pakistani Army personnel laughing and joking together, and sharing water from their bottles. The Blood and Soil fighters were all unconscious.

One of the Pakistani soldiers – obviously a senior officer, judging by the markings on his epaulets – walked over towards Bex.

'I thank you for your help,' he said, saluting. 'We were not expecting to be attacked, not in our own country, and we were unprepared. If you hadn't arrived things might have gone very differently, but I do need to ask who you are and what you are doing in Pakistan.'

'That's a very good question,' she said. She glanced past him, at Anoup. He was waiting for her signal. She nodded, and he instantly turned and whistled a handful of notes at Bex's team.

Still laughing and joking, they raised their vortex ring guns and fired them at the Pakistani Army personnel. The Army men fell to the ground, unconscious.

'I'm afraid the world is safer if that nuclear weapon is in our hands, rather than yours,' she said to the Pakistani officer, who had whirled around in shock at the noise. As he turned back, raising his own pistol, she shot him with her weapon. He fell.

'We'll secure the bomb,' Anoup called over. 'I would suggest, with all due deference, that you contact Mr Patel and inform him that we have been successful.'

'I'll do that,' she said. 'Where did you put Trethewey?'

'Over there,' Anoup said, pointing . . .

. . . at an empty patch of ground in the shadow of a large boulder.

Anoup snarled: a sound like a furious tiger. 'He has escaped! I was sure he was unconscious!'

Bex whirled around, scanning the hillside for any sign of the Blood and Soil leader, but there was nothing.

'The helicopter?' she shouted.

Anoup shook his head. 'The pilot and navigator are guarding it. He'll have headed back to those vehicles. He'll be trying to escape back to the border.'

Bex ran around one side of the hill while Anoup scrambled over the top. As she got around to the other side she saw Trethewey in the cabin of one of the vehicles. He held something black in his hand – probably a radio. He was shouting into it.

Anoup came down the hillside in something approaching a controlled fall. He reached the cabin at a rush, slamming into the side before reaching up and pulling Trethewey out. Trethewey flew over Anoup's head and hit the ground just as Bex arrived.

'He's wearing earplugs!' Anoup growled. 'Probably didn't want to be bothered by the noise of the gunfire. That's why the stun grenade didn't affect him as much as it did his followers.'

Trethewey stared up at Bex with malice in his eyes. 'You're too late!' he shouted. 'I've given the order!'

'What order?' Bex turned to Anoup. 'What order? Did you hear what he said? Has he called for backup?'

Anoup shook his head. 'Worse than that.' He turned and kicked Trethewey in the stomach. The bearded man grunted in pain. 'Tell her! Tell her what you said!'

'I know what you want.' Trethewey virtually spat the words at her. 'Your boss told me to watch out for you. He said you were going to try to stop me from setting the bombs off. You think just because we didn't get the last one that the others won't be used? You're wrong! I've given the order. In three hours' time, those other four neutron bombs will explode, and you can say goodbye to the populations of Riyadh, Islamabad, Tehran and Baghdad!'

'You're still going ahead with it?' Bex cried, appalled. 'Millions of people will die – and why?'

'Just to make a point,' he said, and laughed.

CHAPTER THIRTEEN

'Where are you?' Bex's voice suddenly blared from Kieron's earpiece. He instantly turned the volume down on Sam's sister's TV, which he'd set to show the BBC News channel. If anything big was going to happen, that's probably where they'd hear about it first.

Bex sounded as if she was under a lot of stress. Actually, she sounded like those TV reporters in big-budget end-of-the-world movies who had to announce to a waiting world that an asteroid was about to smack into Kansas, or that reckless fracking was causing the Earth to split apart, killing everyone and destroying everything.

He could hear voices behind her. They seemed to be shouting in a different language. Gujarati, maybe? He knew he'd heard it at school, and in the local shops.

Kieron didn't want to answer. The tone of those three simple words made him want to turn the ARCC kit off, curl into a ball under a duvet and just go to sleep until everything went away.

But he answered anyway.

'I'm here. I'm at Sam's sister's place.'

'OK.' She paused. 'Look, things went right, and then they went very wrong.'

Kieron glanced over to where Sam was trying to help Bradley drink a cup of tea. Bradley's hands were shaking. Kieron gestured to Sam to put the tea down and come over to where he sat.

'Hang on a second.' He pulled Sam's head down next to his, so their ears were nearly touching, and pulled the ARCC earpiece halfway out of his ear. 'Go ahead.'

'We've got the fifth neutron bomb, and we got Darius Trethewey, but he managed to steal a radio and send a message to his people.' She hesitated, and Kieron imagined her swallowing. 'He told them to launch the drones to blow up the other four bombs. I'm sorry – I think we failed.'

Kieron felt like the world was slowly tilting beneath his feet. His stomach twisted as if he'd eaten something past its sell-by date. 'Nothing's been on the news,' he said. 'If four neutron bombs had suddenly blown up above four major world cities, we'd be hearing about it.'

'Nothing on Facebook either, or any other social media.' Kieron felt Sam shrug. 'Disasters like this go viral immediately.'

'Trethewey said it would take three hours,' Bex said in Kieron's ear.

Sam shook his head, banging against Kieron's ear. 'That doesn't make any sense. If he gave the order then his people should send the signal straight away, just in case your people get to them first.' He seemed to stiffen. 'Unless they can't,' he said urgently. 'If they want the signal to go to all the bombs

233

at the same time they'll probably want to use a satellite, and they'll want control of the satellite to stop anyone blocking the signal. Maybe they have to wait until its orbit carries it over the Middle East.'

'Mr Patel said the same thing,' Bex said.

'Who?' Kieron asked.

'The friend I was with earlier.'

Kieron sighed. 'Blood and Soil aren't going to have access to their own satellite communications,' he pointed out. 'They're a bunch of fascist political thugs, not –'

'Not a satellite communications company?' Sam interrupted. 'They have their own TV station, remember? Bradley and I saw them watching stuff on it when we were prisoners. They'll use the satellite from that to transmit the signal – I guarantee it!'

Everything seemed to pause, hanging suspended in the air. Kieron knew what he had to say, but he didn't want to say it.

'Blood and Soil are based in England,' he said eventually. He quickly gestured at the ARCC glasses, bringing up screens and databases as he spoke. 'Yes, they do have a satellite of their own, a cheap one that launched earlier this year, piggybacking on a Russian satellite mission. Their TV studios are in Manchester, but the satellite control centre is in the Pennines, near a place called Skirwith. Clearer skies there.' He paused, and took a deep breath. 'It's about eighty miles away. We can be there in maybe ninety minutes if we use the van.'

'We can be there inside an hour,' Sam murmured, 'if the roads are clear.'

'No!' Bex said instantly. 'I forbid it! I –'

'You know it's the only option,' Kieron said. 'By the time you've got in contact with anyone and persuaded them of your story it'll be too late – assuming they even believe you. We are your last hope.'

'You're my best hope,' she said quietly. 'I can't tell you to go, but go, and go quickly. And be careful!' She hesitated. 'I'm going to take this nuclear weapon and Darius Trethewey back to Agni Patel's island. To be frank, I'm not sure which is more dangerous.'

They made sure Bradley was comfortable, and ran to the van. Somewhere along the way Sam had picked up a duvet cover, which he carried rolled up.

'What's that?' Kieron shouted breathlessly.

'Something that might come in useful,' Sam responded. 'I'll tell you later.'

'Look, do you think you can drive all that distance safely?'

'I think I have no choice,' Sam called back. 'This is something we have to do. Whether we want to or not doesn't matter. Whether we *can* or not doesn't matter.'

'How did you know about Skirwith?'

'Outdoor education. Hillwalking.'

The van was still where they'd left it, which was a relief. It would have been ironic if millions of people died because of a motor-vehicle theft. And it had enough diesel for the journey. And it started first time. Sam threw the rolled duvet cover into the back of the van and they set off.

For the first half-hour they stuck to the A69. The sun sank towards the horizon ahead of them as they drove. To their right the dark bulk of the Pennine Hills was a constant oppressive presence on the horizon.

At the small town of Hayden Bridge they came off onto the narrower, more winding A686, cutting through the Pennines themselves. There was hardly a level stretch of road: they were either heading uphill, engine grinding, or coasting down. Now the hills were looming up on both sides: grey battlements of rock set among long stretches of black forest.

It was virtually night now. The sky above them – a ribbon between dark blocks of hillside – was a deep violet colour. One star shone in the sky. Kieron knew it was Venus – the morning and evening star, first to come out at night and last to vanish in the morning – but he kept thinking it might be the Blood and Soil satellite, moving inexorably along its orbital path towards the Middle East, and carnage.

A constant thought ran through his head, like that digital tickertape that scrolled underneath the picture on news channels. What are we doing? What are we doing? What are we doing?

This was stupid. When he glanced sideways at Sam he could see the same thoughts were going through his brain.

They were teenagers, for heaven's sake! They were emo teenagers!

The fate of the world shouldn't depend on what they did in the next two hours.

But it did. That was the problem. It really did.

Sam suddenly threw the van into a sharp right, turning them almost entirely around with a squeal of tyres. Kieron's head banged against the side of the van. He was about to shout 'What the hell –?' when he noticed that they were now on a different stretch of road, parallel to but lower than the one they'd just been on. They'd slewed around a hairpin turn on a steep hillside.

'Well spotted,' he said.

Sam looked grim. 'This isn't easy,' he muttered. 'I shouldn't be driving this fast.'

'Yeah, I know, but –'

'Yeah. Exactly.'

The sun had vanished completely now, and the sky was black. Other stars were coming out. A meteor flashed across the sky: a straight slash of light, gone almost as soon as it appeared. Under other circumstances Kieron would have been thrilled to see a meteor, but not now. Meteors were supposed to foretell tragic events, weren't they?

One of them might not survive the night. Maybe both of them.

But if they failed in their mission then millions of people wouldn't survive the night. People they didn't know, but that made no difference.

Another sudden turn and they were heading across an old stone bridge. The van left the road momentarily as they zoomed over it, then crashed back to the tarmac, sending a jolt up Kieron's spine.

A small village flashed past: just a handful of stone houses clustered against the road. Somewhere off to the right the trees and the rocks had been replaced by a stretch of deepest, darkest black. Kieron had a feeling it was a river, but a few seconds later they pulled away from it.

'Do those Blood and Soil goons actually know how to operate a satellite TV station?' Sam suddenly asked over the growl of the engine.

'They can't all be stupid,' Kieron replied. 'There must be some university graduates, or engineers, who believe in their sick ideology.'

They were getting to the area where Kieron knew they were going to go off-map: on a small track heading towards where the Blood and Soil satellite control station was located. He called up the map function on the ARCC kit. Fortunately it was still getting a GPS signal, so it provided him with a translucent yellow arrow overlaid on the road, pointing straight ahead.

Up ahead the arrow veered off to the right.

'Slow down,' Kieron said. 'The road either turns sharply right or we've got to take a side road.'

Sam obediently slowed down. Still they almost missed the turning: a dirt road that was obvious only by the fact that the low stone wall that they'd been driving alongside suddenly vanished for ten feet or so.

Sam slowed almost to a halt, turned the wheel carefully, and began to head down the dirt road. Almost immediately the ground rose: shallowly at first, but then getting steeper and steeper.

'How much further have we got to –?' Sam started, but the tyres suddenly began spinning in the wet soil, and the van started sliding downhill. Sam slammed it into four-wheel drive. The tyres engaged with the ground, but it was still laborious. The engine whined like a tied-up dog.

'Pull over,' Kieron said. 'We can walk the rest of the way. I don't want anyone hearing the engine.'

'Walk?'

'Well, climb.'

A rain had begun to fall, and a chill wind blew down the hillside and into their faces. They secured the van, making sure the headlights were turned off, and began to hike up the road – Sam still carrying the duvet cover he'd retrieved from his sister's place. Within moments their faces were wet from a mixture of the cold mist and warm sweat from their exertions.

'What's the plan again?' Sam asked as they trudged.

'Find the place; break in; set fire to it,' Kieron answered breathlessly. 'Or: find the place; break in; find the main fuse box and break all the fuses.'

Ahead of them, and above eye-level, the cloudy sky was obscured by a series of regular blocks of darkness. Buildings. Maybe prefabs. As they moved, Kieron saw a slowly flashing red light in the sky above them. For a moment he thought they'd been discovered by some kind of drone or silent helicopter, but then he realised: it was a mast with a warning light on top to make sure that no aircraft crashed into it.

Sam grabbed his shoulder and pointed. Up ahead, and off to the right, the regular blocks of darkness gave way to a huge black circle.

'Satellite dish,' Sam whispered. 'We're in the right place.'

The dirt road curled to the left but something loomed up in front of them: a wire-mesh fence with a gate in it, right across the road. Open ground between the trees and bushes and the fence meant that anyone crossing it was vulnerable. Just beyond the gate, several Land Rovers had been parked.

Sam started across the open space, but Kieron pulled him back, into the shadow of a large spiky bush.

'What's the problem?' Sam hissed.

Kieron pointed towards poles that had been stuck in the ground behind the fence. On the top of each pole sat a white globe. They looked like street lamps, but they weren't giving out any light.

'I think those things are sensors. Not cameras, obviously, because they're opaque, but they might be infra-red detectors. They'll pick up your body heat instantly.'

'So how are we going to get in?'

A door opened, spilling out a waterfall of bright light. 'Did you hear something?' a voice said.

'Probably a fox. Or a pine marten. Vicious things, pine martens.'

Kieron risked a glance around the edge of the bush. Two men stood outside what was obviously a doorway into one of the buildings. The glare made silhouettes out of them, but they were both dressed in bulky clothes and holding objects that were almost certainly guns. Semi-automatic rifles. They sounded quite young. Behind them, a repetitive thudding sound drifted out of their guard room. Kieron supposed it was music, but not anything he would have chosen to listen to.

'We'd better do another round of the fence,' the first guard said.

'Do we have to?'

'You know what's going on. For some reason the schedule's been changed. Tonight is the night. One hour from now, that signal goes out and the world changes. We need to be alert to anyone that tries to get in.'

'And if they do?' the second guard asked.

The first guard hefted his weapon. 'Fire and forget, as they say.'

Each guard started off in a different direction, walking along the length of the wire fence. Kieron noticed that they stayed directly underneath the poles with the white globes on top. He'd been right: they were sensors.

'Any ideas on how we get through the fence?' he asked, glancing at his watch to establish the time. One hour to go.

'Oh, I can do that,' Sam said confidently. 'I just need to be able to get to the fence.'

'Oh,' Kieron said, surprised. 'So – you first.'

Sam partially unwrapped the object in the duvet he was still holding and took something out.

'What's that?' Kieron asked, intrigued.

Reluctantly, Sam held it out. It looked like a pair of garden shears with a sideways kink about halfway along, but there was something more clinical, more brutal about it.

'Bone shears,' he said. 'From my sister's little collection of medical tools and equipment. I thought we might need to get through a fence, so I took them and rolled them up in one of her old duvet covers so no one could see it. If these things will cut through bones they'll cut through wire.' He glanced at the fence. 'Of course, if that thing's electrified then we've got problems.'

'It's not – no insulators on the top or the bottom.'

'Great. So – what's your idea?'

'Give me the duvet cover and I'll show you.'

Sam handed it over, along with the bone shears. Kieron stowed the shears in his belt, unrolled the duvet cover and laid it on the ground. The rain was heavier now, and within a minute the duvet cover was drenched with water. Kieron picked it up and threw it over his shoulders like a cloak, drawing it over his head as well. 'This thing's now at the same ambient temperature as the rain,' he said, voice muffled by the material. He pulled his fingers in, curling them so they couldn't be seen by the sensors. 'If I move fast enough, my own body heat won't escape or heat the water up before I get to the fence.'

'Better move then,' Sam urged.

Kieron sprinted across the space between the bushes and trees and the fence, keeping as low as he could. Nothing seemed to happen: no alarms went off.

Once he got to the fence he set to work snipping through the wires. Sam had been right – the design of the shears meant that whatever force he applied seemed to be multiplied. He could cut through someone's arm with this thing! Within a few moments he'd created a gap large enough to crawl through. Once on the other side he sprinted to a point beneath the thermal sensors, balled the duvet cover up and threw it back to Sam. Thirty seconds later Sam was by his side. He took the shears away with an apologetic shrug.

'Got to get them back to my sister,' he said. 'She'll kill me if I don't.' He raised the shears. 'With these, probably.'

They moved quietly between the buildings. Some of them seemed to be dormitories, judging by the sight of bunk beds and dirty washing through the windows; some were storage areas and one, a large one, was a kitchen and dining room. Another one, almost as large, was probably a relaxation area – there were sounds of a film being shown and flickering light on the thin curtains. The centre of the maze of buildings was the massive satellite dish, which sat on a concrete pillar.

Kieron glanced at his watch. Forty-five minutes.

The satellite control centre was on the far side, overlooked by the dark bulk of the hillside and the distant, almost invisible fence. Its identity was clear by the air-conditioning units sitting on the roof, which transferred the heat away from the computing equipment. Steam rose off them into the cold night air. There were no windows. He supposed there was no need for them.

They moved around the outside of the building until they found the main door. It had an electronic security system attached: the kind where you had to slide a magnetic card through and punch in a set of numbers before it would unlock.

'What now?' Sam asked.

Kieron looked around, hoping for some kind of inspiration to strike. 'Got a lighter?'

'No.'

'I know you smoke. You must have a lighter.'

'I stopped.' Sam paused. 'I've got a vape. Would that do?'

'Don't be stupid.'

'Actually, we don't need to start a fire. We just need to make them think that a fire has started.'

'You mean, set off a fire alarm?'

'Yeah.'

'I like it.'

Kieron nodded decisively, although he didn't feel decisive. 'OK, you go and look for a fire alarm in one of the other buildings that's near enough to a door for you to be able to get to it easily, and set it off. I'll wait here until everyone clears out, then I'll go in and break everything I can see.'

'What with?'

'A fire-axe? Bone shears? If I have to I'll pick up a chair and smash all the servers with it.'

Sam gazed at Kieron, and there was a look in his eye that suggested there were things he wanted to say, important things, but that this wasn't the time or the place. Kieron felt the same way. He wanted to tell Sam how good a friend he'd been, just in case they didn't see each other again, but he knew that Sam knew, and Sam knew that he knew. That's what being a friend meant.

Sam nodded, as if they'd said all that out loud. He punched Kieron's arm – gently – and then slipped away into the darkness.

Kieron counted seconds. One . . . ten . . . a hundred . . . what was Sam doing?

An alarm suddenly blared out: an electronic *whoop-whoop-whoop!* Kieron braced himself, ready to run in through the doors as soon as everyone inside had left. He quickly checked the time again: thirty-five minutes left until the signal was transmitted. Just thirty-five minutes!

The alarm stopped mid-*whoop!* A second later, a voice on a tannoy system announced: 'This is Security Control. Ignore the alarm. Repeat: ignore the alarm. This was a false alarm, caused by an intruder. There is no fire. Repeat: there is no fire. Remain at your stations until further notice.' After a pause, the voice went on: 'Remember, we've got a job to do. The future belongs to us, people. Nothing will stop us!' Another pause, and then, almost apologetically: 'Control out.'

Kieron slumped against the side of the building. A wave of despair washed over him. Sam must have been taken captive. Not only was he on his own, trying to complete the mission by himself, but he had to rescue Sam as well. He knew what would happen if he didn't. The people in Blood and Soil were brutal. They wouldn't hesitate to hurt Sam, and hurt him badly, to find out who he was and what he was doing there.

What could he do?

The rain coursed down his face and into his collar. It sneaked into his closed eyes and trickled into his ears. He'd never felt so helpless. Sam's life was just the tip of the pyramid. There were all those people in Tehran, Riyadh and the other cities. It was all up to him. Everything weighed down on his shoulders, like a pyramid in reverse.

He wished he could just go back to the van and drive away into the darkness.

The van.

Something snagged inside his brain, some random scrap of memory catching on a sharp spike of desperation. The dirt road they'd driven up had gone past the main gate, and further up the hill. That same hill loomed over the control centre. If he could get the van up that narrow, winding, muddy, sloping road and above the control room, then possibly, just possibly, he could drive it over the edge and onto the building's roof. And if luck was really with him then the van would crash through the flat roof and into the main control room, smashing the controls and stopping the signal from being sent. If he could drive it in the first place. If, if, if. All he could do was try.

A quick look at his watch. He had half an hour.

He retraced his steps through the maze of buildings to the fence, and the hole he had cut. The duvet cover was still there, lying on the ground, soaking wet. He threw it over himself and slid through the gap. Within a few moments he was half running and half sliding down the dirt road towards where they had left the van.

It was only when it came into sight, just off the road, that he realised Sam might already have told his captors where it was. They might already be there.

He stepped out of the shelter of the bushes and grabbed the door handle. Nothing. No noise; no movement.

He pulled the door open and heaved himself into the driver's seat. It wasn't the same as being in the passenger seat. There was less space: pedals knocked against his feet and the wheel blocked his arms and chest.

He tried to remember how Sam had started the van. Two wires, dangling beneath the dashboard. But then what did he have to do? Foot on the brake while he put it into drive, then foot off the brake to move. At least it was an automatic; a manual would have been far too much of a challenge.

Treating it like a problem in logic, he went through all the steps that he'd worked out. With his foot on the brake he touched the wires together. Thank God – the engine sprang to life immediately, sending a shudder through the van's frame. He did what he'd seen Sam do – used the projecting stem on the left-hand side of the wheel to move the van out of park. He suddenly realised that he couldn't see the dashboard; he turned the indicator stem until the headlights came on, almost blinding him. The dashboard lit up: just in time. He saw that he'd put the van into reverse; quickly he selected drive, two slots down. And took his foot off the brake.

Gently the van moved forward. Kieron turned the wheel, judging how much it had to be turned in order to get the van to deviate from its crawling course. He fed a little more power to the wheels, but they started to spin on the wet grass so he slowed down.

According to the van's digital clock, he had twenty minutes to save the world.

He twisted the wheel until the van started moving onto the dirt road, then turned it back so he was going straight.

Gently, tentatively, he guided the van up the dirt road towards Blood and Soil's satellite control facility. Just as he went around the final bend before reaching the facility he remembered to turn the headlights off. He breathed a panicky sigh of relief. The last thing he wanted was the guards seeing his headlights and coming to investigate.

In the darkness it was hard to navigate. He cautiously steered the van past the main gate and up the dirt road as it vanished into the woodland, heading ever upward and circumventing the base.

The tyres kept slipping on the mud. He quickly learned when to apply power and when not to, in order to keep the van moving. Progress was slow – painfully slow – and in his mind he kept seeing images of what might be happening to Sam. Each time he pushed them away: he was where he was, and the only way he could help was to keep going.

His gaze caught on the van's clock. Ten minutes to go. Ten short minutes. He wasn't sure he could do it in time.

He had to.

Off to the right Kieron suddenly saw the lights of the buildings. He was above them now, just about on a level with the flat roofs. The position of the satellite dish gave him a good idea of where he was. If he'd started off at six o'clock on a clock face and he was aiming for twelve o'clock then he was roughly at the ten o'clock point.

Distracted, he very nearly made a fatal mistake. The ground sloped away from him to the right, towards the buildings, and the van started sliding before he realised what was happening. He tried feeding power to the wheels, but they just spun in the mud. He desperately tried pressing the brakes down as hard as he could, but the van kept sliding. He saw the lights of the buildings getting closer, down past a black edge that had to be the hillside. He knew that the plan was for him to crash the van down on the control building, but if it went down now it would hit the kitchen and dining area. That wouldn't do anything! Worse: that might be where they were keeping Sam! He might end up killing his friend!

The side of the van hit the wire mesh fence – almost invisible in the darkness. It bent under the strain, but it didn't give way. He'd forgotten about the fence, but thankfully it slowed the van's slide to a halt. Gently, hesitantly, he fed power to the wheels and steered left. Maybe there were twigs beneath the tyres, or maybe the ground there was drier, but the treads engaged and pulled him away before the van got to the edge. Kieron heard the wire scrape along the vehicle's side as he went.

Five heart-stopping minutes later the van reached a clearing overlooking the back of the site. Twenty feet below him was the satellite control room.

He glanced at his watch, but time had lost all meaning for him now. The numbers were like Chinese ideograms and the hands seemed to be hardly moving. It might already be too late.

It didn't matter. He was where he was, and he had to follow through – if only to save his friend.

He pointed the nose of the van at the point where the hillside dropped away, put it into park, pulled the handbrake up and climbed out, leaving the engine running. Exhaust fumes drifted towards him from the back of the vehicle. He looked at the whole setup like a problem in trigonometry:

working out where the van would go if it moved forward – how far forward, and how far down.

He needed it to be going as fast as possible, otherwise it would just fall down the hillside between the fence and the control building, achieving nothing.

He needed to make sure the wheels didn't spin helplessly in the mud. Remembering what had happened a few moments before, he quickly grabbed as many fallen twigs from the ground as he could and stuffed them in front of the wheels – front and back.

He looked around for a branch long enough for what he needed. It took a few moments, but he found one that had fallen from a nearly dead tree nearby.

Holding the branch he gingerly climbed back inside the van, leaving the door open. He closed his eyes, gripped the steering wheel tightly with one hand and put his foot on the accelerator pedal, pressing it down hard.

All four wheels spun, splattering twigs and mud backwards into the forest. The van lurched and bucked – desperate to launch itself forward, into the darkness.

Kieron jammed the branch down onto the accelerator pedal and wedged the other end beneath the dashboard. It held: replacing his foot and still transmitting power to the wheels.

Offering up a quick prayer to a deity he didn't believe in, he released the handbrake with his left hand and flung himself sideways, out of the open door.

The van sprang forward like a greyhound released from a trap. Kieron's foot caught in the flapping seatbelt as he fell, and for a split-second he thought that he was going to be dragged away and carried over the edge along with the van, but he twisted in mid-air, pulling his foot out of the constraining loop of material. His shoulder hit the ground, sending a spike of agony through his body, but he was too busy watching the van to care. It reached the edge of the hillside, travelling faster every moment, crashed through the fence and launched itself out into space. The weight of the engine pulled it down, heading in a perfect arc. He scrambled to the edge of the hillside and watched as it fell, almost as if in slow motion –

Directly into the centre of the control building roof.

The van plunged straight through the flat surface, smashing through whatever building material it was made of, sending the air-conditioning units flying. Rafters jerked upward out of the hole like huge ribs surrounding a wound. Sparks flew. Flickers of arcing electricity illuminated the scene with a stuttering blue light.

And then, moments later, several explosions sent the van flying upward on a cushion of fire and flame, almost as if it was backing away in horror from the devastation it had caused, before it fell forward again into the inferno.

That same alarm he'd heard earlier started to blare again – *whoop-whoop-whoop!* – but it sounded more desperate now, more like there was a real emergency. He thought he could see people running away from the control building, but the chaos below made it difficult to tell.

Job done, Kieron thought grimly. He didn't know if he was in time or not, but he'd done what he could.

Now to get Sam back.

Going back around the dirt road would have taken too long. Instead he half slithered, half fell down the muddy hillside, sliding until he hit the ground. He moved cautiously through the buildings, trying not to be noticed by any of the Blood and Soul technicians and guards who ran around, panicking, but also trying to see into every doorway and every window, trying to find his friend. Hoping it wasn't too late. Terrified about what he might discover.

'Hey!'

Kieron was so fixated on rescuing Sam that it was Sam's voice he heard behind him. He turned, a half-smile already forming on his lips.

It wasn't Sam.

It was Kyle Renner – the thug who'd been in charge of taking Bradley away from the shopping centre; the thug who'd threatened Sam with torture; the thug who'd led the discussions with the MI6 traitor at the Baltic Centre. The thug who'd been there all along, in the background of Kieron's life for the last few days.

'It's the kid from the industrial estate,' he said wonderingly. 'You didn't sneak inside the car, did you? Hide in the boot, like they do in the movies? I hope not – my dog's been sleeping in there, and she's got stomach problems.' He frowned, thinking. 'You must have followed us, or overheard us talking about this place.' He looked around, at the chaos Kieron had caused with the van. 'I have to say, I like what you did with the place. It's full of nerds and techies – you've brought a bit of action.'

'Glad to oblige,' Kieron said. He felt his fingers twitching as his subconscious mind tried to wish into existence some kind of weapon, but none appeared. He glanced around the area between the buildings, illuminated by the flickering fire, but he couldn't see anything he could use.

Renner reached into his jacket and pulled out an automatic pistol. Kieron immediately recognised it as a Sig Sauer P229C. He'd fired that weapon thousands of times – but only in first-person computer games. He'd also been shot by it thousands of times – in the same games. Now it looked like he might finally discover what it felt like in real life.

Real life sucked. It was dirty, noisy and painful. And it ended.

'I dunno if you've inflicted so much damage that it can't be repaired, at least not quickly,' Renner said, clicking the safety catch off with professional deftness, 'or whether you're more of an irritant than a danger to the cause, but either way I don't think anyone'll care if I kill you right here.'

He brought the pistol up so he was looking along its matt grey length, and pulled the trigger without any hint of emotion . . .

. . . just as something exploded inside the control room, sending a fountain of flame and sparks into the night air.

Either Renner flinched, or the ground shook. His hand moved slightly, and instead of hitting Kieron in the right eye the bullet fizzed past his temple, crisping his hair with the heat of its passage. Kieron flung himself left before Renner could fire again, rolling into the shadow of the corner of a building. He sprang to his feet and sprinted down the length of the wall. As he got to the middle another bullet hit the painted breeze-blocks, scratching a long mark through the paint before it ricocheted away into the darkness. Kieron tasted concrete dust as he sucked air into his lungs.

He didn't have enough time to get to the far end before Renner fired again.

A window by his head had been smashed by the force of the exploding control room. An old, corroded drainpipe clung to the wall next to it. Before his conscious mind could come up with a plan, Kieron's subconscious was forcing his hands to clamp on the drainpipe and his feet to scrabble around until they got a grip on the brackets holding it insecurely to the wall. He hauled himself up with all his strength until he could get a foot onto the windowsill and transfer his weight across. As shards of glass shattered beneath his boots a third bullet passed right through the drainpipe and drew a line of fire across his vision, left to right. Fragments of rusty metal peppered his face. He closed his eyes reflexively, feeling the sting as one went into his left eye. Before Renner could fire for a fourth time he half rolled through the broken window. Glass sliced through the denim of his jeans and scored the skin. He fell forward, leading with his right shoulder and desperately trying to turn so that he hit the floor with his right side rather than his head.

Thick carpet broke his fall. He scrambled back to his feet and ran towards a dimly illuminated door. Through it he found himself at the middle of a T-junction, with corridors running left, right and straight ahead. It was lined with offset doors – one on the right, then one on the left, then one on the right again and so on. Emergency lighting had come on, and the occupants – if there had been any – had already evacuated.

He had to choose quickly. If he ran straight ahead and Renner climbed through the window after him then he'd be immediately visible down the corridor. If he went right instead and Renner ran ahead to the far end of the building to find a door, then they'd bump into each other. Left was his only option – running back down the inside of the building to reverse the run that he'd made down the outside.

As he sprinted, with no clear idea in his mind of what he might do next, he realised that hiding in any of the rooms he passed was pointless. He'd just be trapped.

He'd passed a door before he registered the red cross painted on it, and the sign saying 'First Aid Point' that had been screwed into the corridor wall so it projected out where people could see it. People who needed a first-aid kit. First aid that involved sharp knives, maybe scalpels.

He grabbed the door knob and flung the door open. Again, it was illuminated only by harsh green emergency lighting, but he could make out two beds, base units running along the wall forming a work surface, cupboards attached to the wall above them, and a table. The cupboard doors had labels stuck to them. He ran along, trying to wrench them open, but every single one was padlocked shut. He pulled at them in turn, bracing himself against the wall with his feet, but the doors wouldn't budge.

He heard a sudden *bang!* from the corridor. He thought Renner was kicking in the doors, looking for him. Or maybe he was just shooting through the doors. Only a few minutes before he got to the first-aid room.

Kieron snarled in frustration. He quickly looked around for anything that might be used as a weapon. Just below the work surface running along the wall and above the cupboards he saw drawers that weren't padlocked. He pulled them open, spilling their contents on the floor. Plasters, bandages, packs of aspirin . . . nothing that would be of any help.

No – the bandages! He could make a makeshift slingshot – use it to fire something heavy at Renner's head.

But there was nothing heavy there. Nothing he could use as ammunition, even if the bandages would function as a slingshot without tearing.

Another *bang!* from the corridor: closer this time.

Kieron smashed his fist down on the table. He was running out of options.

No point staying here. He had to check some other rooms, just in case there was something he could use.

Moving to the doorway, he edged his head around the frame and looked along the corridor. He caught a glimpse of Renner's shoulder and back as he moved into a room two doors down, looking for Kieron.

Kieron glanced across the corridor. The room opposite had a sign on the door saying 'Workshop'. That sounded good. A workshop had tools. Chisels. Hammers.

Before Renner could emerge from the room he'd just entered, Kieron scooted across the corridor. For a terrible second he thought the door was locked, but it was just stiff. He threw his weight against it and it opened, spilling him into the room. He quickly sprang to his feet and shut the door. That would buy him, oh, maybe another second of life.

Everything he needed was here – sharp things, heavy things, blunt things. For a moment he was paralysed by choice, and paralysed too by the fact that he'd have to get up close and personal with a man who was bigger, stronger and more vicious than he was – and then he saw the car battery on a metal workbench. And the jump-leads beside it.

Bang! That was the next room along.

He felt as if he hadn't taken a proper breath for hours. His heart was pounding so fast that the individual beats seemed to blur together into a dangerous vibration. Ignoring them, ignoring everything, he clamped the red and black leads to the terminals of the battery. For a second he stood there, mind blank. What should he do next? What had they said in motor-mechanics class about the dangers of working with car batteries?

Yes – the other end of the black lead should be earthed. He clamped it onto a leg of the metal bench that the battery rested on. Holding the red rubber grip on the remaining lead he moved to the side of the door, then realised that when Renner kicked it in it would hit him in the face. He skidded across the door to the other side, flattening himself against the wall.

Just in time. The door smashed open as Renner's boot

caught it and smashed against the wall where Kieron had been standing less than a second earlier.

Renner stepped into the room, gun raised. He seemed to realise with some sixth sense that Kieron was there. His head started turning even as Kieron reached forward and clamped the positive lead onto Renner's gun, completing the circuit.

Renner's eyes opened wide. His hands started to shake. Smoke began to rise from his hands, his neck, his face. His muscles clenched, making the veins in his temples and his neck stand out and, crucially, locking his hand on the gun so he couldn't drop it or throw it away.

Kieron watched, horrified, as Renner took one, two, three tottering steps into the room and fell forward, still twitching. He could smell something burning, and he knew what it was. Tendrils of smoke emerged like questing tentacles from Renner's collar and sleeves.

Despite a terrible, almost unconquerable urge to stay and watch to the bitter end, Kieron slid past Renner's twitching body, ran out of the workshop and along the corridor. The smell of burning followed him until he got to the open air, where he suddenly had to bend over and throw up until his stomach hurt.

'Was that you?'

He turned, feeling his heart sink, but this time it was Sam. He had a bruise on his cheek, and blood running from a cut under his eye, but in the flickering flames of the burning control room that he was pointing at he looked defiant rather than injured.

'Yeah,' Kieron said, feeling relief run through him like a cool breeze. 'Had to do something.'

He checked his watch. Thirty seconds before the transmission had been due to take place. He felt as if a band that had been fastened tightly around his heart had suddenly been cut. 'Thirty seconds left, Sam. Thirty seconds.'

Sam gripped his arm and together they sank to the ground, backs resting against the wall.

'Out of interest –' Kieron started to say, but Sam held up his right hand. The bone shears dangled from it. Blood dripped from the blades.

'They didn't search me properly. They're useless.'

Kieron started to laugh. 'Yeah, I think we can agree on that.'

'I suppose you've crashed the van,' Sam said.

'I have comprehensively and completely crashed the van.'

'So how are we going to get home?'

Kieron tried to bring his laughter under control. It was threatening to take over, like the firestorm sweeping through Blood and Soil's satellite control centre. Hysteria, he supposed. He'd never experienced it before.

He tapped the ARCC glasses, which he was still wearing despite the fact that he hadn't needed them or used them. He'd completely forgotten that he had them on. 'I could call up the local bus timetables on these. What do you think?'

Sam shook his head. 'I think we should steal one of those Land Rovers down by the main gate before they're all taken. Sometimes the low-tech solution is best.'

259

Kieron looked around at the flames, the sparks, the devastation. 'Low-tech does have its appeal,' he said. 'And I'm not even sure the buses are running around here at this time of night.'

CHAPTER FOURTEEN

'How are you feeling?' Bex asked.

The weather was hot and humid, but the cocktail in her hand was cold enough to make up for it – especially when she pressed it against her forehead – and the view from Agni's island out across the Bay of India was spectacular.

'I've got a ringing in my ears that wasn't there before,' his reassuring voice said, 'and my vision is still blurry, but apart from that I seem to be OK. I don't think I should spend too long on this thing though.' He paused. 'How are you feeling?'

Bex glanced at the cocktail. 'I'm OK,' she said.

'Your friend Mr Patel's taken control of the neutron bomb from Pakistan?'

'Yeah. He's also got Darius Trethewey locked up in a comfortable but very secure bedroom and is questioning him about the locations of the other four. He's sending teams out to Riyadh, Tehran, Islamabad and Baghdad in advance, with orders to retrieve them from whatever Blood and Soil facility they're located in, along with the drones. That's four more weapons of mass destruction to add to his collection.'

'Do you trust him?'

She took a sip of the cocktail. It tasted of mango and coconut. 'I think I do,' she said. 'Yes, I definitely think I do.'

'But you don't trust our bosses at MI6, from what I hear.'

'One of them is working with Blood and Soil, and we need to know who it is.'

'And expose them?'

She smiled. Maybe it was the effects of the cocktail. 'That, or we let Mr Patel take whoever it is and put them in the next bedroom to Darius Trethewey.'

She heard a voice in the background, asking something. 'Is that Kieron?' she asked.

'No.' Bradley seemed unusually embarrassed. 'It's Kieron's friend Sam's sister. She's asking if I want a cup of tea.'

'Very cosy.' Bex felt a sudden and unexpected flash of jealousy. She wasn't sure why – Bradley was like a brother, rather than a partner. Maybe she just didn't want to lose him, or even a part of him, to someone else. 'I'll need to have a talk with Kieron,' she continued, trying to suppress the unwelcome thoughts. 'He can't use the ARCC kit any more. It was fun while it lasted, but it's too dangerous. He'll get himself hurt, or killed.'

'The kid did well,' Bradley said gently. 'Destroying that station took some guts. He picks things up quickly, and he doesn't get scared. Or, if he does, he doesn't let it stop him doing what has to be done. I think we ought to consider keeping him close by.'

'You just want to spend more time with his friend's sister,' Bex said before she could stop herself. She bit her lip, wishing she could call the words back.

'Hey!' Bradley sounded offended. 'It's not like we get many perks in this job. We need to grab them whenever possible.'

Bex took another sip of her cocktail and gazed out across the glittering waves at the distant horizon.

'I wish we could keep him close,' she said. 'I've got to really like Kieron, even though I've never met him. But that means I want to look after him. I feel protective towards him. The trouble is, we're still in danger. We're going to have to risk our lives in order to expose the Blood and Soil spy within MI6, and I can't let Kieron share any of that risk.'

'I'm not sure he's going to go that easily,' Bradley said.

Bex sighed. 'Is he there?'

'Yeah. Do you want to speak to him, or shall I give him the bad news?'

'Let me do it. We've shared so much, Kieron and me, that I think he deserves hearing the goodbye from me directly. Get ready to pack up any stuff you've got there and leave. Find a safe house somewhere you can lie low.'

'OK,' Bradley said, but even over the thousands of miles that separated them he didn't sound happy.

CHAPTER FIFTEEN

'So we saved the world?' Sam said. He and Kieron were sat on Sam's sister's sofa. She was working, and the two of them – well, three including Bradley – had pretty much cleaned her fridge out while she was gone. They were going to have to do a run to the shops before she got back otherwise there was going to be trouble. The problem was that now Bradley had recovered – more or less – from his injuries he was starving hungry all the time.

'We did,' Kieron said. For a moment his brain flashed up an image of Kyle Renner, twitching on the floor of the Blood and Soil workshop, smoke actually coming off his skin. That really wasn't a memory he was happy keeping. 'But at what cost?' he added quietly.

'The least they could do is buy us some upgraded computers, and throw in some of their ARCC kit as well. That stuff's well cool.'

'I've got a feeling,' Kieron said thoughtfully, 'that we'll be lucky if we get to keep the pens they make us sign the Official Secrets Act with.' He'd been thinking about the situation obsessively, and he kept coming to the same conclusion – whether Bex and Bradley returned to MI6 or whether they went rogue, looking for the double agent in their own organisation – they weren't going to want to risk the lives of two teenagers. And no matter how he tried, he couldn't work out any convincing argument for letting him and Sam stay involved.

'And I've never even met her,' he said quietly.

'Who?'

'Bex.'

Sam shook his head. 'Don't get your hopes up, mate. You know, like people say, "Oh, be careful online, because that person you're talking to that you think is another teenager might be a fifty-year-old truck driver trying to groom you"? Well, Bex might be like that. You've built her up in your mind as being some young, beautiful female version of James Bond, but she's probably hideously overweight and ugly.'

'You know what?' Kieron tried to keep the irritation out of his voice. 'It doesn't matter what she looks like. I know it's a cliché, but I've got to know her, and I really like her.'

Sam opened his mouth to answer, but Bradley appeared in the doorway. He held the ARCC kit in his hand.

'Kieron? I've got Bex on the line. She wants to talk to you.'

'Here we go,' Sam muttered. 'We've all been on the receiving end of this conversation before. "I just want to be friends." "You're like a brother to me."'

Bradley smiled and stepped forward, but his legs seemed to crumple beneath him and he fell forward onto the carpet with a thud that must have echoed through the block of flats.

Kieron and Sam got to his side at the same time. Sam

checked his pulse while Kieron gently raised his right eyelid. His eye had rolled up so that only the white and a thin curve of iris was visible. Kieron wasn't sure, but it seemed to him that the iris was twitching.

He heard a voice coming from the ARCC earpiece. Scooping it up, he inserted it into his own ear.

'Kieron?' Bex was saying. 'Are you there?'

He sighed. 'Bex, I think we have a problem . . .'

Andrew Lane

Andrew Lane is a popular and much-loved writer for teens and young adults. He is the author of the Young Sherlock Holmes series, which has been published in forty-four countries. He has also worked extensively in the extended universe of BBC TV's *Doctor Who*, and has written three adult crime novels under a pseudonym.

Before becoming a writer, Andrew spent twenty-seven years working for the Ministry of Defence on the fringes of the Intelligence and Counter-terrorism communities. He has been inside several classified intelligence headquarters in the UK and US (and not as a tourist).

WIN
A SPY FOR A DAY
EXPERIENCE!

Do you fancy stepping into Bex or Kieron's shoes for a day? Then enter the AWOL competition before 31 December 2018 and you could learn a whole lot of skills and techniques used by real spies. Skills taught on the day, introduced by ex-surveillance officers, include code-breaking, laser agility, shooting, fire-lighting and building a shelter.

TO ENTER, VISIT:
www.piccadillypress.co.uk/SpyForADay

Please note:
1. The competition is open to UK residents only
2. You must be aged between 10 and 16 to take part in the Spy for a Day experience.
3. An adult over 18 must enter the competition on your behalf (ask a parent or guardian).
4. A parent or guardian of the winner must remain on-site at all times.
5. Experiences take place on Saturdays and Sundays between March and November.
6. You must make your own way to and from the experience venue near Milton Keynes, Buckinghamshire.
7. The competition closes on 31 December 2018 and the prize is valid until November 2019.
8. For full terms and conditions see www.piccadillypress.co.uk/SpyForADay

Look out for more spy action from AWOL

A new mission has come in.
Several deaths have occurred at a secret research facility,
but Bex needs help to investigate.
Should Kieron go undercover?

Turn the page for more . . .

'What's the problem?' Kieron asked from one of the bedroom doorways.

'Whatever's wrong with Bradley is affecting his ability to use the ARCC equipment,' she said. 'I don't know if it's neurological or psychosomatic. We need to get him looked over.' She held the glasses up. 'But I also need to see if MI6 have sent through any messages. It's been a while since we checked in, and I should give them an update.'

Kieron walked across the living area and took the glasses from her. She noticed that he was holding the earpiece. He must have taken it from Bradley's ear. 'Look – you sit down. I'm used to the kit. I've used it more recently than you. I'll check for messages, and then you can talk me through any response.' As she hesitated, he went on: 'You've been travelling, you're probably jet-lagged and you haven't stopped since you landed. Just sit down and have your cup of tea. You don't have to look after all of us. Let me look after you.'

It was the mention of jet lag that did it. Bex had been keeping it at bay, trying to pretend that it didn't exist, but she'd not slept a wink on the flight, and by now she'd been awake for longer than she wanted to think about.

'OK,' she said. 'I give in. Just this once.'

As she sank into the chair that Bradley had recently vacated, Kieron sat on the sofa and slipped on the glasses. His hands immediately sprang to life: moving in the air as if he was assembling some complex invisible machine. Watching him, Bex found herself amazed at the ease with which he used it. Bradley was competent, but Kieron seemed almost . . . intuitive.

'Right,' he said. 'I've got the classified email program up and running. It needs a separate password obviously.'

'TAG-LOL-GID,' Bex recited automatically. 'It's a randomly generated set of three single-syllable sounds. It avoids people using the names of their pets or the road where they used to live. All of those things can be researched.'

His fingers twitched. 'Got it. Right – OK! Wow – no spam!'

'Of course not. You've accessed an MI6 server. It's separated from the public Internet, and it's got all kinds of firewalls.'

'I know – I've been taking a look at them. Very impressive.' He paused, reading. 'There are a couple of queries about how your mission is progressing –'

'Where do I start?' she muttered.

'And an email with a new mission! It says you should confirm receipt and give an estimate on when you can start.'

'Who's it from?'

'There's no name – just what looks like a job title: "Dep-Director, SIS-TERR".'

Bex took a deep breath. She'd have to debrief her bosses

on what had happened in Mumbai of course – although as she was supposed to have been undercover, luckily they were used to waiting until she was clear so that she could update Bradley. But this new assignment – was it real, or was it a trick to lure her and Bradley out of hiding?

'What's the mission?' she asked.

Kieron nodded. 'According to this,' he said slowly, 'there have been several deaths of members of staff in something called "The Goldfinch Institute".' His fingers danced in the air. 'Yes – there's a link to more information on it. The Goldfinch Institute is apparently a research facility based in Albuquerque but with facilities around the world. It manufactures highly classified weapon systems for the British Army, MI5, MI6 and SIS-TERR in the UK, as well as the CIA, the NSA and the FBI in America.' He paused. 'Hang on – I'll move back to the email. OK, the briefing note says that the deaths appear, on the face of it, to be natural, but the fact that they all occurred at roughly the same time is raising suspicions on this side of the Atlantic. What this Dep-Director wants you to do is to go to Albuquerque and covertly investigate to see if there is any threat to British interests. Basically, find out if these deaths really are natural or whether they might be murders.' He frowned. 'Albuquerque. That's in America, isn't it? Somewhere down south? New Mexico . . . ?'

'New Mexico,' Bex confirmed absently. 'Your geography is surprisingly good.' Most of her mind was consumed with poring over the contents of the email that Kieron had read out. Investigate deaths at a classified American research institute? She and Bradley had done similar things in the past, but never in America. In fact, there were rules in place in the intelligence community that specifically prohibited members of what was known as the '5-Eyes Community' – the USA, the UK, Canada, Australia and New Zealand – from spying on each other. It was fairly common knowledge that the Americans at least flagrantly ignored that prohibition, while everyone else pretended not to notice, but for her to be asked to operate in the USA . . . it must be important. And that meant it was the kind of thing that she really shouldn't turn down. And the money would be good, which was what they were particularly short of at present.

'I didn't learn that at school,' Kieron replied. 'I know it's in New Mexico because my favourite band record their albums in a studio there.'

'Lethal Insomnia?' she said hesitantly.

He smiled. 'You *do* listen. Sam said you don't, but I knew he was wrong.'

'Anything else?' Bex asked.

'A couple of attached files – looks like autopsy reports on the dead staff members – plus some maps of the area. Oh, and there's a budget. If you need to go above a certain amount of money then you need to seek approval. And that amount of money is –' he gasped – 'a *huge* amount! I'm not surprised you can afford an apartment like this!'

Bex shrugged, feeling strangely defensive. 'It's not that much, in the scheme of things,' she said. 'We've got to pay for all our own travel, and sometimes we have to go undercover, so we have to stay in good hotels and buy stuff to back up our story, like . . . wristwatches and . . . er, cars.' Even as she said the words, they sounded weak. 'And there's danger money as well. It's a risky job. If something goes wrong, the British government will claim they know nothing about us and leave us to our fate. That's one of the reasons MI6 uses freelance operative teams like us – we're eminently deniable.'

'Yes, but –' Kieron's eyes were wide behind the glasses – 'this is an *incredible* amount.'

'We have to sort out our own pension schemes and healthcare insurance,' Bex said in a small voice.

'My mum could buy her own flat for this amount of money.' Kieron's tone wasn't accusatory – more like sad. Maybe even wistful. The kind of tone that someone might use if they were describing the perfect Christmas present – one they would never, ever get.

'Look –' Bex said, wanting to try to explain the realities of the world to Kieron, but he interrupted her before she could get the words out.

'Oh!'

'What is it?'

'Apparently there's a time limit on this mission. It needs to be completed within a week, which means that you have to accept it or reject it pretty much within the next hour or they'll pass it to another team.'

'That,' she said, 'gives us a problem.'

Kieron nodded. 'Bradley can't help you.'

'But if I reject the mission then SIS-TERR will go to a

different team, and we're not going to be top of the list for the *next* mission that comes along. If we're out of action as a team for too long then we'll slip off the list altogether.'

'There's only one answer then,' Kieron said. Maybe it was the lenses of the ARCC glasses, but his eyes seemed very wide.

Bex nodded. 'Fancy doing some temp work?' she asked heavily.